# Through the Land of Cloud and Leaf

Book 2 of the
Scions of the Aegean C series

A novel by

Terry L. Craig

Through the Land of Cloud and Leaf
Book 2 of the Scions of the Aegean C series
Published by Wild Flower Press, Inc.
P O Box 2532
Leland, NC 28451
www.wildflowerpress.biz

This is a work of fiction. Although some of the situations
portrayed were inspired by life situations, the story and
the characters are fictional.

Images on front cover, used under license from Shutterstock.com

Paperback Version:
ISBN: 978-1-946549-02-0

Library of Congress Control Number: 2017910935

## Dedication

To my beloved sister JoJo who flew away to heaven long before I was ready to let her go. My comfort is in knowing that the deep fellowship that God forged between us here will flow into eternity.

To my Bill.

## Acknowledgements

Many thanks to those who helped me in the polishing stages of this book—especially Tonya Brown, and Ethella Seyler.

## Backstory for the Series

In 2044, a spacecraft BX-9, christened the **_Aegean C_** left Earth on a mission with nearly 2,000 people aboard. The majority of the travelers were people of the Genon race—_terraformers_ tasked with transforming the New Hope settlement into a fruitful habitation for future generations. The Genon carried with them the tools, seeds, livestock, and special skills for molding this wild, new settlement. They had the expectation of carrying out their mission with little, if any input from the soldiers who were tasked with their safe delivery before departing the settlement. Others on the mission—technicians, biologists, doctors, and engineers— were expected to remain at New Hope for several years and be available when their expertise was requested, but their primary objective was to observe and record specifically _how_ the Genon were so successful in their endeavors.

The spacecraft suffered catastrophic damage shortly after takeoff, but the skill of the flight crew kept the craft intact as it reentered the atmosphere. The flight deck officers were killed when the ship crash landed on a shelf in a mountain range, not far from the equator. Miraculously, most of the passengers (soldiers, technicians, and Genon) survived and much of the cargo was salvaged but they landed in such a rugged and remote area, they knew rescue would be difficult.

Something noticed by the military in the first hours which became a source of growing concern: There appeared to be no signs of other human life on the planet. There were no responding radio transmissions, no visible roads or trails, no lights in the distance, no satellites moving through the night sky. And the constellations were different.

In the months to come, the people of the _Aegean C_ came to the conclusion that they were not on the same Earth they'd left—they'd catapulted through either time or space and come to a different place. They eventually reconciled themselves with the fact that no one would be coming to rescue them and determined to make a life in this new world that was as wild and dangerous as it was bountiful.

The "Firstlanders," as they came to be called, soon realized that they were extremely fortunate to have landed on a plateau where the land was suitable for growing crops and the climate was moderate year-round. Had they crashed into the icy slopes above the plateau, many would have quickly succumbed to exposure. Had they landed in the vast jungle below the plateau, they would have died in a tangle of toxic plants, poisonous insects, and huge predatory creatures. The plateau, which they named Aegea, could be transformed into an oasis where future generations could live.

The people of Aegea knew their technology would eventually fail, so those in the First Generation set about writing down all they knew about science, medicine, technology, and the world they left behind. The spacecraft was dismantled so the materials could be repurposed.

The soldiers on the original mission had weapons and a mandate to "protect the passengers and cargo." Not long after they crashed, large predatory animals posed an imminent threat to the people and the livestock, and the military assumed a continuing command with the same general mandate. The professionals on the flight were considered on a social par with the military. The Genon, despite the fact that their labors made long-term survival possible, became a race of laborers. Over time, families from each segment of society started to hoard the knowledge of any useful skill in order to keep from slipping further down a system increasingly skewed in favor of the military and the professionals. The ways and means of life for the people of Aegea became a mix of early industrial technology and secret recipes.

During the second generation after the crash (sixty years ago), a few of the older Genon workers led a rebellion demanding equality in governing, assets, and living conditions. All who participated in the rebellion were rounded up along with their immediate family members while a tribunal was held. Military leaders knew a lasting example must be made, but they also realized they couldn't simply slay the rebels. Neither could they expend the resources needed to imprison and feed so many in a community still struggling to survive. After much debate and a divided vote, the General, the leader of all Aegea signed an order. Each of the rebels was brought out to the settlement's main plaza—one by one. Any of their kin who publically disowned them was cleared of wrongdoing. Any who refused to disown them would share their fate: Banishment.

The guilty, some with their small children, were taken down the mountainside, deep into "the poison forest," where even some of the most experienced among the Genon hunter/gathers had perished. The rebels were there with no weapons or tools and told that any of them seen attempting to return to the plateau by any means would be killed on sight. They quickly vanished and no one was ever precisely sure what happened to them. Even now, in the fifth generation, there are whispered rumors that descendants of "the Exiles" live on in the jungle. These stories inspire some of the Genon and cause the military concern.

In Book 1, the aging leader of Aegea, General Fairmont dies shortly after selecting a replacement. On that same morning a servant of the new leader, Shaye Penway, ran away from his home by climbing into a large wooden box that she believed would be transported to town. Also on that day the only daughter of the new leader, Jariel, was abducted. She was sedated and placed in the same wooden box where the servant hid, then secretly transported to the Poison Forest. But the men carrying the box through the jungle were killed by a giant predatory creature, leaving the women alone in a place of great danger.

# List of Main Characters

**Basil**—Grandson of Old Menoh

**Ben**—one of the Exiles who discover Shaye and Jariel

**Chessie**—a gleaner (the lowest status) of Aegea

**David**—one of the Exiles who discover Shaye and Jariel

**Dell**—assistant to the inventor, Sage Dooley

**Duana McClaren**—Jubal McClaren's wife

**Fiona**—Old Menoh's wife

**Jariel McClaren**—the only daughter of Jubal and Duana McClaren

**Jubal McClaren**—the newest General of Aegea

**Kosh**—Son of Old Menoh

**Lemon**—former houseman and servant for Jubal McClaren

**Menoh**—"Old Menoh," considered the patriarch and Elder of the Genon workers in Westland

**Mosely**—Colonel Grayson Mosely was the chief rival of Jubal McClaren for the office of General of Aegea

**Mosha**—a cook in the service of Jubal McClaren for thirty years

**"Mule"**—Samuel, one of the Exiles who discover Shaye and Jariel

**Nathan**—a patriarch and Elder of the Genon Exiles

**Pearl**—of the Penway family, a Great Aunt to Shaye

**Peony**—Nathan's wife (Homeplace)

**Sage Dooley**—Chief inventor of Aegea

**Shaye**—daughter of Cpt. Frank Penway and his wife, Elle.

**"Seph"**—Joseph, General McClaren's aide

**Tressa Dooley**—Sage Dooley's wife

**Ty**—Tyrone McClaren, the only son of Jubal and Duana McClaren

**Willow**—Nathan's sister in (Homeplace)

## Locations

**The Aegean Plateau (Aegea)**
- **Oldtown**—the location of the first settlement, now old
- **Midtown**—west of Oldtown with finer homes for officers and upper class
- **The Outpost**—an outpost with a small settlement and facilities for the military, in the central portion of Aegea
- **Westland**—a military post on the western end of the plateau. The Great House of Jubal McClaren is here.

**The Poison Forest**—the jungle below the Aegean Plateau, but known to the Genon people as the **Great Forest** or the **Land of Cloud and Leaf**

**Homeplace**—the home of the Exiles

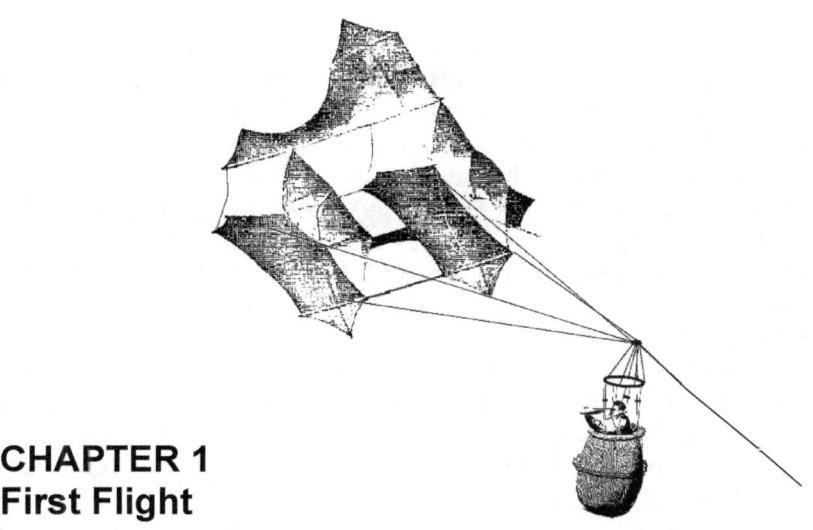

# CHAPTER 1
# First Flight

"It's possible to fear so much for your own life that you waste all of it in a safe place."—*Hal Dobbin, just prior to boarding the final flight of the spacecraft Aegean C, one hundred nine years ago.*

## In Aegea

The country's most important inventor, Mr. Sage Dooley, perches in a large basket near the edge of the precipice, his pulse racing. The draft of warm air rushing up the cliff face snatches up the giant kite carrying it aloft. The harness and basket attached to the kite lurch upward. The kite line shoots off the large spool of cord—one hundred feet, two hundred feet, and climbing. With his hands clenched on the rim of the creaking basket, Sage lets his gaze sweep over the widening vista. Trees on the plateau grow smaller. His lanky assistant, Dell, looks like a tiny stick figure in a child's drawing. Sage gasps with exhilaration.

He selected this very spot on the wall for the kite experiments for two reasons: First, because it's far from any populated settlement (away from nosey onlookers). Second, it's one of the few places where the wall sits at the very edge of the plateau. On one side of the wall, solid ground is just thirty feet away. On the other side, however, is a drop of several thousand feet!

In recent months, Sage Dooley and Dell ran multiple experiments on the updrafts here, using larger and larger kites. Last week, they used this rig with stones in the basket to simulate the weight of a man. Today, he told Dell they were only going to test the kite again, but at the last minute he got into the basket and told Dell to push the large kite off into the updraft. Even though Sage is a small man and the kite is capable of carrying him, it's a risk that no one in the military would have let him take. Truth be told, he's been plotting to do it for months.

Sage knew his window of opportunity had arrived last night when there was a flurry of military activity and all high-ranking officers were called to gather at General Fairmont's house in town. Although no one said so, Sage was relatively certain it was a "death watch."

With everyone's attention focused on the final moments of Aegea's current leader, Dooley knew it was his best chance to slip away from his guarded home, travel to the northern edge of the plateau with Dell . . . and attempt to fly! It was an opportunity he couldn't pass up—after all, he would be thirty-three years old in a few days. Shouldn't he be able to celebrate it in a grand fashion?

Although he's only a few hundred feet above the *plateau*, the jungle at the bottom of the cliff is nearly a mile down. Does he dare lean forward in the basket and look down to see what it feels like to dangle from a kite thousands of feet in the air? Not yet. Instead, he turns around to look at the vast expanse of wild green jungle that the soldiers call the Poison Forest. It stretches out from the bottom of this cliff as far as the eye can see.

He thought he would be frightened, and he knows he probably *should* be, but he's not. Never in the entirety of his life has he felt so energized . . . so free! He would be willing to continue his ascent if not for the limitations of the line keeping him earthbound. He turns again in the basket and looks at the line.

*It's like a navel string, an umbilical cord,* he tells himself. *I wonder what would happen if it broke . . . or if I cut it?* Several scenarios spring to mind—none of the imagined endings involves a safe landing on the plateau.

A wisp of a low cloud briefly engulfs him and he whoops with delight. When it moves on, he dares to glance down the cliff that drops away for thousands of feet and he's *almost* dizzy. Then he looks back up to the expanse of the plateau and a realization hits him. He is the first person to see such a view from the air in more than a century! The last time anyone saw the world from the air was the day that the spacecraft *Aegean C* crash landed there with his ancestors and nearly 2,000 other people. The revelation is both inspirational and sobering. *I wonder if anyone on the craft thought they'd survive while they were streaking toward the ground.*

A hundred years ago, the plateau was mostly covered with stands of ancient trees, meadows, and boulders that had tumbled down from the mountain peaks over the eons. Today the plateau is crisscrossed with fields, pastures, orchards, and roads etched into existence by five generations of people. To his left, at the eastern end of the plateau, is a sprawling tangle of buildings, alleys, fountains, and streets that were built not far from the wreckage site of the Aegean C. Over time, the settlement became so large that it spilled out beyond the original wall (built to keep inhabitants safe from the large predatory creatures that killed more than a few Firstlanders). The site of the oldest dwellings on Aegea is called *Oldtown*—a jumble of crumbling structures that are mostly occupied by Genon people now. The newer part, called *Midtown*, is a sprawling settlement of larger homes with private gardens where military officers and professionals of high standing live.

The basket jostles in the wind and the small telescope fastened to a lanyard around his neck swings back and forth. *Oh yes,* he remembers, *I have a spyglass!*

He braces his feet against the sides of the basket and slowly loosens his grip on the rim to hold the spyglass. He looks to his right, out into "the country" out where there are orchards, fields and pastures—flanked by the military outpost of Westland. The bright golden hue of the Great House of Westland is easy enough to spot. Far behind the post he can see a great waterfall cascading down the mountain, but he cannot see the mill his father designed, churning away at the base of the falls. As he slowly sweeps the lens of his telescope across the view before him, he sees several of the aqueducts which now provide water for people, livestock, and field irrigation—even during the dry seasons. His great uncle was the one who planned the aqueduct project.

What else can he see? Sage turns his head to the left and focuses the lens toward town. The movement of the kite makes it difficult to use the telescope, but he finally manages to spot the three-story, bright white house of the general, standing out against the earth-toned houses and green trees that surround it.

*And, what is that?* The basket bobbles. He repositions himself in the basket and braces his feet again before he can give it a better look. A large flag flaps in the breeze above the general's house. It's a black flag. *The general must have died.*

The tense voice of his assistant, Dell, drifts up on the breeze and interrupts his thoughts. "Are you all right? Should I pull you in now?"

Dooley lets go the telescope and grabs the lines of the harness.

"Yes!" he calls back, "Reel me in!"

Dell is understandably nervous. Sage Dooley is considered "one of the most valuable living assets" on the plateau. Beginning with Hal Dobbins, a scientist who survived the crash of the Aegean C, Sage's talented ancestors were among the small contingent of technicians and scientists who vastly improved the living conditions (and survival chances) over the generations, and Sage seems to have inherited their genius. Years ago, when he crushed his left foot in an experiment that went haywire, the military decided that he must be "protected" so that he could live a long—and hopefully inventive—life. They are now doubly concerned because the line of Sage's family may end with him. He and his wife, Tressa, have been unable to bear children.

That's his lot in life: a hobbled foot and the constant presence of guards. Often, Sage feels as if he's trapped—and it drives him to take risks. Dell understands. That, in and of itself, would be enough to make them friends. Add to that Dell's loyalty, physical strength, and his rarely given (but generally practical) advice and the two men are less like professional and assistant, more like brothers who alternately try to get each other into—or out of—trouble.

Sage wrote a letter early this morning stating that he alone was responsible for his actions—that Dell was unaware of his plan and therefore not accountable for the outcome of the flight. Even so, if he got badly injured again or died in an accident, Dell might stand before a tribunal and face consequences. The look on Dell's face when Sage jumped into the basket communicated that he knew it could be trouble . . . but he didn't refuse to help. He understood.

Dell is heaving on the crank with all his might to wind the line for the kite back on the large spool, but the increased tension on the line causes the kite to momentarily rise.

Sage wants to observe the operation of the ratchet on the side of the wheel, but something in the distance catches his eye. He turns his head and squints at it. *Yes, there is definitely something moving at the top of the wall that surrounds the plateau.* It's only because he's up in the air that he can see it at all. He raises the spyglass and tries to quickly focus in the correct location. *There it is.*

It's a tram car leaving the wall and swiftly gliding down its cable into the jungle below, carrying one of the large crates the military uses. He can see there is an insignia on the crate, but from this distance, it's just a smudge. He wonders, *Who would be doing this? And why would they be doing it today?* His focus travels back up the tram cable to the wall. At least two men are there. Possibly in uniform. The kite bumps him around again and he loses his sighting.

Although test runs of the tram he invented to transport people and goods down to the jungle were successful, General Fairmont changed his mind and shut it down within a week of its completion. Like so many other of Sage Dooley's inventions, the tram will remain a secret project that will collect dust unless an "urgent need" for it arises.

Dooley frowns and looks again. The tram car has disappeared out of view . . . and he can no longer see the two figures who were watching it from the wall. Perhaps someone *else* is using the events unfolding in town to do things unnoticed.

# CHAPTER 2
## Runaway Servant

"**Y**our fortunes can change in a single day. Who knows? Be faithful, for today may be your last day of mourning, or your last day of prosperity."—*A proverb of His own People.*

### Westland, on the Aegean Plateau

Her questions rush out in an angry torrent. "What do you mean, *'Shaye ran away?'* Didn't I tell you to stay with her? How could she have run away? Why didn't you *stop* her?"

Raymond stands, rigid as a wooden post in the center of the salon, knowing his fate may hang on his answer. Sweat from the back of his head trickles down a crease in his leathery neck, past his loose collar, and down between his shoulder blades, but he doesn't dare move. If Duana McClaren, the ishi (the matriarch) of the Great House of Westland would persecute Shaye, a servant with *many* years of service, what could happen to him? A dismissal and a *dis*-recommendation from Duana could echo over the entire plateau with *dire* consequences. He might very well end his days as a *gleaner*, living in temporary shelters, surviving only on food that could be scraped out of orchards and fields already harvested.

Wringing a tired old hat between his hands, he clears his throat and begins. "Well, ma'am, I took her to her room just like you said, and I stayed right there by the door, and I didn't go anywhere while she packed her things." He pauses to clear his throat again, and she takes a step closer to him.

Sensing the very air around him filling with the static charge of her ire, the cadence of his speech speeds up and words fly out of his mouth in one long sentence. "And after a while I felt some concern, so I knocked and then I opened the door, but she wasn't there and I saw how she must have gone out the window on the other side of the room and I never would have expected anyone to do that and she was gone like a bird and," he stops, to swallow and inhale. "Of a truth, ma'am, Shaye is vanished and I don't know where she went."

He pulls his elbows even closer to his body while he waits, eyes shut, head already tilted against the expected volume of her response. Who would have thought he could be in so much trouble so early in the day?

But she doesn't say a word. Instead, her eyes search the room until she sees a vase on the table between the two upholstered chairs, not far from the fireplace. It's only inches away from her hand. She slowly leans over, wraps her fingers around the slender neck of the container, then hurls it with all her might into the empty hearth.

Raymond's eyes pop open and his shoulders involuntarily jerk up at the sound of the delicate vessel crashing against the cold stones. But he doesn't leave his spot—even though several shards of the vase have flown out, striking the legs of his baggy work pants before bouncing to the floor near his sandaled foot. His gaze remains riveted to the floor, but within his field of view are two additional fragments near the hem of the ishi's long, dark dress. He makes no move to retrieve them, while his anxiety intensifies with each passing moment.

She folds her arms and slowly inhales. It's been years since she last gave into the urge to smash something . . . but it's so satisfying, she must fight the urge to find more objects to throw. Fortunately for Raymond, another idea pops into her mind and she turns to ask him, "Where is Shaye's roommate?"

This is a totally unexpected turn in the interrogation. She might as well have asked him to lay an egg! Completely dumbfounded, he shrugs. "I don't know, ma'am. Keepin' track of her isn't part of my job."

"UHH!" she cries, throwing her hands up in exasperation. "Go across the road to the office on the post and tell the duty officer I need to speak with him right away."

It's almost as if her words are bouncing around in his head. He needs to slowly replay them in his mind so they can sink in. He starts to nod, but Duana continues.

"And once you've done that, go and bring that girl back here."

His mouth drops open. "Shaye? I told you I have no idea where—"

"No! Her roommate, Raymond, her *roommate*! That round, sort of ugly little woman. What's her name?"

"Chessie?"

"Yes, that's it. After you tell the duty officer I need to speak with him, find out where Chessie is supposed to be today, then go fetch her and bring her back here."

"Yes'm." His head bobs up and down, but he's waiting to see if there are further orders.

Duana closes her eyes. "Now, Raymond. Go right now."

Once he's absent from the scene, one could imagine that the elegance of the room would reassert a sense of dignified serenity there. Situated just beyond a lavish dining room, this dark-paneled salon, or "sitting room," has wide windows, a high ceiling, fine furnishings, and a large fireplace. Indeed, Duana herself reflects as much refinement as anything in the room. Everything from her perfectly coifed brown hair, to the beads hanging from her slender neck, to the embroidered shoes peeking out from under the hem of her dress bear testimony to her high standing. But elegance and serenity aren't partners here. Not today.

After a minute of steaming back and forth across the rug, mumbling arguments to herself, Duana walks to a window. Her feet have stopped moving, but her clenched right hand continues to strike an angry cadence against the window sill. Staring at the trees in the distance she wonders, *Where could Shaye have gone? She can't have gotten far, and certainly nobody will dare help her once word gets out. We'll find her wherever she's hiding and she will deeply regret laying a hand on the daughter of a colonel.*

*For seven long years I've waited.* She turns away from the window. *Certainly no one could accuse me of being unkind. When I moved her out, didn't I arrange for her to share one of the rooms in the new building where other servants would gladly sleep? Perhaps I was too kind.*

Duana now replays the words of her written communique, already on its way to her husband at the other end of the plateau.

*Jubal*

*You need to know that something happened which requires your immediate attention. If I had been allowed to signal you about the situation, it might have been resolved by now, but the captain left in charge at the post wouldn't allow me to have a signal relayed through the tower, so don't be shocked that you are finding this out via a written message that will have taken hours for you to receive via a rider.*

*This morning, Shaye attacked Jariel, struck her, and knocked her down! Jariel was very traumatized.*

*I know that you and Mosha both have a sense of duty regarding Shaye, so I decided to simply trade the girl instead of punish her.*

*Remember when Nob the butcher approached us and asked to have her as a match for his son? I know you opposed the trade, but under these new circumstances, I thought it would be the wisest thing to do. I was willing to set her transgressions aside and let her walk away. I sent word to Nob, but as soon as Shaye was informed of the trade, rather than being grateful, she ran away! Now that she's thrown off all restraint, she may very well be plotting some sort of vengeance upon us.*

*Shaye's years of privilege have led her to think she is above all rule, and her open rebellion sets an example for others that cannot be tolerated. She knows you are away, and if we don't mount a search for her, I fear she will return to the house and attempt to inflict harm on us. I want your men to help find her, and I want you to draw up charges against her. Please come home as soon as possible.*

*Duana*

# CHAPTER 3
# A New Leader for Aegea

"There can only be one leader. It is, therefore, decided on this day, exactly four years after the crash of the Aegean C according to the calendar of Earth, that in order to insure our continued safety and survival, the military shall retain the right to protect and govern all people through a central command while we continue to hope for rescue. There shall be one general, with four colonels who will serve directly under him. If the general, with witnesses present, selects one of the colonels prior to his death, that colonel shall become the next general. If a ruling general doesn't select a colonel, there shall be a vote from among all officers from the rank of captain and above, to determine which colonel will serve as the next general."—*From the Official Constitution of the Aegean Plateau, duly signed* **one hundred seven years ago.**

Ty McClaren is awake early. Again.

Was it the chilly night air that woke him . . . or the dark dream he knows he's had before, but can never quite remember?

Giving up on sleep, he stands, but stops to wrap his blanket around his shoulders before he closes the shutters on the window to his room. After lighting the lamp on his desk, he sits down while holding his hands near the flame to warm them. The leather-bound book he was reading earlier is still on the desk and he opens it, but he has no desire to think about his studies right now. After several minutes of staring blankly at the words, his eyes gravitate to a small wooden box sitting just within the circle of lamplight, at the far right-hand corner of the desktop. He purchased the intricately carved container at the market of Oldtown after he didn't make it home for his first leave from the academy. It sits there like a fancy little fortress, guarding a small symbol of hope.

He rubs his eyes and endeavors afresh to concentrate on the book, but a conversation he overheard between two cadets last week starts to replay in his head the same way it has a multitude of times.

*"No, I'm not going anymore."* One of them says, lowering his voice. *"Can you imagine what our parents would say? What they'd do to us?"*

*"What do you mean 'our' I'm just having a good time, you're the one who let that girl think she actually meant something to you. And now you're as dull as geometry while you hole up here avoiding your Genon girlfriend."*

*"She wasn't my girlfriend and I'm never going to see her again."*

*"Come on. We can go some new places. Even if we see her, just ignore her. You didn't promise her anything, did you? Even if you had, what would it matter? What can she do to you, what could she say that would matter? How many times do you think this very scenario has played itself out since the beginning? Unless she's really stupid, she knows how it works. Just move on, man."*

In an effort to stop the replay, he pushes his hands forward and accidentally knocks the box off the desk. He drops to the floor and crawls toward the box. It opened upon impact and the hand-carved comb it held is nearly a foot away.

He lunges to pick up the comb, and inspects it for any damage. Holding it in his hand, he wonders, *Why didn't I insist on going home? What must she think? That I lied when I said I loved her? That she doesn't matter?* For a moment, he pictures her in his mind—her long black hair and the golden eyes that captured him, even as a young boy.

He places the comb in the box and sits on the floor. "I must get home."

*And do what? What possibility is there that this could ever end well? How can I make this up to her?*

### 

Two hours later, all the cadets waiting for morning classes gather in the open courtyard that occupies the space between the dorm and classrooms where instructors are preparing for another day of lessons. Several young men employ their energies kicking around a small ball made of animal hide. Onlookers watch two cadets engage in a wrestling match that may or may not remain friendly.

Brilliant sunlight breaks into every crevice of the stone courtyard while Ty McClaren leans back to stretch out along the top of a short wall near the front steps to the dorm. It's one of the few places freshmen cadets are allowed to sit in the courtyard.

"Hey, move your feet," his friend, Carl, commands.

Ty doesn't move or open his eyes. "My feet were there first."

"Tough."

Ty looks up, squinting at the silhouette of his friend in the bright light. "I just got comfortable."

"Tough."

The young McClaren swings his legs back over the wall, and as soon as he does so, two more cadets hop over from behind and perch in the space.

"Hey!" Carl complains.

Ty shrugs. "Tough."

Soon, the bell signaling the start of the day's classes will ring. Ty turns so he can straddle the wall and lean against the end post. His head finds a perfect balancing point on the stone cap topping the post, and he closes his eyes again. His lack of sleep and the warmth of the sun quickly melt into sleep.

> *He's walking out of the back of the house in Westland, Shaye and Mosha are buzzing about in the kitchen, planning their day. Outside, fresh laundry is flapping on the lines, ready to be gathered and folded by women sharing the day's gossip. At the tables behind the house, the workers are sharing a meal. He and Basil will soon be off for a day in the woods and fields . . .*

Ty jolts when Carl shakes his shoulder. "Ty!" he says in an urgent but low voice, "Have you heard?"

The two cadets nearby stop their conversation and turn to listen.

"Heard what?" Ty asks. Looking around, he realizes that all the activity in the courtyard has stopped. Cadets are milling around in groups having serious discussions—and many of them are glancing in his direction.

Carl brings Ty's attention back into focus when he speaks again. "All the colonels have been summoned to the old man's house. Robert says it means Fairmont is dead or dying."

An older man in uniform comes out of one of the classroom buildings and rings a hand bell, shouting, "Three minutes to get to class!"

The collective groan usually heard at First Bell is absent. Instead, the cadets slowly move toward the classrooms, still speaking quietly in small groups, occasionally turning to look at Ty. They all stop talking and watch when the teacher of his first class enters the courtyard and walks directly up to Ty.

"Your father has requested that you return to your room until further notice," he says.

### 

All he knows for certain is *all* senior officers have been summoned to the home of General Fairmont, and he and Liam Wexler (the only other son of a colonel at the Academy) were both told to return to their quarters during morning classes. He assumes rumors of all sorts are swirling around the campus by now.

As much as he'd like to be able to walk about outside and find out more, he understands the reason for seclusion. Truth be told, he isn't sure that he could stay out of all the speculations that are surely growing by the moment. Cadets would all be fishing for any tidbit he might know, asking for his input. He can imagine their questions.

*"Is it true that your father is at the General's house?"*

*"Do you think the General is dying?"*

*"Will your father be the next General?"*

*"If no one is selected as the successor, what do you think will happen?"*

No matter *what* happens, he's aware of the real potential for trouble. There are four colonels, and only one of them can become the next leader. If General Fairmont selects Ty's father as successor, the supporters of Col. Mosley, his father's chief rival, may make trouble. If the general selects Col.

Mosley, those who support Ty's father (including most of the officers and cadets here at the Academy) will be up in arms. If one of the two "weaker" colonels (Wexler or Krayton) is selected, there will be a power struggle. The worst-case scenario would be if the general names *no* successor before he dies. There could be civil disruption on a large scale.

Ty sits down at his desk, but it's impossible to think about his studies right now. His eyes gravitate back to the wooden box, and he lightly places a hand upon it. *If Father is made General, who knows what might become possible?* The thought gives him a hope that he hasn't dared to feel until just this moment.

His door opens and Carl leans in. "*Ty!*" the young man yells breathlessly. "They've raised the black flag at the General's compound! He's dead! What do you think will happen next?"

Ty tries to appear calm. "Have you heard anything else?"

"No! But Frank says that the flag went up just minutes ago!"

There's a sudden surge in commotion. People run past Carl in the hall. They hear loud shouts on the stairs and outside the window.

"I've got to go see," his friend says before he bolts from the doorway toward the stairs.

Ty runs to the door. Cadets continue to pour out of the building and he can't hold himself back from finding out what's happened. He joins the throng rushing down the stairs. It's an old building, dating back to late in the Second Generation, so the whole staircase bounces with the footsteps of dozens of cadets.

When he gets to the ground level, Ty joins a sea of young men streaming out the door toward the large courtyard where many of them hang out between classes and after hours. He can hear a rising chorus of male voices singing the anthem of Aegea as he exits the building. Hundreds of cadets and soldiers are there.

"There's Ty McClaren!" somebody shouts and fellow classmen rush in to surround him. Some of them are giving him playful shoves, others are shouting excitedly. He has no idea what to make of it.

Carl presses through the crowd and shouts above the din, "They've sent for our battalion flag! They're taking *our* flag to the general's house!"

The blank expression on Ty's face says he has no idea what this means.

"Your *father* is general now! The riders have been dispatched and they're going to raise our flag—*your father's* flag—at the general's house!"

The Academy is Jubal's stomping grounds. His battalion headquarters are here and he has oversight of everything that happens here. His appointment may not be met with joy throughout the land, but for the vast majority inside these walls, it is welcome news.

Amidst a frenzy of shouting, the anthem starts again. They hoist Ty up on their shoulders and begin marching around the courtyard with him aloft while they sing.

*Of course,* Ty realizes. *That's what happens. They raise the flag of the new general.*

# CHAPTER 4
## Missing Daughter

"When loyalty holds the highest rank—above truth, love, and justice . . . calamity is sleeping in your house."—*Cora McClaren, great-grandmother of Gen. Jubal McClaren*

She hears voices on the bottom floor of the house, then the sound of someone coming up the stairs from the kitchen. Duana looks over at the landing, expecting to see the girl Raymond was supposed to fetch—Shaye's former roommate, Chessie. But it's not Chessie. It's Mosha, the cook who has worked for the colonel for more than two decades.

Certainly Mosha will have heard the news about Shaye and Jariel, and she will now attempt to plead Shaye's case in the matter. The old woman takes several steps toward the salon but doesn't cross the threshold. She stands in the dining room, hands smoothing the front of her old apron. "Ma'am."

The ishi wants to make her point first. "I suppose you've heard that Shaye attacked my daughter."

"That's not exactly what I heard, ma'am. Is Miss Jariel all right? Where is Shaye?"

"Jariel is in her room and she'll recover . . . eventually. As for Shaye, she is hiding someplace, but we'll find her soon and she's in serious trouble when we do."

Mosha's brow furrows and she opens her mouth to speak, but Duana quickly fills the silence. "I tried to be kind to Shaye—for your sake more than anything else. Nob the butcher asked me to trade for her *months* ago in order to make a match for his son, and I turned him down. Even after the incident this morning, I still wanted to be mindful of you, so—rather than having her detained and charge her with striking Jariel—I accepted the trade."

Mosha gasps, but the ishi forges ahead with her statement.

"Of course, she wouldn't have been welcome at the Great House any longer, but you would still have been able to go and visit with her on occasion. *However*, despite the continuing mercy I've tried to show to the girl, she ran away. Who knows what sort of thing she might be planning. It was the final stroke, Mosha. I sent a message to the colonel and when he gets here, I *will* bring charges against her."

The happy demeanor normally radiating from the old cook's countenance is gone. Mosha takes another step forward. "Whatever has happened, ma'am, I'm sure there has been some sort of misunderstanding. Shaye has seen a lot of changes in her life recently and she's not been quite herself."

"Oh! So now it's *my* fault for moving her into a nice room in the new building?"

"That's not what I was—" Mosha blurts out before stopping. She makes an effort to sound reasonable. "She's a *good* girl, ma'am, and I find it hard to believe she would 'attack' Miss Jariel. Maybe we could all just cool down and talk about what actually happened."

"Are you calling me a *liar?*" Duana barks.

Mosha lowers her eyes. "No, ma'am. . . . I'm asking you for a personal favor." she says, her voice starting to quaver. "I'll never ask for another. Please don't harm my girl like this."

"But she's not really *'your'* girl, is she? She's a cast off, an orphan who should *never* have been allowed to live in this house in the first place. She *never* understood her position in life and if she's been harmed, she's done it to herself." The ishi turns her back to the cook, before saying, "Shaye is responsible for this mess, not me. My mind is made up and the message has been sent. There is no more to discuss and you need to go back to the kitchen."

The old woman steps into the salon and speaks again, but this time there is a tone in her voice that the matron of the Great House has never heard before. "You've poisoned Miss Jariel's heart against Shaye for years now . . . and this is going to end badly for *everyone* if you don't stop."

Duana spins around. "What are you saying? Are you making some sort of *threat?*"

The old woman straightens her stance and she looks Duana in the eye. "No ma'am. I'm saying your poison will harm us all."

Duana points at the stairs and says, "Go downstairs where you belong. You can look for a trade if you'd like, but you're not going to be able to play on anyone's heartstrings. Not this time. Your days of petitioning for Shaye are over."

### 

An hour later, Duana is still in the small salon, sitting in a chair. *Nothing* seems to be going her way today. No one can find the runaway, Shaye. The girl's roommate, Chessie, was of absolutely no help at all in figuring out where she might be hiding.

There's an eerie quiet in the house.

She turns to look toward the window. The patch of sunlight on the floor doesn't seem to have moved from where it was the last time she looked at it. She turns back around in her chair and stares at the broken vase in the fireplace while she waits for her daughter to come downstairs. The shards fade from her focus as she recalls the argument they had last night.

> "How do you <u>know</u> that Gilbert Lot is 'never' coming to visit me?" Jariel blustered. "He said he would be back and he was quite sincere! He <u>cares</u> for me."
>
> She took Jariel's hand. "Your father thinks the young man is anything <u>but</u> sincere. He's forbidden Gib to return to Westland or to court you."
>
> "And I suppose you're taking Father's side."
>
> "Well, I heard recently that he has been chasing a number of girls in town."
>
> Jariel began shouting. "How would I ever know for sure? You keep me trapped out here where no one will ever visit me! If you and Father had your way, you'd lock me in this house and never let me escape until you made some sort of political match for me! Then I could marry some awful man and be as <u>miserable</u> as you are!"

*Duana stood and slapped her daughter. "How dare you! You won't leave the upper floor of this house until you apologize."*

*Jariel crumbled into a chair and began to sob.*

*After Duana left the room, the girl ran to the doorway and shouted, "You just proved it! I am a prisoner here!" before she slammed the door.*

As the memory of her daughter's accusations rumble around in her head, Duana lets out an exasperated sigh and leans back in her chair. Right after the incident with Shaye would have been a perfect time for Duana to gloss over their own little tiff and let the demand for an apology slide.

*That may have been a tactical error, since we need to present a united front to Jubal.* She tells herself. *But we'll work things out before Jubal comes home.*

The servant went to fetch Jariel quite some time ago. What could possibly be taking so long? She glances again at the patch of sunlight on the floor and then at the wide entrance to the room and mutters under her breath, "Beth where are you? It can't have taken that long for you to waddle up the stairs. How long does it take to fetch my daughter?"

Looking back at the window, she tells herself, *Jubal could be on his way home within another hour or so.*

With one hand on her back and the other under her large belly, Beth enters the room and says, "Excuse me, madam."

Duana cannot help but stare at the huge bulge in Beth's dress. *Soon we'll be so shorthanded, I'll have to get more servants for the house and the kitchen . . . although there is that little girl . . . what's her name? Ana. Perhaps Ana might do as a replacement helper for Mosha. She's about the same age that Shaye was when she started working. . . . But who knows what we'll do for a few days when Beth delivers her baby. ANOTHER one! What will I do?*

"Excuse me, madam," the servant says again.

"What is it?"

"I cannot find Miss Jariel."

Duana rises from her chair. "Where did you look?"

"Everywhere. I looked in her bedroom and in her weaving room. I even looked up on the roof, although I know she rarely goes there. And when I came down the stairs, I noticed that the door at the bottom of the stairwell at the back of the house on the ground level was left open. Should I look outside?"

### 

The young captain re-fastens the top button on his double-breasted uniform tunic, then sweeps his fingers through his sandy brown hair before he places his hat squarely on his head. As a matter of habit, he looks around. Does he need anything else? No.

"Okay," he says to his fellow officer. "Let's go then."

They step outside and stride in the direction of the home of Col. Jubal McClaren, also known as the "great house of Westland." This is the *second* time this morning Capt. Fleming has been summoned to the home. Sensing some sort of power play in the works, he's bringing his friend Lt. James Bowes. James can serve as a witness to what is (or is not) said.

As the two men walk across the smooth, stone-paved road that separates the cluster of soldier's quarters from the colonel's compound, Captain Fleming squares his shoulders and rolls his head around to ease the tension in his neck. Both men pause at the gate and glance at each other before they return the salute of the soldier posted there.

Fleming steps up and pulls the gate open without waiting for assistance. *Might as well get right to it.*

Once they're through the gate and around a corner in the pathway through the hedge, Fleming squints in the direction of the enormous house. A row of large, arched windows with shutters on either side are the only break in the golden yellow color of a building which is so bright in the morning sun that it actually hurts his eyes. It's been said that the idea for the structure was copied from a plan for a grand edifice that the colonel saw in the archives, and then spent nearly a decade building. Towers at either end extend beyond the roofline and give it a fortress-like appearance.

The two men travel through the garden surrounding the house, and Fleming leads his friend along the path past giant ferns and a pool where water lilies serenely stand in dark water. When the two men round a corner, brilliant-feathered birds from the Poison Forest squawk at them from fancy cages, and continue their clamor until the men are quite a distance away.

Fleming stops once he arrives at the main staircase for the home, waiting momentarily for his companion to catch up. Normally, he'd bypass these stairs and follow the path on around to the right of the building where the colonel has offices for staff and several meeting rooms, but the colonel isn't here . . . and the summons came from inside the home.

The two men ascend the stone steps to the home and Fleming knocks only once before a male servant opens the door. They are escorted past a spacious, paneled entryway with a vaulted barrel ceiling then beyond a formal dining room to the home's smaller salon. The colonel's wife is standing near the fireplace. At their earlier meeting, she acted as if she had the right to send a signal to the colonel, but he knew better. He reminded her of the "rules" regarding signaling and politely refused her request to ignore them, then offered to send a swift rider to town with a written message. The vexed ishi made him wait until she wrote one and sealed it, handing it to him with a hand as cold as it was pale.

Her eyes dart from one man to the other. "Captain Fleming . . . and Lieutenant Bowes is it?"

"Yes ma'am," Fleming says as they remove their hats in unison and stow them under their left arms. "I'm sorry but we haven't received any response from the colonel yet."

"That's not why I requested your presence. We have an urgent situation here which requires that I send a signal to town."

The captain's brows come together. "Is someone gravely ill?"

"No."

"Is this a life-or-death situation?"

She considers the two uniformed sentinels standing several feet apart before she focuses her attention on Fleming. "I'm not sure what to call it, but I assure you this is *very* serious. The colonel would want to be informed of this situation as soon as possible."

Fleming makes an effort not to roll his eyes. "I'm sorry, ma'am, but as I told you earlier, I've been given the *strictest* orders about signaling. Unless somebody is 'dead, nearly dead, or the compound is under siege,' I cannot authorize a personal message to be signaled from the tower."

"I'm *certain*," she responds, "that if Major Ratliff were here, *he'd* send the signal."

She has a reputation for steering into areas where she doesn't have authority and Fleming has been warned not to *ever* let "the colonel's missus" manipulate him into a career-altering breach of protocol.

He keeps his firm posture. "But the major isn't here, ma'am. He was called to town at dawn, and he still hasn't returned. Perhaps, if you could *tell me* what the problem is, I could better decide."

Duana doesn't move for several moments while she weighs the embarrassment of laying the family's private life open (possibly to be repeated around the tables in the soldier's mess hall) against her mounting panic. "My daughter—the colonel's daughter, Jariel—isn't in the house."

Fleming can't grasp why this would be such a big deal. He knows the colonel's daughter is pale, skinny, and not often seen—but then, the compound is surrounded by a *very* tall hedge so who would ever see her anyway? Who would know what the girl's habits were? Given the girl's plain looks, *who would care?* A look of skepticism settles on his face before he asks, "And . . . she *never* leaves the house? She couldn't be out in the garden or taking a stroll somewhere on the grounds?" He can see a vein beginning to pulse on Duana's temple so he stops talking. He should take care not to annoy her, but he can already imagine the grilling he would get from the major *and* the colonel if he caves in and gives this woman what she's demanding without a very good reason. He must have evidence of a genuine emergency.

"Well, it's not *just* that she's out of the house," Duana says, standing taller. "I didn't share this when you were here earlier, but she had a violent altercation with a servant this morning—"

"Was your daughter seriously injured?" he quickly asks.

"Well, no. But then the servant ran away."

In his frustration, Fleming squeezes one eye closed as he makes an effort to connect Duana's rambling trail of logic. "So . . . you think your daughter might have gone out to look for the servant?"

"No! I think the servant may have come back in the house and . . . done something."

"Is the servant a large man? Could he have carried her away?"

Duana's chin drops to her chest. "No. The servant is a young woman about my daughter's age and size—"

"Don't you think your daughter would have made a *lot* of noise and struggled if she were being dragged out of the house against her will? Wouldn't someone have seen or heard this and intervened?"

The ishi splays out her fingers and pushes her hands down as if she's attempting to keep a lid on a wildly boiling pot. "I know it sounds like a silly thing, but I *forbade* my daughter to leave the upper floors of the house last night and I know she wouldn't have left without my permission."

It only takes a split second, but she sees the *Aha!* gleam in his eye and the short glance he shoots at his fellow soldier, before he asks, "And . . . was this the result of some sort of disagreement you had with your daughter?"

Duana knows that Mosha, Raymond, and Beth were all in the house last evening. An interview might yield the fact that she and Jariel argued, and Jariel shouted down the stairs about being a prisoner here. "Yes."

"And you forbade your daughter, a young woman of *seventeen seasons*, to leave the upper floors of the house?"

She exhales, "Yes."

"And you still maintain that she didn't decide to . . . say for instance, go for a walk without telling you?"

Rapidly closing the distance between them, she leans into his face. *"Listen to me! I'm her mother and I can sense something is wrong!* I want you to send a signal to my husband and I want you to help me find my daughter. *Now."*

He considers his answer before he locks his gaze on the far wall and says, "I'm sorry, but I'm not authorized to use the signalman in the tower to send a message unless something more substantial has happened than that your daughter 'isn't in the house.' I can send another rider to town with a written message and we can organize a search of the house and the grounds, but that is all I will do until we have some sort of evidence that this is more serious or unless the colonel signals us from town ordering us to do more. Meantime, I will be happy to have several soldiers check the grounds for your daughter."

### 

Young Capt. Reginald Fleming is back behind the desk, and so far, it's been a tough day to be the one left in charge—certainly, he isn't in the mood for any more teasing from the likes of James Bowes.

"I did what was necessary given the circumstances, *Jimbo*," he says, squinting at his sometimes friend. "So just drop it. Okay?"

The wooden chair creaks as James suddenly takes his feet off the other side of the desk and sits up. "Don't call me *Jimbo*, and no you didn't. You caved in. She wanted you to devote some troops to finding her daughter, who—as far as anybody knows—could just be out for a stroll, and you couldn't find a way to say 'No.'"

"I'm sorry I let you come with me," Fleming mutters before sliding a stack of paper over from one side of his desk to the center. "Obviously, you don't know how to navigate the political hazards of the upper echelon. Probably why *you're* still a lieutenant." Then he adds, "I have work to do. You're dismissed."

"Ah. I get it. This conversation is officially over."

Fleming doesn't look up. "Sure is."

Bowes rises from his seat. "Fine."

As soon as James is out the door, Fleming leans forward and rests his head on the stack of papers. *If only the major had asked someone else to be the duty officer today.*

It's barely past midday, and his career could be in ribbons. Two times he's been summoned to the colonel's house to be pressured by the colonel's wife to send signals to town regarding domestic affairs—something that is *strictly* forbidden. But the second time, he did agree to have several soldiers begin looking for the colonel's daughter. He hasn't worked out how he will explain it to his superiors yet, but he's certain that Duana McClaren will complain no matter what the outcome, and he's also pretty sure she'll have the last word.

###

Two soldiers on horseback arrive at the front gate of Westland and pull to a stop. After gaining entrance, the riders wearing the Signal Corps insignias urge their horses to resume their gallop down the road until they arrive at the stone courtyard where the offices for the post are located. One of the men has an urgent message for the duty officer and he hurries into the wooden building with the sign stating it's the main office.

"Sir!" the rider says as soon as his eyes light on Fleming. "I'm Spec. 5 Riley of the 1st Signal Corps. I was dispatched from the Outpost because your signalman isn't responding. The General sent a message two hours ago and no one has acknowledged. We've tried repeatedly since then and there has been no reply, so I was sent to deliver the message directly to Mrs. McClaren and to investigate why there has been no return signal. I am to deliver this message then go into the tower and signal if everything is in working order."

Fleming's heart flounders around in his chest before he finds the words, "The *General?*" He'd been under the impression that the aging general was so feeble he couldn't leave his house. *Why would he be signaling to Mrs. McClaren? . . . And why was there no acknowledgement from our man in the tower? If there was some sort of malfunction preventing acknowledgement, I should have been informed immediately so a rider could be dispatched with details of any repairs needed here. Of all the days for a signalman to be taking a nap! And on* my *watch!*

Captain Fleming quickly scans the paper on the top of the stack to see who is supposed to be on duty in the tower. "Spec. 5 John Grimes," he says aloud. He tries to remember anything he knows about Grimes as he stands and locates his hat. Truth is, he can barely remember what the man looks like.

Once Fleming and the messenger are outside the office, he tells the horseman who accompanied the messenger to wait, ready to ride back with details if there is some problem with the signal tower. He then calls for a sergeant and a private to accompany them across the road to the colonel's compound.

This is the messenger's first time to Westland so he's never seen the grounds of the Great House before. Once they're through the gate, he realizes the stories *weren't* exaggerations. If he could, he'd stop and admire the sheer grandeur of it all—but there's no time for that now.

When they reach the front stairs of the house, Capt. Fleming stops and speaks to him. "Go up to that door and knock on it. Someone will see you in and you can put the message directly into the hands of Mrs. McClaren. I'll head around to the tower to see if I can find out what's amiss. You can join me there shortly and send a return signal." Fleming points at one of the soldiers who accompanied them. "Reese here will go with you and then show you the way to the tower when you're ready." He looks at the fourth soldier in the group. "Harper, come with me."

As the messenger and his escort ascend the stairs, Fleming and Pvt. Harper walk swiftly to the right side of the house where there is a single wooden door. Inside is a small office for the colonel's aide (when he is here) and a stairwell in the tower that leads to the colonel's office and the signal room at top of the tower.

Fleming tries the door. He pushes the latch down, but the door won't move. He tries knocking on the door.

"Inside! This is Capt. Fleming. Open the door!"

There is no response and they hear no movement inside. The wooden shutters on the bottom-floor windows are closed, so they can't see into the office or access it.

Fleming steps back about twenty-five feet and looks up at the open windows at the top of the tower. He cups his hands around his mouth and says, "Hello! Grimes! Can you hear me?"

There is no response. He tries again. "Hello! Grimes! This is Capt. Fleming and I order you to open the door at the ground floor level! Respond if you can hear me!"

After several seconds of silence, Fleming looks at Harper and says, "I don't care how you do it, get that door open. Go get an ax and chop the door to pieces if you must, but keep working on it unless I tell you to stop!" With that, Fleming runs back to the front stairs of the home, and mounts them three at a time. Without knocking, he opens the door. The messenger and the sergeant are waiting in the hall but he doesn't stop to talk to them. He walks through the hallway that leads to the main rooms of the house.

"Hello!" Fleming shouts. "Mrs. McClaren! Come quickly!"

She appears in a doorway with the opened message still in her hand. He moves toward her and starts talking. "Mrs. McClaren, we need to go through the house to the other side where the colonel's door to the tower is. Something is wrong and we need access to the tower immediately."

Before she can speak, he brushes by her and begins running toward the other side of the home. He knows the way.

She follows behind him, "What's wrong? Is it Jariel? Is she in the tower?"

He's so intent on getting into the tower, he doesn't respond. When they arrive at the tower door, he tries the latch and realizes this door is bolted from the inside as well. With too much adrenaline flowing to care about Duana, he turns and says, "Quickly, ma'am! Is there another way to get into the tower?"

She turns and swiftly leads them back through the house, stopping near a small door off the dining room. "There. That is a stairway that goes to the roof. Some of the windows of the tower face the roof so you might be able to climb up to them."

"Come with me," Fleming says to the men.

They all climb to the roof and run to the tower. Two of them let the signalman climb up on their shoulders so he can crawl into a tower window. He quickly reappears in the window and says to them, "There isn't anybody in here. I'll go down the stairs and unlock the doors."

Fleming closes his eyes and holds his breath while he considers what to do next.

### # # #

Within ten minutes, they send a signal to inform headquarters that the soldier who should be manning the tower at Westland is AWOL. Jubal McClaren is to be personally informed that his daughter Jariel McClaren is also missing along with a female servant by the name of Shaye. The messenger who came by horse will wait in the tower for a response.

Within twenty minutes, a reply is signaled to Wesland and the alarm bell on the post sounds. The bell is the signal for all soldiers to muster in the courtyard and every man on the post has three minutes from the first sound of the bell to get there, dressed and ready to receive orders.

There are forty-six men stationed in Westland, and all but the missing signalman answer the call of the bell. Also present, at the request of the General himself, is Basil, a Genon man whose family has worked in service of the McClaren family for three generations. Basil and his father are the best trackers in all of Aegea—and until his father arrives, Basil will lead the search for Jariel.

Capt. Fleming stands on the porch of his office, facing the men. He raises his voice so that all of them can hear him.

"Listen up! A lot has happened and I need ALL of you to pay attention. Early this morning, General Fairmont died and Jubal McClaren became General of Aegea."

A few whoops go up from the crowd, but he quickly silences them.

"We have no time to mourn the loss of Fairmont *or* to be glad for McClaren. Sometime this morning, McClaren's daughter, Jariel, went missing. Also missing are a female servant *and* the signal officer for the first shift in the tower, Specialist John Grimes.

"Does anyone assembled here have ANY information that you suspect would have a bearing on these disappearances? Any clues, conversations, or things you've seen that you think might help us? If so, now is the time to speak up!"

He waits momentarily for any response, but there is none, so he continues, "At this time, we suspect that all of these disappearances are connected in some way. Until further notice, there will be two men on each gate of the post and two men in the tower at all times. Before sunset, we *will* question every person who lives or works at Westland. If anyone on this property has *any* information that might be pertinent, I want to know about it. We will also begin to search every building from roof to root cellar, and then every inch of ground, if necessary.

"We will work on emergency status until further notice. With the exception of the signalmen, *anyone* not on a scheduled sleep shift or actively manning the gate will be involved in locating Jariel McClaren, Specialist Grimes, and the servant girl . . . what's her name again?"

Basil steps closer to him. "Shaye is her name."

"The servant's name is *Shaye*," Fleming repeats. "She is a seventeen year old Genon with gold eyes and long black hair. All men are to arm themselves and be on the alert for any clues. ANYthing you find is to be brought to my attention immediately. All sergeants will report to Capt. Bowes for details on shifts and assignments. Within twenty minutes, I want every soldier on this post working his assignment."

### 

Inside the house, the colonel's wife is sitting alone on the floor of the salon staring into the cold fireplace. A message from her husband is on the floor nearby. It reads:

> To Duana McClaren.
>
> Pack enough clothing for a week. An escort will bring you and Jariel to town, departing at the ninth hour tomorrow. Have much more to tell you when you arrive.
>
> Signed, General McClaren.
>
> End of message.

In addition to everything else, the pregnant servant, Beth is in labor.

# CHAPTER 5
## The Latest News

As he promised earlier, General Jubal McClaren sent for his son to come to his office at the Academy. Until now, there has been no time for private conversation. The younger McClaren is so excited, he feels almost as if he could *float* to the office. His father is the general! It could change *everything*.

Once Ty is through the door of his father's office, however, he's swallowed up by concern. Jubal is standing by the window with a solemn look on his face. It's as if he were standing beside a grave.

"What's wrong, what's happened?" Ty asks.

Jubal steps closer to his son, but his eyes watch the door until it closes. "Ty," he begins. He has to stop and take another breath before he can say it. "Something has happened to your sister."

"Tell me! What is it?"

"Someone has taken her and no one has been able to find her."

Ty shouts, "NO!" before he steps within inches of his father and asks, "When did this happen? Are we mounting a search? Who would do this?"

Jubal touches the pocket where Duana's note sat for several hours. "I'm not certain," he says, then looks directly into his son's eyes. "We have to be *very* careful not to panic or to reveal our plans. All I know for certain is that Shaye and Jariel had an altercation this morning and Shaye struck Jariel. No one can locate *Shaye*, either."

Ty finally finds the air to ask, "What? What are you saying?"

The general turns away. "I'm not sure, Ty. It's like pieces of data are scattered about . . . and I don't know what to make of them yet."

Jubal's aide, Seph, knocks twice before opening the door a crack. "Sir. It's the signal officer. He's here with another message."

Jubal replies, "Send him in," before he looks at Ty and points to a chair in the corner. "Sit right over there. I'll let you stay, but don't say a single word or make a move."

Ty seats himself before the signal officer enters the room.

The officer looks at Ty and then to the general but doesn't speak.

Jubal nods and says, "Go ahead."

"Sir, here is a message from Westland that I received and decoded just minutes ago."

The colonel takes the message and reads it aloud:

Code Delta.

For Signal Officer and McClaren only

Body of Westland signalman found near the stables with a fatal blow to head. Uniform missing. Other packages not located. Capt. Fleming organizing a thorough search of the compound and surrounding area. Your trackers Basil and Tre are now working to follow leads until help arrives.

All soldiers at Westland on emergency alert. Per orders, extra guards have been posted in the Great House, all gates to the compound and the post.

Awaiting further instructions.

# CHAPTER 6
# A Ride in a Coach

The horses pulling the coach gallop down the stone-paved road at full speed, the man with the reins continues to shout and drive them on. Instead of the stately ride the general planned for Duana and Jariel tomorrow morning, Duana must make the trip today, and no one is with her. She's bouncing around inside the carriage like a dried bean dropped in an empty jar.

A full military escort with weapons at the ready ensures that the general's wife will arrive in town without incident before dusk. At this dizzying rate of speed, she will traverse nearly the whole length of the plateau to join her husband at the academy in less than two hours. Despite the discomfort, if the wheels wouldn't break and fall off the coach, Duana would have the men go even faster. She's almost grateful for the jarring ride—it's helping to keep her mind off the horrors that may have befallen her child.

She must speak to Jubal. She must see for herself that their son is safe. They must find Jariel.

*We should be there soon. We've reached the edge of Midtown.*

Reinforcements have already traversed the plateau in the opposite direction and arrived at Westland. Among them are more armed soldiers, a doctor, and Kosh—a Genon man whose family has worked with Jubal McClaren's for three generations. Kosh and his son, Basil, are reckoned to be the best tracker/hunters in all of Aegea and both of them are already searching for Jariel.

### 

A soldier arrives at the office of General Jubal McClaren with a message: The coach carrying his wife has been sighted on the road leading to the Academy. Throngs of well-wishers have already gathered on the road that leads to the Academy. Duana's arrival will not be a private one.

Jubal leaves his office and hurries to the cobblestone driveway just outside the entrance to his apartment. The McClaren family won't be moving to the home reserved for Agea's leader until the family of the former general moves out. Until then, his quarters at the academy will be their home in town.

Cheers go up as the coach approaches the gates and soldiers swing them open. Horses clatter into the courtyard before the driver hauls on the reins, bringing them to a full stop. A young soldier quickly opens the door as the new general approaches, and Duana practically falls out of the carriage compartment into his arms. His tense smile is a visible reminder of the message he sent her earlier, warning her not betray anything that has gone on in Westland. She's pale and obviously shaken, but she manages to smile back.

Jubal continues to hold her in his arms. With all the calm he can muster, he says, "I know it was a rough ride, but you're here now and you can relax." He turns to speak to the soldier holding the door. "My man will take her bags inside, but stay with them until they are picked up."

The young man salutes as Jubal turns and carries his wife into the apartment.

Just days ago, Duana wouldn't have dreamed that such a triumph could turn out like this. Under other circumstances she would have glided out of the carriage and coolly grasped Jubal's extended hand. Once inside, she might have allowed him to briefly embrace her, and she would have warmly congratulated him. But now, she has no words . . . and she doesn't want him to let her go.

As soon as they're inside the door, Jubal sets her on her feet and their son, Ty, rushes to greet her. He's never seen his mother look so disheveled, and as soon as Duana sees him, she starts to sob. Another first.

Jubal quickly picks her up again and carries her into the drawing room.

"Duana," he says when he sets her down on the sofa. "I know this is hard, but please, until everyone else is out of the house—"

There is a knock at the door.

"Ty," Jubal says, "stay here with your mother until I return." He takes long strides to the entryway and closes the door to the drawing room before letting the soldier with the bags enter the apartment.

Once the general is back with his wife and son, he pulls a chair close to Duana and says, "Now tell me. Tell me everything that happened. Try to remember every detail."

The young captain at the post will undoubtedly report all that Duana told him in an attempt to defend his own actions, so she might as well say it now and get it over with.

"Jariel and I argued last night. I told her that young man she's been infatuated with—Gilbert Lott—wouldn't be coming to see her. She had a tantrum and said some very ugly things." Duana stops short of telling Jubal that she slapped Jariel, but she's not sure why. It isn't as if Jubal doesn't believe in discipline. "I told her she couldn't come downstairs until she apologized for the ugly things she said."

"And what happened this morning?"

"I wanted to send a signal to you about what happened with Shaye, but that awful captain wouldn't let me."

"I'm sorry Duana," her husband says quietly. "You know all the men have standing orders not to allow family members to send signal messages unless it's a dire emergency. I can't fault him for doing what he was told." Jubal leans closer in and says, "Now, is there anything else that happened in the past day . . . any odd detail, any unusual happening that you can recall?"

She slowly rubs her temples. "I keep going over it in my head. I can't think of anything else. . . . It all happened after Shaye attacked Jariel."

"Shaye 'attacked' her." Ty repeats with skepticism.

"Don't say it like that. Why is everyone so quick to assume Jariel was at fault? Shaye was cleaning in Jariel's weaving room and did something mischievous. When Jariel confronted her, Shaye struck her and knocked her down before running out of the house." Duana's eyes moisten again. "I'm certain Shaye's had a hand in all of this. She knows that the two of you are easily swayed by Mosha so she's been skulking around for months now and stirring up Mosha's sympathy."

"Stirring up Mosha's sympathy for *months* now? About what?" Ty asks.

Duana looks back and forth between her husband and her son. "I assumed your father told you. It was time we moved Shaye out of that dark, cramped little storeroom in the house and into a nicer room in the new servant's quarters."

Ty glares at his mother. "And what prompted you to do that?"

"This isn't the time or the place to worry about Shaye's room," his father says.

Ty leans in toward his mother. "Wait. This doesn't make sense. If moving Shaye to a new room was such a blessing to her, why was she 'skulking' about? What makes you think she was trying to stir up Mosha's sympathy? I've known Jariel her whole life and Shaye since we were toddlers. Over the years, I've seen Jariel do *plenty* of things to provoke Shaye, but even in the depths of anger or sorrow Shaye would never do something like this."

"You're right," Jubal quickly interjects. "We won't jump to conclusions. The last thing we need is to be influenced by assumptions made in a swirl of emotion."

Duana's posture stiffens but Jubal attempts to return to his line of questioning. "Is there anything else? What did you do after the incident with Jariel and Shaye?"

Duana glances at Ty and looks away. "I've already told you."

Jubal puts a hand on hers. "Please. Indulge me. We need to be certain we haven't missed something. You sent for Nob the butcher, and then what? Did he come right away? Who did you speak to, did you see anyone else?"

Duana takes a deep breath and stares at the floor. "As you know, Nob made an offer for Shaye months ago. He hoped to make a match between her and his son, so he wanted her to come and work for him, but we turned him down. After Shaye attacked Jariel, though, I thought it would be best if she finished paying off her debt working for Nob. I sent for him and he came to the house right away. He was still anxious to make a deal, so I agreed."

"Why did you do that?" Ty asks. "Shaye wanted to move to town. She was trying to find work here and live with her aunt . . . you could just have let her make a trade *months* ago. But you did something like that to her instead? Everyone in Westland knows that Nob's son is a vile person! Why would you do that to Shaye? How could you do that to Mosha?"

Duana turns to glare at her husband. "She was looking for work in town? You had to have known! Why didn't you tell me? One word from you and she'd have been hired by anyone in town in the blink of an eye. For seven years I endured it while you let that girl live in my home. You never should have let Mosha bring her into our house. . . ."

She stops talking when Ty stands up, fists clenched and says, "NOW it makes sense. This isn't about placating Mosha, is it, General?" With mounting defiance, he says, "You made sure Shaye couldn't leave Westland, and you made sure I didn't leave the Academy. Always a man for details and the 'long term plan,' you arranged it all . . . even dinners with Lindsey—because you knew, and you thought you could *fix* everything." He stares into his father's eyes. "That's it isn't it?"

Jubal shrugs. "I did it for your own good."

"Knew *what*? Did *what*?" Duana demands.

Ty is shaking with rage. "I've loved Shaye nearly all my life. I love her . . ."

Until this moment, Duana thought things couldn't possibly be worse. She sits in stunned silence, as her son's words sink in. They convey a truth as terrible to her as any news she has received thus far today.

Ty's focus is so centered on Jubal, he doesn't see anything else. ". . . but I let you sweep me into your grand plan."

"Son, love is not enough when the world is at war with you—"

"Stop it, *stop it!*"

Jubal tries to speak in a calm voice, "Just calm down, Ty."

His son takes swift steps to the door, but turns before he opens it. "You've told me more than once that you were preparing me for something greater. You said I should wait until I could get to a place of authority, and *then* work to make the world better. . . . But it occurs to me that if I lack the conviction or courage to do what I know is right—in *this* time and *this* place—then I can't be trusted to do what is right in the future. I will do whatever it takes to find her."

Duana can barely eke out the words, "You don't know what you're saying."

Ty pulls on the door latch. "Unless you lock me in the fort, you won't stop me."

# CHAPTER 7
## Dooley's Dilemma

> "Sometimes, your greatest triumphs will remain secret. If you must always get credit for your work, don't be an inventor in Aegea."—*Reginald Dooley, father of Sage Dooley*

It's the end of his historic but long day for Sage Dooley. Dell, steers the long-bed wagon through the back roads of Midtown carrying a spool of rope, the large basket, and the kite that Sage flew this morning. Shadows stretch before the men as they weave their way around to the south side of the hill. They travel up and around several hairpin turns and are nearly at the top of the hill when Dell slows the horse and pulls the wagon to a stop.

After he and Dell dismount the wagon, he helps carry the kite and the basket into the large wooden building that serves as his lab. The spool with all the rope is too heavy for them to lift without help, so they'll need to cover it with a tarp for the night.

While Dell searches for the tarp, Sage wanders over to his desk and sees the small round object he left there yesterday. He grins as he snatches it up and puts it in his pocket.

Once they're back outside, the two men hurry to cover the spool in the fading light, then head their separate ways. Even riding the horse, it will take Dell twenty minutes to get home. Sage's house is just a short walk up a path through the trees. It takes him longer to climb the path tonight. The adrenalin rush that made him feel nearly invincible while he dangled from the kite subsided hours ago and now the foot he injured years ago pulses with pain. He's feeling the weight of every step. Before he clears the trees that border the alleyway that runs behind the wall of his garden he considers what might happen. If sentries spot him, what will they do? Make him live in seclusion, surrounded by guards night and day? The thought amuses him and he moves across the alley.

He approaches the eight-foot tall fence that runs behind his house and fumbles in his pockets for the key to the gate while he talks to himself.

"It's here somewhere. You locked it this morning, so I know you had it." He stops for a moment. "Unless you dropped it over the edge while you were in the basket." He briefly pictures a key slipping from his pocket and falling silently out of sight toward the Poison Forest below.

A voice jolts him back to the present. "Halt! Identify yourself!"

It's a nervous, squeaky sort of voice that Sage doesn't recognize. Someone in uniform is approaching and Sage squints to see a man silhouetted against the evening light. Once the unfamiliar face comes into focus, he smiles. *This one looks like he just graduated from the academy yesterday.* He gives the kid a wry smile and stands with his hands slightly raised. "You're new. I'm Sage Dooley, and this," he says, pointing at the gate, "is my house." He can tell by the expression on the young man's face that further explanation will be necessary. He points back to the path he just took through the trees, "I'm coming up from my lab. It's down there."

Another soldier trots up, and says to his comrade, "That's Sage Dooley. Let him pass."

"I'm sorry, Mr. Dooley," the young soldier offers. "They just assigned me today. We're here to protect you—to keep out intruders and such. You can go ahead."

Sage fights the urge to smirk as he considers what just happened. *That was incredibly easy. Should I pride myself on my escape this morning . . . or be worried that nobody figured out I was gone?* He checks the right front pocket in his trousers and finds the key, then waves at the two soldiers and unlocks the gate. "Well then. I'll be going in now."

Sage steps through the gate into the small garden at the back of a two-story stone home and begins to whistle as he limps along a stepping-stone maze through the tall plants, stopping twice to pick flowers. Just as he makes the last little turn in the maze, he hears her voice.

"I *thought* I heard someone whistling . . ."

His wife, Tressa, stands in the middle of the wide porch, arms folded.

"I could be a dangerous man with a weapon or a wild creature." he replies. "Do you have a knife handy?"

She flips dark blond hair behind her slender shoulder and tries to muster a fierce expression. "Are you saying you could *have* a wild creature . . . or that you might *be* one?"

He steps onto the porch and holds out the flowers. "Neither. But you should always be prepared." She hugs him and he continues, "Especially, since they've started 'protecting' us with green recruits." He lingers in her arms for a moment and inhales the fragrance on her skin before he pulls back to look into her pale blue eyes. "You know, I got clean away this morning, and just now I walked right up to the back gate . . . and until that moment, I don't think they realized I was gone. The kid they had watching the gate didn't even know who I was."

She nods. "It's because they've pulled the regular guards to use them elsewhere. General Fairmont died this morning."

"I know."

"Who told you?"

"No one. I could see the flag." He leaves out the part about dangling from a kite way up in the sky when he saw it. "I wonder who'll be the next general," he says. I sure hope it's not Mosely. If he had his way, he'd pull everyone back behind the walls and sit in a tavern with his cronies until everything in the Archives had completely rotted away and the Genon were mad enough to burn down the whole plateau."

She opens her mouth to say something, and he holds up his hands. "I'm sorry. I know he's your mother's second cousin, but—"

"Didn't you see the new flag that's up now?" she interjects. "It's already done. It *isn't* Mosely. Jubal McClaren is general now. His flag is up at the general's compound."

Her husband's eyes widen. "Really? Of the four colonels, I like him the best. He's still military, to be sure," he says, wagging a finger in the air, "but he's got a good mind and he's not afraid of innovation. Maybe we'll be able to save some of the records that are almost in ribbons now." Sage's mind is already whirling toward new projects. "Maybe he'll let me make a few things that Aegea can actually use."

"You mean you want to invent *practical* things—like kites that people can ride . . . or use to plummet to their deaths?"

It takes less than a second for him to process her statement and come to the most logical conclusion. "You *read* my letter?"

She lets out an exasperated sigh and rolls her eyes. "I'm a *woman*, Sage. You slip out of bed while it's still dark, skulk into another room, scribble something down and hide it in the basket on your table before you sneak out of the house. What about this *doesn't* beg for investigation?"

He chews at the corner of his lip as he thinks aloud. "Should I be mad that you read it? Grateful you *didn't* have a knife just now? Concerned by how cunning you've gotten?" He cocks his head to one side and gives her his best don't-be-mad-at-me smile. "Help me out here."

She searches his eyes and places a tender hand on his shoulder. "I know you feel trapped by your life. It's not like I want you to live in a cage . . ." she stops and takes a measured breath. She's not angry . . . she's scared. "I'd like to think you weren't quite so anxious to sneak off and throw yourself at anything that seems dangerous. I love you, and I want you to live, Sage. You're all I have."

His head slumps forward. "I'm sorry. It's not that I don't *want* to tell you. I just can't help myself sometimes and I don't want you to worry." He folds her in a tight embrace and they rock back and forth for a while before he says, "You're all I have, too."

She slips out of his arms and walks toward the back door of the house and he follows. Just when they reach the door, she spins around and says, "So . . . *was it fun?*"

At first he doesn't know how to respond, but she begins to smile.

"Oh *man!*" he says, sounding more like a nine-year-old than an adult, "I was *flying*, Tressa, I was *flying!*"

"Come inside and tell me what the world looks like from up there."

As she watches him walk through the door, she notices his limp is more pronounced than usual. "Did your foot run out of juice for the day?"

"Well, yeah. I did a lot of hopping around I suppose." He chuckles. "Didn't feel it at the time, though."

They walk through the bottom floor of their home and Tressa leads him to a large sofa in a room laden with odd gadgets and half-finished projects. Once he's seated, she kneels down and carefully removes his shoes. His left foot is definitely swollen.

"Mary," Tressa calls out, "will you bring a basin of water please?"

A young woman soon appears with a basin of cool water for what has become a nightly ritual when Sage is keeping "regular" hours. The rough bottom of the bowl makes a gritty noise when Mary sets it on the tile floor and Tressa maneuvers it into position.

Once Mary is out of the room, Tressa rolls up Sage's pant leg, peels off his sock, and gently grasps his leg just above the ankle.

He squeezes both eyes shut. "Don't damage me."

She smiles as she lowers his foot into the basin and he makes faces.

"If you didn't abuse the foot so much, it might not try to get all this revenge."

"I know, I know."

She rises to her feet and folds her arms as she looks at him. "And have you eaten at all today?"

"Well . . . I had a piece of bread before I went out the door this morning."

"And you starved poor Dell all day, too?"

He shrugs.

"I swear," she says, "I don't know why Dell is so good to you."

He pulls on her arm until she falls onto the sofa next to him. "I don't know why you are so good to me either," he says softly, "but I'm grateful."

She kisses him on the nose and hops up before she says, "Hold those sweet sentiments in the spot where you file 'essential' information and I will be right back with food."

### 

An hour later, their dinner plates are littered with sooshi hen bones, vegetable skins, and bits of bread are resting on a small table near the sofa.

He suddenly remembers something and he starts to root around in his front right pocket. "Hey. I have something for you."

"A bit of a cloud perhaps?"

"Nah. I gave that to Dell."

She squints and gives him *the look*. "Well you can sure make a woman feel special."

"No. Really. This is *way* better."

She leans closer. "What is it?"

"I was going to tell you that this is what I worked on all day."

"You planned on *lying* to me?"

"Well, yes and no. I would have buckled as soon as you asked me anything and blurted out the truth. But I *have* spent a lot of time on this. Henry figured it out from the archives . . . but we had to wait for the ingredients from the forest."

Henry, a chemist, is probably the only man in Aegea considered on an intellectual par with Sage and he's one of Sage's few friends. He lives around the corner from them, happily abiding on "the dark side" of the hill, since he spends much of his time indoors and mostly works at night. Sometimes, the two men won't see each other for a month or more, but then they'll spend round-the-clock days together alternately investigating some new concept, arguing about it, laughing about it, or experimenting with it. Apparently, they've come up with something new.

"What is it?"

With no shortage of drama, her husband thrusts his hand forward and opens it as if it contains a jewel.

A short laugh with snort escapes before Tressa pops her hand over her mouth. "It's a ball, Sage. It's small, I'll grant you, but people have been using balls for games since . . . since forever." She laughs again and says, "You need to get out and mingle more." Now she straightens her posture and prepares to be wowed. "So. What did you *really* bring me?"

He moves the ball closer to her. "This."

She looks confused. And disappointed. "*That?*"

"This! Watch!" He quickly flings it toward the floor—and just as fast as it went down, the object bounces back up and he grabs it again.

Now she looks stunned. "What *is* that?"

He holds it out to her again. "I told you. It's a ball. But *this* one is made of something called *rubber*," he says, flinging it down again and catching it, "which makes it *bounce*. I made it with sap from a special tree that grows in the forest." He smiles while he rolls the ball between his finger and thumb. "Henry read about the substance in the Archives more than a year ago and we've had gatherers scouring the forest for the right kind of tree and a particular vine ever since. The substance has enormous possibilities."

Wanting to hold the ball, she tosses her napkin over toward the table with the plates, but she miscalculates the trajectory, so the napkin arcs right over the table and onto the floor instead.

Sage frowns for a moment as he watches the napkin disappear behind the table. "You know, I saw something weird today."

Accustomed to his odd leaps in conversation, she merely asks, "What was it?"

"When I was up in the kite, I saw someone using the tram. They were sending a crate down into the Poison Forest."

"I thought the General Fairmont closed down the tram."

"Yeah. So far as I know . . . he did."

Sage closes his hand around the ball when they hear a gentle knock in the doorway. It's Mary.

"May I clear out the dishes and the basin?"

"Yes, thank you. Just put them in the kitchen and go home. I'll clean up later."

As soon as Mary is out of earshot, he says to his wife, "Why do we have a servant if you do the work?"

The serene look on Tressa's face disappears. "Despite what many are saying now, you and I both know that among the Firstlanders, the women did all sorts of things—they were soldiers, and scientists, and technicians. But in order to preserve life itself, women were placed on "protected" status. Well, that is, unless they were Genon women. Genon women were still expected to work stride for stride along with men. For all these generations now they've worked, planted, harvested, *and* given birth to children that they are expected to ignore when one of us demands it. Mary has two small children to care for, and if she were in *my* place, caring for those children would be about the only thing she was *allowed* to do. I have no children, but I'm expected to preside here and smile at fancy dinners while she's treated like a pack animal that has to work in order to eat. My great-grandma was a member of the 2nd Jump Battalion—yet I'm expected to sit here with an empty womb in a large house. Somehow—*somehow*, we have to find some middle ground in our world, Sage. Even if we had children, I'm *more* than a baby factory. And Mary is *more* than a servant. She's also a mom with hopes and dreams, too." Tressa shakes her head. "I'm right here, but, by all means, go call Mary back and we'll make her clean the dishes."

Scooting closer to her, he sweeps some of her hair behind her ear. "How can I be so in love with you and yet manage to scuff your heart so much?"

She wraps her arms around his neck. "Despite what others might think, I wasn't meant to live in a cage, either. I long to fly outside of it, too, Sage."

He leans forward till his forehead touches hers. "So where would you like to fly?"

"I want to fly out into a world where each of us is more than an object with just one use."

### 

Hours after Sage and Tressa Dooley finished their dinner in their home in Midland, the only son of Aegea's new general, Ty McClaren walks up the stairs to his quarters at the Academy feeling completely spent. After the argument he had with his parents, his father followed him outside and they talked. While the gulf in their relationship remains, his father did promise to keep no more secrets and pledged to provide any resource needed as they worked together to unravel this frightful mystery.

Ty doesn't like the fact that he has an armed escort, but realizes it may not only be necessary at this point, it's probably *expected* since Jubal is now the leader of Aegea. Above all, Jubal convinced him that they need to be fully aware of the fact that—if Jariel can be plucked right out of the Great House of Westland—none of them are completely safe. If they have *any* hope of getting her back, they must keep up the appearance that things are proceeding as they should. The family needs to appear calm. Secrecy may be the only thing keeping desperate people from desperate measures.

He opens the door to a dark room, but he sees the dim outline of a folded piece of paper on the floor just inside the threshold as one of the guards enters the room with a lamp. At first, he figures the paper is one of the notices about schedules and grades that are commonly slid under doors here.

While the guard quickly searches the small room, Ty stares at the note thinking, *At this point, who cares about a change of venue or schedule for some class?*

Before exiting the room, the guard picks up the note and hands it to him. Ty lights the lamp on his desk before he closes his door then tosses the paper near the lamp and sits down. After a few moments, however, he picks it up and reads it.

> *To the McClaren family:*
>
> *We have her. You can waste time looking for her, but you won't succeed. If you know what is good for HER you won't make any announcements to the other officers. We will contact you shortly with our demands.*

Ty stands and quickly tucks the note in his pocket before he goes out to the guards and asks to be taken back to his father.

# CHAPTER 8
# In the Land of Cloud and Leaf

"In the world of men, wherever you find great beauty, danger and darkness are not far away."—*A proverb of His own people*

## The Great Forest

Thousands of feet below the plateau where soldiers are just beginning their search, thunder rolls in the sky above the dense growth of jungle, and the shade of the forest grows even darker. First, Shaye and the others hear the applause of rain drops tapping upon the canopy of leaves above them. Next, a cool mist begins to float down from the canopy. In the first minute, despite the sound of a storm above, surprisingly little of the water hits the ground. Then, the travelers feel tangible spritz of moisture on their skin. As the downpour continues, broad leaves on some of the trees, turn into rain gutters that collect drops of rain, then tilt to spill streams of water below.

With claps of thunder shaking the ground around them, the men quickly weave together lattices of hard vines, then snap off the stems of long leaf plants, and pull them through the grid work to make umbrellas. Soon, the group resumes walking.

As the shock of all that's happened today wears off, grief grows in Shaye's heart. Every step takes her farther away from all she's ever known, from every person she's ever loved, from the sacred ground where her mother and her father are buried with the kin of four generations. When Shaye hid in a cargo crate to get away from Duana McClaren, she felt certain it was on its way to town. She *never* would have guessed that the box was destined for the place her people call "the land of cloud and leaf"—the Great Forest that sprawls away from the mountains.

This place is just as her mother described it: full of fearsome beauty and the potential for sudden death at every turn—a place where few from Aegea would *ever* dare to come. For five generations "gatherers" from the Genon race have come here on short expeditions to harvest valuable plants and animals.

Six decades ago, more than two hundred Genon were taken deep into this forest and exiled. They were abandoned with no tools, supplies, or food—because they dared to challenge the rule of the military. They were told that if any one of them was seen again, he or she would be slain on the spot. Even with their knowledge of the forest and formidable survival skills, they disappeared, seemingly without a trace. It was presumed by the ruling military authorities that the Exiles eventually fell victim to the fearsome predators, toxic plants, and many diseases of the forest.

Throughout the generations since then, however, rumors persisted among the Genon in Aegea that "the Exiles" had survived and that their offspring *still* inhabited the forest, killing any soldier who saw them. When Genon gatherers sent into the forest to do the military's bidding occasionally disappeared, the military maintained that they, as well, had fallen victim to one of the many dangers there.

But some of the Genon on the plateau held out the hope that their disappearing relatives hadn't died and chose to hope, instead, that they'd joined the ranks of the Exiles. To this day, among the Genon people stories about the Exiles are still whispered around fires at night and they ask themselves, *If the military really believed the Exiles no longer existed, why did they keep such a wary eye on the trails that snake down the cliff into the forest below the lofty plateau? Why do they still guard the gates at the wall that surrounds the plateau?*

Shaye's grandfather, a gatherer many years ago, told her mother that an Exile saved him once. And her mother also said she'd seen one in the Great Forest once, but neither encounter involved talking . . . lending credence to what others whispered about the Exiles: that they wouldn't suffer anyone who lived on the plateau to speak to them . . . and they didn't allow any soldier who saw them to live.

As a child, joining the Exiles in freedom was a wish that Shaye never believed would come true. Her imaginary quest was framed in the golden light of a young girl's mind—a dream of escaping her sorrows and going to a place where lasting joy and freedom would abound.

How different reality is from the perfection of dreams.

Shaye steps over a skinny, fallen tree. *I've dreamed of being with the Exiles nearly all my life. I dreamed of being an upright woman, free to walk among my own people. Yet here I am with the Exiles—and it may be the worst day of my life. In a single day I have been ripped from nearly all that I love, faced sheer terror, killer creatures, and now a trek to some faraway place.*

They're traveling, as much as possible, in single file. As she carefully steps behind the man in front of her, she chides herself. *Everything could have turned out differently, if I hadn't made such terrible mistakes, if I hadn't told myself I was in love with Ty. I wouldn't be here if I hadn't allowed myself to believe that he loved me, too. If I hadn't been so desperate, I wouldn't have struck Jariel . . . and been traded. I wouldn't have been forced to run away.* For a while, Shaye is actually grateful for the cold rain that allows her tears to mingle with the trickles of water that run down her face. No Genon should be seen crying.

*If only I could make the sun and moon go backwards until the night it all started and live it over again. . . . If I hadn't gone out to meet Ty on the roof, I could have worked until my time of service to the McClarens was up and left with no regrets, no shame. Instead, I've endured all these months of sleepless nights, and fearful days. For what? I should have known he'd never come back. And then I gave Mrs. McClaren an excuse to trade me—to Nob the butcher!* A picture of Nob's brute of a son rises in her mind. *I had to run away . . . and hiding in that crate seemed like an answer to my prayers . . .*

She remembers the weight of a heavy object being dropped into the crate on top of her, having the wind knocked out of her lungs, gasping . . . and then falling into a gas-induced sleep. She awoke in a daze, and while she was still reeling with the effects of the fumes, she crawled out of the box to find herself in—of all places—the Great Forest. It was then she saw a man appearing out of the jungle mist and walking toward her. He was smeared with the orange clay soil of the jungle, his clothing, weapons, and countenance made him seem like an ancient Genon warrior—like the ones in stories she heard as a child. She immediately knew he was an Exile. He spoke to her urgently in their common, ancient tongue, reminding her that the Maker was watching—that she would be responsible for the life of the other woman with her. *"What woman?"* she'd asked.

No one could have been more surprised than Shaye when she found out that the object thrown into the box on top of her was Jariel.

She just can't figure it out. *Why would someone take Jariel and hide her in a box? Why did they send the box to the forest?* In her wildest dreams she couldn't have imagined this turn of events.

The warrior made it clear that Jariel's life was in her hands. From what her mother told her, Shaye already knew the Exiles would kill any non-Genon who saw them, or anyone who might report back to the soldiers about their presence. Maybe the warrior overheard the conversation of those who brought the crate into the forest. Maybe he heard them say Jariel was a soldier's daughter. In any case, he seemed to know the other Exiles wouldn't accept her . . . and that they would either kill her or leave her there to die if they knew the truth. The warrior said it was Shaye who would decide if Jariel lived or died.

*And so you lied. You lied—to preserve your enemy! And now the Exiles—whom the soldiers would destroy—are doing all they can to rescue her because you told them she is one of our people.*

Shaye looks at Jariel's limp body on the stretcher the Exiles made to carry her. Even though the old man did what he could to treat a spider bite on Jariel's neck, the girl is unconscious and pale as death. *She may not survive.*

None of the Exiles invited her and Jariel to tag along . Since the women were taken into the forest as prisoners in a box, it seemed obvious that it was for some evil purpose. The men *assumed* Jariel and Shaye would *want* to come away with them—and live.

Shaye stops walking when she realizes that, if she and Jariel survive this journey, their fates will be forever intertwined.

*If she lives, how long will it be before they find out about her? What will they do when they find out she's not really from the clan of Nashe but the daughter of an officer? How can I tell them I never intended any harm? No one will ever believe another thing that I say.* Shaye takes a breath.

Despite the makeshift umbrella, her clothing is soaked right through by the tropical downpour. She's getting cold but the Exiles press on, driven by the need to put distance between themselves and that crate. They move fast as they can go with two men carrying Jariel on a stretcher followed by a weak and weary Shaye. They all know that, any moment, soldiers could be descending upon the scene where the box still sits.

They take hope in the fact that every hour that passes will bring further decay to the scene where they found Shaye and Jariel and saved them from a savage *k'mosh*. The Exiles press on and hope that the remaining clues will work in their favor. If soldiers find the mauled remains of the men who brought the crate into the forest, they'll also see the discernable evidence of the *k'mosh*—the giant creature with teeth and claws that killed their comrades. As long as scavenger animals don't carry off the bodies of the slain men, it won't take a leap of reasoning to see what happened and assume that the missing women were killed as well. The Exiles took care to bury the *k'mosh* and hope anyone searching will fear the beast is still lurking nearby. An Aegean with any sense at all would be afraid to remain in the vicinity where a beast such as this was on the prowl. Perhaps they will give up and go back where they belong.

The rain now washing over the forest will slow any searchers down *and* cover most of the signs of the Exiles' trail. Since there are still no indications of soldiers in pursuit, the

Exiles entertain the growing hope that they will get away with what they've found.

They've only stopped once to rest and reapply insect repellent provided by a brisk rub of certain leaves on all exposed skin. Shaye had to apply it on her own skin and Jariel's. The greenish tint from the leaves on Jariel's pale skin makes her look like the featured attraction at a funeral. The girl is very ill. Seeing her like this, Shaye realizes that, as much as she hates Jariel, she's actually afraid the girl might die.

*If only Jariel could have been taken somewhere safe where anyone searching could have found her. If only the girl hadn't seen the Exiles. . . . But there may be no safe place for Jariel and she has seen the Exiles.*

The increasing flow of water down the sloping forest floor slows their progress. The need to thread their way around dense, thorn encrusted bushes and tangled curtains of spider webs delays them even more. Water continues to topple over rock formations and widen old gullies in the ground. The orange-red clay in the soil makes for slick going, and the muck that forms as it mixes with the rotting vegetation from the forest makes progress difficult.

She doesn't know how long they've been walking, but Shaye has no energy left. Two of her toes already have cuts, and she has a long scratch on her ankle. She steps over a mucky puddle, but the slick clay under her sandals denies her any footing and she begins skidding down the sloping ground.

A man walking behind her grabs her arm before she falls and says "*Eh, eh!*"

It's the first sound of a human voice since they left the box, and the men in front of the line turn to see what's going on. The hem of Shaye's shabby gray dress is drooping down with the weight of the water. Her long hair has fallen out of the customary knot, and now looks like a shiny black scarf draped over her head and shoulders, down to her waist.

The expedition's leader sees Shaye is soaked, cold, and exhausted. Although one of the men continues to shield Jariel's head from the rain with an umbrella, her dress is so wet it's completely molded to her bony frame.

The old man looks around and above before he gives two sharp whistles. Within a moment there is an answering whistle echoing through the trees. Everyone waits until one of the men who was scouting ahead comes back. After a brief conference with the old man, he leads them on a new course. Within minutes, they reach an outcropping where several large boulders sit, stacked upon one another as if a giant child had placed them there. Two of the boulders on the top of the stack lean together, leaving a space large enough between them for the travelers to shelter out of the downpour. Two men enter first to make sure it is safe, then the men carrying Jariel take her in and set her down on one side the space. Including the old man, there are only six men now. The others are out scouting or watching behind.

Shaye moves through the opening, and after she sees that Jariel is still breathing, she steps to the doorway and wrings some of the water out of the hem of her dress. Her fingers are wrinkled from the water and her teeth are chattering. Thunder booms above the trees and the sound of water continues to sizzle all around. The old man moves closer to her and speaks in their ancient Genon language. Although she's had trouble understanding the younger men, it's easier to understand him. *Perhaps*, she tells herself, *it's because he talks slower . . . or that he speaks a version of Genon that's closer to mine.*

"What is the name your mother gave you, child?" he asks.

"I am Shaye," she answers in Genon. Even as she says it, her mind is echoing, *I am Shaye . . . the liar.* She shivers.

The old man says. "I am Nathan, son of Peter, who was a Firstlander."

She nods in respect. *Oh, the stories of our people he must know. His father would have known my great grandfathers! His father would have lived in the time before Aegea and would have walked in the other world that Aunt Pearl spoke of . . .*

"You rest," Nathan says kindly. "We will wait for a while." He leans out of the small cave to peek up at the tops of the trees. "The rain will pass soon."

She looks at him—all determination and sinew, not an ounce of fat on him—with skin so leathery a mosquito probably couldn't succeed at getting a meal from him. His hair and beard are gray with streaks of pure white, and there is more hair on his chin than on his head, but his golden-hazel eyes are still bright and clear.

Everyone else in the cave is quiet, but it seems to her as if they are pulling closer, watching, listening. Aware that her soaked dress is clinging to her skin, she once again pulls on the hem, and then folds her arms across her chest and inches back toward Jariel. She's not accustomed to such close quarters with men.

*It would be rude,* she tells herself, *for men to stand so close to a woman at home.* And then she realizes, *I have no home.*

As if he can sense Shaye's discomfort, Nathan says, "Stand back," to the men. "Don't trample the girl."

They move a step back, but one of the men elbows through the group, closer to Nathan, then nods in her direction as he speaks. The only words she understands clearly are "Why is this? These are wrong [unknown words] for plateau Genon. They don't have [unknown words]?"

She fights the urge to panic. *Has he decided something is suspicious?* Given that Shaye can speak a good bit of Genon and has the classic black hair, and golden eyes of their race, there can be no question of her lineage . . . but could this man be wondering if they are some sort of spies? Is there something the Exiles were expecting she and Jariel to have that they *don't* have?

Nathan points to Shaye's bag and speaks to her, "Of the people who joined us over the years, most had [unkown word]. Do you have some in there?"

Her heart skips a beat. *Is this some sort of test?* She shakes her head and reminds him, "I don't know all your words." She glances over at Jariel wondering, *What will become of us?*

"*Hmmm,*" he says. He attempts to describe what he means. Holding one hand out and then making a fist with the other and moving it in a stroking motion over the first hand. "Carved with a knife. Uh . . . shoes of wood."

Shaye finally exhales. "Oh. I understand," she says, picturing the clogs most servants wear. The shoes she has on are leather sandals and Jariel doesn't have any shoes at all.

"No, we don't have them," she answers. "I have only these. The owner of the house where I served hated the sound of the wood shoes on his floors." She looks at Jariel and shrugs, "I guess she wasn't wearing any shoes when the men took her."

Nathan nods before he speaks to the man who inquired about the shoes. "You and Mule will help with the shoes."

Shaye frowns with the effort of concentration before a picture of an animal comes to mind. "You have a mule?" she asks. "Where is it?"

The men laugh as they poke one man in particular. He has the darkest hair of all the men.

"Oh. We have forgotten how it would sound to new people," the old man says when he nods in the direction of the man they were teasing. "His name is Samuel . . . but he was very stubborn as a child, so his father shortened his name to '*Muel,*' and so we've always called him Mule."

She looks around at the men and attempts a smile.

They turn as Jariel stirs, then sits up—but only long enough to have dry heaves. "Home," she moans as she flops back down.

Shaye kneels down beside her and says, "She needs water."

Several of the men simultaneously offer bottles made of animal skins. She takes the nearest one and props up Jariel's head. "Take a small sip at a time. Your body needs water."

Jariel takes several sips before she leans back and pleads, "Are you taking me home? *Please* take me home."

Shaye leans close and says, "But you *can't* go back. Remember?" She tries to hold Jariel's gaze. *Whether it is by accident or on purpose,* she tells herself, *Jariel will end up letting them know who she is . . .*

"I believe I understand," Nathan says.

Shaye looks up, ready to plead for their lives. Before she can throw herself at his feet and confess, he says, "My father told me that my mother never stopped grieving. Not until she went to be with the Maker, just a few months into the exile. He said that she wept for her mother and her sisters. She longed for dry ground, and the wind on her face . . . and seeing the sun. For many of them, it was like this. Even after we journeyed to our new home far away, they would come back here to find Genon brothers and sisters who *wanted* to join us—yet after they came, some of them still grieved for many days. I understand, daughters. Don't be ashamed of your sorrow. We've learned that, after the Exile, our people on the plateau decided it was bad to reveal emotions . . . but we are a people with deep hearts, deep passions. It's *because* we know the Maker that we feel so much."

The old man squats down and touches Jariel's face with the back of his hand, then holds her hand for a few moments before he peers at Shaye. "And I can see you are afraid when you look at her. Yes, the spider that bit her was a bad one. He could kill." The old man looks back down at Jariel and gently places her hand across her waist. "But this girl has a strength you cannot see. She will spring up again."

Shaye feels shaky and sits down on the cave floor, leaning her back against the side stone. Several of the men offer her a drink of water and some fruit. She drinks the water and gladly eats some of the fruit, and once she does, she feels remarkably better.

Within minutes, the sound of the rain diminishes and Nathan sticks his head out of the cave. He looks back at Shaye and asks, "Can you go on now? We have much ground to cover and very little time before it gets dark."

She stands up and nods. As they exit the rock enclosure, the old man offers her a hand so she can step back down onto the forest floor. Now that the rain has stopped, clouds of mosquitoes are on the prowl.

"We need more than the leaves to keep them off," Nathan tells her.

The group stops beside a small stream, swollen with water from the downburst. Several of the men start excavating mud from the bank of the stream and Nathan scoops up some of the red soil. "Rub this on," he says, plopping a large glob of it in her hands. "It works better than the leaves."

She watches as the men rub it on their exposed skin, and then does the same for herself and Jariel. When she stands up, Nathan bids her to stand still while he completes the task of smearing mud on her face.

"We will camp by a tree that the first exiles found," he tells her as he smears the last dab close to her mouth. "We call it the widow tree."

*Perhaps,* Shaye surmises, *one or more of the husbands died on the way there.* She finds her voice and asks, "Did you stop and mourn there?"

Nathan thinks for a moment before he realizes what she is thinking. "No child," he says, once again showing her his semi-toothless grin. "You will see. There is more in the world than you know now, and there is much to learn."

Within minutes of their departure from the cave the rain stops completely, but it's replaced by steam, rising from the forest floor. Insects continue to swarm in the oppressive air around them. Some of the more aggressive mosquitos are even biting her through her dress! Soon, it's time to rub more of the mud on her skin and Jariel's—and this time she even rubs some on their clothes. The clay on her dress seems to double its weight, and in this steam, their garments will stay damp for the rest of the day. She can only hope the clothes in her bag are still dry.

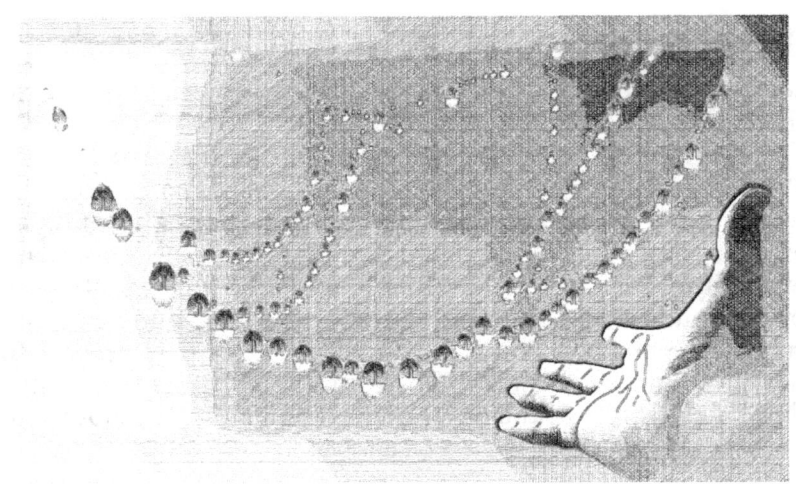

# CHAPTER 9
# The Widow Tree

"When you feel abandoned, you can know it is a test. You can know He is waiting to hear your heart singing to His in the midst of the darkness, as one would sing to a beloved in the night."—*Great Aunt Pearl, quoting the Tell*

It's as if they're in a deep cavern with only burning torches to illuminate the way. She must ignore the shifting shadows and the glints in small pairs of eyes reflected in the trees around them. Her ears are tuned to the soft roar of the torch she carries while she carefully steps behind the man in front of her. The last light of the day drained from the sky long hours ago, and a darkness she's never experienced before hovers just outside the flames. There is no moon, there are no stars under this deep canopy.

Shaye reminds herself, *Mama used to say, "Don't think about how frightened you are. That only makes it worse."* She has no idea which direction they've traveled or how far, but she's bone weary. In her heart, she hears something her mother used to say often. *"The Maker is everywhere, and you must trust that he knows where you are going, even when you do not."*

She hears voices up ahead, and then—finally—she sees the larger glow of a campfire where those who came ahead await them. Walking before her in the line of travelers, the two men carrying the litter with Jariel stop near the fire and set the litter down.

While greatly relieved that they've finally arrived, she rushes forward to look at Jariel. *How does she look? Is she still alive?* Shaye kneels down and takes the girl's hand to see if it's still warm. Much to her relief, Jariel's eyes open. *Perhaps she really will recover.*

The group around the fire watches the two young women while several more men straggle in from the trail. Once she's satisfied that Jariel is alive, Shaye realizes how completely spent she feels. Even if a great beast of the jungle dropped into their midst, she doesn't think she could flee from it.

The man who asked about Shaye's shoes earlier in the day and one other man—the one the old man Nathan called "Mule"—are diligently rubbing long plant fibers between their hands and making what appears to be thick twine. One of the men near the fire throws green leaves into the flames and the air fills with a smoky haze.

Nathan draws near to Jariel and says, "We should get her up now."

Several of the Exiles move in to help the girl sit up and she moans.

The brown-haired man who seemed as if he might cut Jariel to ribbons earlier (if she wasn't "one of His people"—a Genon) kneels beside her and tries to give her some water to drink. After she starts drinking, she puts both her hands on the bottle and upends it. It looks as if she might drain the whole thing.

"Wait," he says. "Drink slow! You will be sick."

Jariel doesn't know the Genon language and she doesn't care what he's saying. She keeps drinking.

The man looks at Shaye. "Tell her she should not drink all this." He uses simple words in Genon since she's had trouble understanding the rapid-fire speaking of the young men. The Exiles haven't seen newcomers from Aegea in nearly ten years, so Nathan had to remind the men that the language problem was common among new arrivals in the past. Over time, the Genon in Aegea were forced to abandon their native tongue and use only Command Dialect. New arrivals among the Exiles knew less and less of a language their people had spoken for millennia. Some of them knew only common phrases or a few words in Genon. Shaye has a basic understanding of the language, but she will need to adjust and learn more, as others before her have. Jariel will have to start from the beginning.

Shaye kneels beside Jariel and speaks in Command Dialect. "If you drink too much, you may get sick again."

Jariel stops drinking and reluctantly hands the nearly empty goat skin bottle back.

Several men simultaneously offer Shaye a drink. She accepts the closest bottle and takes several swallows of it before handing it back.

"Come now," Nathan tells her. "You should help your sister. . . ."

Shaye tries not to flinch at the term "sister" being used in reference to Jariel. He is still speaking so she concentrates on his words.

". . . so of course you both will want to tend to your *personal* needs before sleeping. But don't wander," he says, taking off a belt with his knife in a sheath on it. "Put this on," he says, handing her the belt. "You can dig a hole with the knife, and use it for a defense if need be. And come right back."

Another man points to a gigantic tree, standing like a sentinel near the camp. "I cleaned the ground behind that root for you just now. No spiders. No bad snakes. Go there. Don't walk far from it."

Shaye takes the belt from Nathan and looks around. It's hard to imagine that she woke up this morning on the Plateau . . . *how could this be?*

The brown-haired man and Shaye help Jariel to her feet. She's wobbly so Shaye slips an arm around her waist.

"Come with me. We must relieve ourselves," Shaye says.

Jariel frowns before a light of recognition comes into her eyes. She puts an arm around Shaye's shoulders and takes her first, faltering steps. As they leave the bright light of the fire, objects lose their color then assume monochrome tones as dim light envelops them. When they step behind the gigantic root that extends like a wavy tentacle from the trunk of the tree, Shaye can't see a thing, but when she turns around, the light of the fire can be seen above the top of the root. After several seconds, a few objects begin to take shape.

Jariel wobbles and tightens her trembling grasp on Shaye. "Please don't let go of me. Please."

Since they're a good distance away from the men, Shaye dares to whisper, "Do you remember any of this day? Do you remember what I told you earlier?"

After a short silence, she hears Jariel's weak response. "Yes."

"Just don't say anything that could reveal who you are. We don't know how many of them know words in your language. The old one, Nathan, remembers some."

Jariel stares in the direction of Shaye's voice, "Just don't let go of me, please don't let go."

"Don't think about how frightened you are," Shaye tells her. "That only makes it worse. We're alive—and yes, it's dark, but that's only because it's nighttime. We're only steps away from the firelight and we're among people who have already saved us more than once today. Just think about those things."

Jariel takes a deep breath. "What is that awful smell?"

"One of the men scraped the ground clean to be sure there were no spiders or other nests here. You smell the decaying, moldy leaves from the tree that he swept aside."

"Oh."

"I need to bend down and dig a hole," Shaye tells her, "If you must lean on something, the tree is on your left—but I wouldn't recommend keeping your hand on it if you can stand on your own." After one more attempt to look around, Shaye digs a hole with the knife and then helps Jariel turn and squat down and keeps holding onto her hands.

"Where are they taking us?" Jariel whispers.

"I don't know," Shaye whispers back. "We've been travelling downhill since they found us, and Nathan—the old man, the one who treated your spider bite—told me the trip would take 'many days.' We will be far away by the end of the journey."

After a few moments, Shaye feels Jariel's shaking arms take on a rhythmic pulse before she hears her crying. When the girl pulls herself up, her thick voice is inches away. "Please, Shaye, I beg of you, don't let them take me away. Find a way to make them take me back."

"A soldier came into your house, took you, threw you in a box, and sent you down the mountain where more soldiers brought you miles into the forest. Even if someone could take you back where they found us, would you be safe near the box? No. Would you be safe if they took you to the edge of the forest? No. Even if someone could get you back to your home in Westland . . . what makes you think you would be safe there now?"

Jariel doesn't respond.

"We have no idea what has happened on the plateau," Shaye tells her. "We have no idea what the soldiers wanted when they took you. A trade of some sort? Revenge on your father? We don't know. What I *do* know is that Nathan and the other men in this camp weren't part of whatever plan it was that took you from the plateau. These men think they *rescued* us—and they *did*. If they hadn't found us, we both would have been swallowed up by the things in this forest. All we can do is trust the Maker."

"Why would I do that? My people have no maker, and your maker obviously cares nothing for me."

Now it is Shaye who doesn't have an answer.

###

When the two women return to the light of the small fire, Shaye notices the men using small handfuls of water to remove some of the mud from their faces and hands in preparation for a meal, and Nathan tells her that the smoke from the fire should keep the bugs at bay for the night. That's when she notices the mud on her own arms looks like a cracked landscape. So does the mud on Jariel's face. *What must my own face look like?*

She and Jariel both wash off their faces and hands before Nathan offers them some sort of meat that one of the men skewered on a branch and seared over the fire. Shaye pulls a piece off the small carcass and sniffs it before she takes a bite. It's a bit gamey, but she knows she needs nourishment so she eats it. Jariel refuses to even taste it.

Nathan, speaks to Jariel in the broken speech of a language he hasn't needed in many years—the Command Dialect of the plateau. "Come, daughter. Eat." He points at the sizzling meat. "Him eat good!"

Once Jariel makes it clear that she won't eat, that she only wants to lie down, they hoist her up into a thick layer of green leaves they've placed on a frame of branches nestled in a tree, about six feet off of the forest floor, and instruct Shaye to tell her that it's a safe place to sleep.

Nathan studies Shaye's face in the firelight before he says, "Do not worry. She is mending now. She will wake up feeling much better tomorrow." He stands up and says, "You come now and I will show you something."

She's exhausted, but it would be considered very rude to say "no," so she complies. They walk to the very edge of useful fire light and he points to a looping latticework of branches, standing in a tall, hollow column that extends up into the darkness. "This is a widow tree."

Shaye knows better than to put her hand on anything unknown in the forest. "May I touch it?"

He smiles. "Yes, but don't put your fingers inside the holes, there could be creatures inside."

She reaches out and feels the cool, smooth bark and realizes that it is not a dead plant. She looks back at him, puzzled. "It is a *hollow* tree . . . yet alive?"

"Oh yes. She lives on. Tomorrow you will see she has so many leaves that she creates the darkest shade of all beneath her branches."

"So, why do you call her the widow tree?"

"This kind of tree starts up there," he says, pointing to the canopy above them. Birds or other creatures eat the fruit of these trees and then excrete the seeds in other trees, high above. The widow tree, she is very clever. As a seed, she makes a bed up there among the leaves of another tree where it is safe, then she sprouts and begins shooting out her roots—down, down, down," he says this while he demonstrates with his fingers moving toward the ground. The host tree cradles her in his arms and lets her soak up the light, and she likes him so much," Nathan now points to his temple, "she thinks, *I will make this my husband when I am older.*' Then she begins to wrap her branches around him and hold him tightly. For a while, they maybe are equals, but over time, she grows larger and stronger, and so does her grasp upon her husband—until, one day, he is entirely trapped. He cannot escape. Eventually, he dies in her arms and fades away,"

Nathan says, putting a hand on the tangled trunk, "leaving only the widow and her empty embrace."

Shaye gazes at the tree in astonishment. "I have never heard of such a thing in all my life."

"Yes, yes," he says. "You will see. The world is filled with wonders you do not know." He beckons her to walk back to the fire and squats down to chew on his share of the meat. Occasionally, he spits bits of gristle or bone out and places them on a small pile that the men will bury later.

Not wanting to waste any more water, the men rub the dried mud off their arms with their hands. Nathan tells her again that the smoke from the fire will keep insects away for the night. The men look dusty, but slightly better, so Shaye decides to do the same and is pleased to remove the cracked shell off of her arms before she seats herself on the small carpet of green leaves the men have spread on the forest floor.

Her eyes quickly sweep over the group. Most of them appear to be men in their twenties, with the obvious exception of Nathan. Several of them, including "Mule" and the man she mentally dubbed "Brown Hair" have lush beards so they must be in or nearing their thirties, while the youngest ones have sparse or nearly no growth on their chins. Nathan's beard, mostly gray, is quite long. He is undoubtedly an Elder of the people, and perhaps he brought them on this trek to share his vast wisdom about the forest—the same way an older gatherer from the plateau would have trained younger ones—the way her grandfather trained her mother and others.

"Will you tell us your name again?" Nathan asks.

"Shaye."

They all repeat it, saying, "*Shhhaaay,*" before Nathan asks, "What does that mean? Where does it come from?"

It has been so long since anyone has asked her this, she's forgotten how foreign it would sound to a community of Genon. It would be frowned upon for her to tell about her name in Aegea. Would it be a taboo topic here as well? "My father named me. My mother told me that it meant something like "thank you" in a language . . . from the other world."

The young men all turn to look at the old man. He nods. "Shaye. Yes. One would want to give thanks to the Maker for a fine daughter."

"Yes," one of them chimes in, choosing his words carefully and speaking slowly. "A woman with your beauty could even have been a queen in the old world."

"*Eh eh!*" Several of the men say before one of them throws a small stone at him.

Nathan loudly clears his throat before saying, "And what is the sister's name again?" the old man asks, poking his chin in the direction of where Jariel is resting.

"Jariel."

Now Jariel's name reverberates around the group.

"I don't know what it means," Shaye adds when she realizes they're all staring at her. She can feel herself tensing up again, as if any moment she will need to run away. Before there are more questions she decides to ask one of her own. During the course of the day, she's been told most of the men's names, but the only ones she can remember are Nathan and Mule. She asks, "Can I hear each of *your* names again?"

"I'm Enoch," the man farthest from her on the left says quickly. "But they call me 'Tooth'."

She's half expecting that he has only one tooth left in his head, but he smiles and reveals he has a full set of teeth. Before she can ask where he got the nickname, the man next to Tooth chimes in.

"His mother said he was born with a tooth *and* an appetite to go with it. And he is still trying to eat everything!"

All the men laugh and Tooth gives the guy a shove. As the man falls backward, he says, "My name is Philip."

The man Shaye thinks of as "Brown Hair," the one who kept his hand on his knife when he first questioned her about Jariel, speaks up next. "I am Ben."

She allows herself to briefly study Ben. The most muscular of all the men, he's as tall as Mule, but has a long slender face and a long nose . . . which seems just the right size with the added feature of his beard. His eyes are nearly the color of hers—and they seem to take in everything. When he looks back at her, she realizes she's given him enough attention so she concentrates on the next man.

"I am Samuel," Mule says. "You know the story of my name," he says. He has darker hair than Ben, softer brown eyes, broad features, and a mischievous grin.

In turn, each of the men say their own name and she repeats it after them: Jude, Matthew, John, Loash, David, and Avallach. Her eyebrows arch up with the last name and he explains a bit further. "Like yours, my name is from another culture, but it was passed down to me and I don't know what it means. My mother liked the sound of it."

Several of the men say a sarcastic, "*Awww,*" and he shrugs it off.

Now they've come full circle back to Tooth, and Shaye says, "I hope you will forgive me, brothers, if it takes me a while to learn all of your names."

After glancing around the group again, she realizes that the first man she saw when she got out of the crate—the one who looked like a warrior, the one who pleaded for Jariel's life—isn't here at the fire. She asks, "Where is the other brother?"

"What other brother?" Ben, asks.

The sudden silence is palpable as they all lean in for her answer.

She swallows hard. "I thought," she finally offers, "that I saw another man earlier . . . but I don't see him now."

Nathan looks directly into her eyes and says, "You are mistaken, daughter. All the members of our group are here. Perhaps it was the bad medicine in the box with you that made you see things." His tone is serious. After a pause, his voice becomes gentle once again. "What type of work did you do in Aegea?"

Shaye looks around the circle of men. They're all still watching her. Do they think she's crazy? She wants to explain herself, to describe what she saw—but senses this is a bad idea. And, despite her great desire to ask them hundreds of questions she realize *they* want to question *her.*

"I helped to cook, and garden," she begins, "and I served the members of a household."

"Did you work alongside your family?" Nathan asks.

"No. I am an orphan. My father was a soldier," she says, looking down at her hands, then quickly adding, "but he believed in the Maker and he married my mother. The military punished him for standing up with her and made him work on a project that took his life when I was three." Her eyes nervously sweep over the group, but she sees they are all nodding. This squares with the cruelty they've all learned about Aegea.

"My mother, Elle, was a gatherer after her father, Joash. They were from the clan of Zim," Shaye continues. "My mother died of a fever when I was ten and I had to serve in the house where we lived after my father died—the house of a military family—to pay off my debt. Until today. Today I was cast off. . . . I was to be sent to the family of a terrible man . . . and I ran away." She realizes she doesn't have the energy to maintain an outward show of courage, and the weight of all their focused attention is more than she can bear. "I'm . . . I'm very tired."

Nathan nods toward the place where Jariel is sleeping. "Go ahead and rest with your sister there. We will keep watch over the two of you." He looks at each of the men. "No one will bother you while you sleep."

Several of them get up and jostle for the privilege of helping her climb up to the bed, before she hears Nathan say, "And *no one* on this journey will make offers of courtship or marriage before we are home."

Shaye briefly considers the oddness of the comment, but she's too exhausted to ponder it for long. Stopping at the foot of the tree, she reaches for the hem of her dress and realizes it's stiff with the weight of all the mud and the salty sweat embedded in it. She also realizes she's too tired to look through her bag for a change of clothing, much less go behind that tree to do it. She pulls the back hem of the dress between her legs and ties it in a knot with the front hem of the dress, making it look like a pair of baggy pantaloons—the way many generations of Genon women have done as they worked in the fields with men.

Philip and Loash, who both appear to be in their mid-twenties stand on either side of her and offer to help her into the tree. Philip is about her height and has eyes that are almost golden in color and he has black hair. Loash is a little taller and his hair is black, but it's less like hair, more like a wild mane.

"No, thank you," she says, placing her foot on the stub of a branch about a foot off the ground and then her hand on another one that's is even with her shoulder.

They nod but continue to stand there.

"I'm fine," she adds.

"Yes," Philip says, smiling.

She likes the way his eyes crinkle up at the corners when he smiles, like they're smiling, too.

"Don't worry," he says. "We will keep watch for large snakes that hunt at night."

"Do you want to take my knife with you?" Loash asks.

Instantly she recalls the story of how her father stopped a gigantic snake of the forest from squeezing the colonel to death. Her eyes widen and she looks back at Nathan.

One downward wave of his hand shows the old man is skeptical. "Rarely have we found the very large snakes in this section of the forest, but," he spreads out his hands and shrugs, "no place in the land of cloud and leaf is completely safe. Perhaps you should take it . . . just in case."

She takes the knife in a leather sheath and clamps it in her teeth before she clambers up into the bed, realizing she'll need to add human-devouring snakes to the list of things to avoid in the coming days. Once she gets to the edge of the bed, she finally manages to nudge a sleeping Jariel over so she can settle in. She decides to put the knife along her side, near her right hand—just in case. Looking at Jariel, she marvels that the pale oval of the girl's face is almost like a lamp in the surrounding darkness. She can see dark spots where Jariel's eyes, nostrils, and mouth are but the rest of the girl's face nearly shines with an opalescent light.

Smoke from the fire, lazily gathers around the camp and the men grow quiet. After the oppressive heat of the day, the leafy bed they made for Shaye and Jariel is surprisingly cool. Completely exhausted, she closes her eyes and falls asleep. She dreams of Jariel's mother, Duana, reaching through the darkness with long arms to catch her.

### 

Hours later, Shaye's eyes open. What woke her up? Almost by instinct, her hand finds the knife. Engulfed in mist and smoke, she holds completely still until she remembers exactly where she is. *I am in the Great Forest.*

The campfire is more for smoke than light now, so she can see very little. Although she's never heard it before this night, the serenade of frogs and other creatures doesn't frighten her. Her mother always said the forest had a song of its own at night.

Now that she's awake, her thoughts wander back to what Nathan said earlier, ". . . *my mother never stopped grieving. Not until she went to be with the Maker, just a few months into the exile. She wept for her mother and her sisters. She longed for dry ground, and the wind on her face, and garlic, and walking in the sunlight. For many of them, it was like this. Even after we journeyed to our new home far away, they would come back to the Great Forest to find Genon brothers and sisters who wanted to join us, yet after they came, some of them still grieved for many days. I understand, daughter. Don't be ashamed of your sorrow.*"

She stares into the shroud of darkness above her and her eyes well up with tears. She covers her mouth with both of her hands while she weeps.

A humming sound comes to her ears. It's not the hum of a creature, but the low voice of a man that seems to waft down from the smoky mist above her. Afraid Jariel might be awakened by the sound, she quickly wipes her face with her hands. The man's tune is both haunting and beautiful, reminding her of the sacred songs she learned as a child. As the sound gathers strength, she leans over to the edge of the bed and looks down where the men are. Through the haze she believes she can see all of them. Only two men, Jude and Mule, are awake and both of them are sitting near the fire, still working on the twine they were making earlier. Neither of them is singing, and they give no sign that they hear it. They keep working.

*Am I dreaming?* When she leans back onto the cool leaves, the voice begins to sing out in the language of her people.

> Be merciful to me, O my Maker, for I am in distress
> And my eyes grow weak with grief,
> My heart fails with loneliness, for who will take up my
>     cause?
> I am thrown into darkness as though I were dead;
> I am a broken jar that is cast away . . .

It's as if this lament is pouring from her own soul. *Could this be a song of the Exiles? Certainly, it could have applied to them as much as it does to me.   What great perils, mourning and misfortunes they must have suffered.*

The man continues to sing,

> I saw my sister in the Land of Cloud and Leaf,
> And I longed to hear her voice, to see her face
> She was beautiful but full of sorrows, for who will take
>    up her cause?
> Help her to listen, O Maker, to your council
> And walk with you in the garden of your grace.

The man resumes humming the tune, and the sound of his voice drifts away until all she can hear once again are the night creatures in the forest.

And then she feels it. As if something gently brushed against her . . . only from the inside. She puts her hand upon her abdomen and waits.  It happens again, and this time, a small spot on her belly rises up and touches the palm of her hand. Her heart pounds and her eyes well up again. *My child! My very own child!  How can I know such anguish and such joy all at once?*

She holds completely still, waiting for more movement, but eventually, she falls back into a deep sleep.  When she awakens, the sun is up and the men are moving about. They're preparing to break camp and begin the day's journey.

### 

All night, Jariel McClaren dreamed of home, but her heavy heart quiets when she opens her eyes.  She cannot figure out what she's looking at.  It could rival her mother's finest necklace, yet it's draped between two branches, just beyond the nest where she rests.  It has an intricate pattern, and more glistening gems than she's ever seen before.  She reaches out to touch it, to see if it is real.

"Don't touch that," Shaye scolds. "It's a snare, made by a spider."

Jariel jerks her hand away in a panic. "Really? A spider? *Where is it?*"

"Not the same kind of spider that bit you.  That kind of spider lives in the ground.  This one lives in the trees and eats small bugs.  He will leave you alone, just don't molest his trap."

Jariel can't take her eyes off of it. "What are those jewels on it?"

"Haven't you ever seen water in a spider trap before?"

"Those are *water*?"

"Yes."

"Did the spider put them there?"

Shaye groans, "*Ohhh lah.* You are such a stupid thing."

"You can't talk to me that way."

"I'll talk to you any way I want. You have no special position here. Genon believe people are to be counterparts, we work together. We don't try to crush each other."

One of the men lifts himself up on a nearby branch and smiles at them.

"Your name is . . . David, isn't it?"

His face lights up with a giant grin. "Yes, I am David," he says slowly, so that she can understand him.

Shaye glances at his smooth face. He may be even younger than she previously thought. He might be as young as she is. He's got light brown curls that are much lighter than the hair of the ferocious man Shaye originally dubbed "brown hair." David's hair and his dark blue eyes are evidence of a mixed heritage, but the others seem to accept him. It's heartening to think David has a place among these people, too.

"Don't be ill-mannered," Jariel says to Shaye. "You should introduce him to me."

"Why?" Shaye scoffs. "It's not as if you'll be having any extended conversations."

While David doesn't understand the language, the facial expressions and the tone of conversation between the women communicates their displeasure. He cocks his head to one side and smiles at both of them. "The day is new. Arguing already?" he says in Genon. "What kind of women do they have on that plateau now? Do sisters who have found freedom have nothing better to do than argue?"

Happy to keep Jariel out of the conversation, Shaye answers him. "I think the girl has recovered from her bite. At least her mouth works."

Looking back and forth between David and Shaye, Jariel asks, "What are you saying to him?"

Shaye shrugs before looking at her. "He asked if you could walk on your own today. I told him that at least your mouth seemed to be working just fine."

David continues to watch the sour exchanges between them and shakes his head.

"*Eh eh!*" Nathan says from below. "There must be respect for the women in their bed. Come down, David."

The young man frowns but drops out of sight.

Jariel looks at Shaye, and for the sake of curiosity, she's willing to set aside the disagreement. "What does that mean when they say that? I used to think people were clearing their throats, but it obviously has some sort of meaning. What does '*Eh eh*' mean?"

Shaye considers it. "I never gave it much thought before, but it's . . . a sound to get attention or to correct. It's like 'uh oh' . . . or 'no no'."

"Oh. Why was someone saying it to him just now?"

"He isn't supposed to be looking at us up here."

"Oh."

When Shaye sits up completely, she sees a small white flower that was crushed under her weight during the night. She's pretty sure it wasn't there when she went to bed. Someone either tossed it up here . . . or dropped it down from above. She doesn't touch it or draw attention to it, but she looks over at Jariel. "Did you hear singing last night?"

"What singing? Were they singing?"

"Never mind," Shaye says, then occupies herself by pulling the hem from the back of her dress up between her legs and tying it in a knot with the front hem the way she did last night.

"Why are you doing that?"

"We need to crawl down from here and no doubt they will try to help us when they see we're coming down. You don't want everyone to think you're letting them look up your dress, do you?"

Jariel ties her dress in the same way and Shaye finds the knife Loash gave her last night before they begin the climb down to the ground.

As predicted, several men scramble to help, but Shaye ignores them and climbs down on her own. Jariel accepts assistance but is able to stand on her own once she gets to the ground. They all stare at her. It's the first time they've seen her awake and fully upright on her own.

One of the men mumbles "She could turn to the side and even the wind wouldn't find her. It looks as if someone was trying to starve the girl."

A couple of others grunt in confirmation.

Shaye didn't hear the comment, but the silence following it is uncomfortable. "Good morning," she says to all of them.

"Good morning," they answer back.

The old man steps forward with a pair of rope sandals and offers them to Jariel but speaks to Shaye. "You will need to translate. Jude and Mule made these last night for Jar-el."

Shaye lowers her eyes and tries to sound respectful as she corrects him, "Jariel." It's difficult to say, since the name is foreign to them.

"Yes. Thank you," Nathan says, "I would want to say it right. We will all practice it. Jariel."

Some of the others echo it, and Jariel's focus nervously darts around the group.

Nathan holds the sandals closer to Jariel. "They won't protect your feet from thorns—so you will need to mind your step—but they will keep your feet safe from stones and such."

Shaye nods and gives the polite Genon acknowledgement. "You honor her."

Jariel looks at the woven rope pads hanging from long, twine-y straps. It's apparent that she doesn't know what they are.

"They are sandals," Shaye tells her. "Some of the men stayed awake last night making them for you so remember your manners. If you are going to walk at all, you will need something on your feet. Nathan says they won't protect you from thorns, but they should give you protection from most other things."

Jariel takes the shoes and makes a small bowing gesture to express her thanks, then spins the footwear around by the straps, trying to figure out how to work them.

One of the men kneels down in front of her to help before Nathan taps him on the backside with his walking stick and says, "*Eh eh*. Let the sister help her."

"Truly," Shaye says to Nathan, "we need some privacy. Our clothes are still damp from yesterday. I am hoping that some of the other clothes in my bag are dry."

"You go to the tree, then," he answers. "We will wait. *All* the men will wait here."

Shaye looks at Loash and asks if they can use his knife, he smiles and says, "Yes."

Jariel is a little shaky, but manages to walk alongside Shaye until they are behind the large tree they used last night. Shaye looks in her bag, then pulls out one of the three dresses she rolled up and put in it just yesterday. It's not completely dry, but it's drier and much cleaner than the dresses they are wearing. "Here," she says, offering the gray dress to Jariel.

Normally, the young Miss McClaren would have flatly refused to wear the rough, shapeless, gray frock made specifically for servants. But her fine dress wasn't made to wear in a jungle and will turn to ribbons in no time. Besides, it's covered with vomit, mud, and green sap. Shaye pulls out another gray dress and holds it up in front of Jariel like a privacy screen. "I won't look. You change first, and then I'll help you tie up your shoes."

Jariel frowns for a moment before she says a quiet, "Thank you."

When it's Jariel's turn to hold up a privacy screen, Shaye quickly dons another dress while she offers a bit of advice. "When we go back, they will offer us food. I know you don't like eating, but for Genon, sharing food is like sharing friendship. Last night, they understood because you were sick. But today, it would be very rude to refuse to eat. You must try."

"Okay," she answers before she starts rubbing her shoulders then her hip. "My," she mumbles "How can anyone stand to wear this itchy—"

"*What?*"

"Nothing."

###

Within a few minutes, the two women are back in the camp wearing fresh clothes.

Alert for the first time since she arrived in the jungle, Jariel tries to take in all the sights around her. "I never knew there could be so many shades of green," she says in awe.

The fire the men have burning this morning is much smaller and it isn't smoking . . . for smoke might be visible above the trees from a great distance.

Shaye's focus gravitates over to the widow tree that was barely visible last night. The uneven latticework of bark extends more than fifty feet up into the canopy above. Now she can see the multitude of branches that extended down from above like arms and long-fingered hands, slowly enclosing around the host tree that was eventually devoured by darkness, rot, and insects. There are several places where Shaye can see right through the column—where the "husband" tree has been completely demolished. There's an eerie magnificence to the efficiency of this tree in a place where survival is about ruthless expansion and crowding out any competition for light or water. Even now, rope-like tendrils dangle down here and there from the widow's dense foliage and eventually, they will thicken and form support columns for further expansion.

Shaye walks over to the trunk, then around it. On the back side, she sees a large tangle of the widow's branches encasing something. She stops to examine it.

"That's a large stone." Nathan interrupts her thoughts. "We met the husband tree *and* the stone here when I was a boy, on our first journey. The widow was here, too, but she had just begun her hold." He shrugs. "The stone may be the only thing that outlives her."

Jariel joins them and asks, "What *is* this?"

"It's called a widow tree," Shaye tells her. "This kind of tree slowly grows around another tree and then kills it. Look, you can see right through it here. The other tree used to be in there, but it's gone now."

"How frightening." Jariel's eyes sweep up and down the trunk. "And beautiful. Is everything in the forest this way?"

Nathan tries to speak Jariel's language. "I tell yous," he shakes his head and tries again. "I tell your sister Shaye in the night past, there is *much* you never see before. The Maker was very busy. You will see. The world have much more than we know."

Jariel listens and starts to respond to him—but then stops short. She suddenly looks at Shaye and blurts out, "You told them we were *sisters*?"

Shaye glares at her. "It's an *expression*. I know the people you served taught you *nothing* of our ways, but *all* who belong to the Maker are brothers and sisters."

Nathan watches the exchange, smiles, and reverts to speaking in Genon to Shaye. "I can see you have much work ahead of you. She needs to learn our ways and our language in order to live her new life. This poor child has been robbed of the wisdom of our people. Since you brought her, I will trust you to teach her . . . patiently."

Shaye controls the urge to roll her eyes and groan. Instead, she takes a deep breath, and with deliberate calmness says, "I didn't *bring* her to the forest."

Nathan shrugs. "Well, the Maker put you in the box with her. He must have had his reasons for sending you together."

Before Shaye can respond, the old man turns and beckons them to follow. "Come now and eat, we have far to go."

When they return to the center of the camp, they see different items, gathered and placed in piles on top of large leaves—a buffet in the wild.

Everyone stops talking and they all stand still as Nathan says, "We thank the Maker for the bounty of this food and the gift of fellowship with two sisters. We are grateful that *Jar-i-el* is mending. We are grateful that our sisters, who were bound, are free now.

Jariel hears her name and looks around the group. Obviously, solemn words are being spoken. She takes her cue from the others and stands still.

"Just so," many of the men say, and Shaye echoes them.

Nathan looks at Shaye and says, "It is good that her first meal in freedom is begun with thanks to the Maker, don't you think?"

"But, the girl doesn't know our Maker," Shaye says.

A second hush falls upon the men as they listen.

The old man looks upward and shakes his head as if he's heard tragic news, then lets his eyes rest upon Shaye. "Then we shall begin to show her. Please, tell her what I have said."

While she listens to the translation, Jariel just looks down.

Within moments, the men are helping themselves to the food and Nathan bids the women to do so as well.

To her horror, Jariel realizes one the piles of food in the banquet is moving! It's a mound of some sort of grubs . . . or worms! Even though she's so hungry she's shaking, she wouldn't dream of even *touching* one of those things. Instead, she quickly gravitates to something that looks like grapes and grabs a handful of them before she realizes that the small green spheres *aren't* grapes. Each one has a hard, textured peel. Now she's hoping they aren't raw eggs from some creature, for she has three of them in her hand.

Nathan points to the squirming mass at the other end of the buffet and says in Jariel's language. "Jariel, take, eat."

Terrified, Jariel stands completely still and manages to give a small shake of her head in refusal.

"No? Come," he says again in a cajoling tone. He grabs one of the creatures and pops it in his mouth. After he swallows it he smiles. "Him eat good!"

Watching the horror on Jariel's face, all the men laugh.

She picks one of the small green objects already in her hand and eyes it before looking to Shaye for some sort of direction as to what to do with it. Shaye shrugs. She has never seen whatever it is, either.

Ben ("Brown Hair") steps closer to Jariel and she steps back—partly because his sudden move startles her, partly because she fears he might force her to eat a bug of some sort. Instead, he plucks one of the green spheres from her hand, bites through the crisp, thin skin, then pulls half of it off, exposing a gelatinous, translucent, orange globe on the inside. "This is a *ganip*." he says in Genon. He says it again, "*Ganip,*" with a bob of his head, as if he's bouncing the word to her, then waits for her to repeat it.

"*Ganip?*"

Another head bob, "Yes. *Ganip*. It has a stone in the middle," he warns before he sucks the small fruit out of the peel.

Shaye translates the advice about the pit inside before the two women try the fruit.

It's sweet and tart. Both of the women smile and nod as they savor the taste.

He looks at the other men as if he's won a trophy of some sort, then turns back to the women and places a hand on his own chest. "Ben."

They both nod and repeat it. "Ben."

One of the other men quickly steps forward and hands Shaye an oblong, dark yellow fruit, as big as a fist, with deep ridges running top to bottom.

"How do I eat this?" she asks.

He picks up another one that is a lighter yellow and simply bites into it.

She takes a sniff of the fruit in her hand. It smells like a flower. She bites into it, and juice dribbles down her arm as she chews the fruit. "*Mmmm,*" she says. "This is very good."

She offers a bite to Jariel, who looks at the firm, translucent flesh inside, sniffs it, then takes a bite. She holds one hand in front of her mouth when she says, "This reminds me of something. What is it? Roses? Or maybe a sweet tea?" She stops long enough to swallow. "Oh my. This is amazing."

For the next few minutes, the group offers a variety of the collected foods to the women, and they try each item—with the exception of the caterpillars. Within minutes, the fire is put out and their journey begins. Some of the men scatter— some to watch behind, others to scout ahead.

Ben leads the rest of the group to a trickling stream where they wash the sticky juice from their faces, arms, and hands. Jariel can't stop looking around at all the plants that surround them. She points to several brilliant pink blooms, each one on a shaft emerging from the middle of a frosty green plant nestled among rocks or in trees. "Isn't this like the yellow flowers in the corner of the garden, under the trees?"

Shaye considers it. The curved, long leaves and spikey flowers on the plants *do* resemble those in the garden at Westland—flowers which were undoubtedly brought from the jungle. "Yes. It could be," she answers. "Like cousins, maybe."

When they bend down to rinse off, Shaye draws closer. "See?" she says when she knows Jariel is the only one who can hear her. "These are *good* people. Nathan saved you from the spider bite and they all could have perished when they rescued us from the K'mosh. They believe they are saving us from a terrible life on the plateau." Shaye glances around once more to be sure the men are out of earshot. "If the military of

Aegea knew where we were, if they knew the Exiles existed, there would be bloodshed and men on both sides—*good* men who had *nothing* to do with whatever brought us here—might die."

When Ben and another man step closer to them Shaye stops talking and unrolls one of the dirty dresses from yesterday. Now they are away from the fire, the flying insects are biting, and she's fascinated by the fact that hordes of mosquitoes are hovering around the dirty dress she's holding.

"They come to the smell of your sweat in the garment," Ben tells her. "You can rinse out your clothes, but we cannot stop sweating. When there are so many insects we keep the mud on ourselves."

Once again, they scoop up mud from the bank of the stream and apply it liberally to their skin.

When the men are walking away, Jariel points to the one next to Ben and asks, "Which one is that one again? What's his name?"

Shaye frowns as she concentrates on the retreating man. "I think he is called Philip." She wrings out the dress she's holding before she adds, "And you should never do that. Genon don't point at people."

"Why?"

"Most commonly, the only person we point to is the Maker. You can gesture toward an object, but to point at a person is rude. You simply look at them and sort of nod upward. Like this," she says, demonstrating the action.

"Oh."

"Try it."

Jariel looks at Philip and juts her chin toward him. "Like that?"

"No. More like you are about to kiss the air in front of you and gently moving your chin out in the direction you want someone to look."

She tries again. "Like this?"

"Yes. That's the polite way."

"Why would you point at your Maker?"

Shaye considers how she can explain it. "*Ummm.* We use two fingers to point to him. Together, like this. One of them stands for me, the other for him . . . it says only with him do we truly live or move. To touch the fingers to the lips and point to him, like this," she says as she gestures, "is a vow."

Ben calls out to them, "There is no more time for washing! We must be on our way,"

Jariel is obviously undernourished and frail, but she tells them that she can walk for a while, so they all set out on the next leg of the journey.

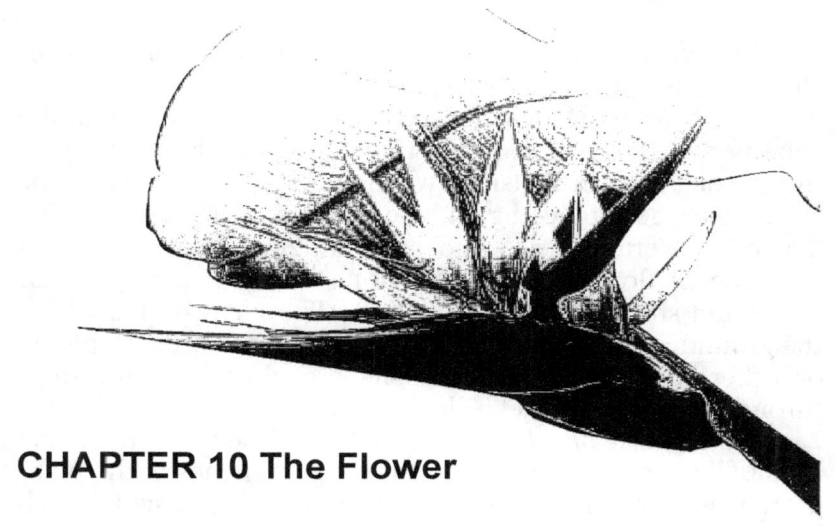

# CHAPTER 10 The Flower

"Wherever you find great beauty in the world, danger and
darkness are seldom far away"—*An ancient proverb of His
own people.*

They've been in the forest for several days now. Jariel has
regained much of her strength and every day the Exiles
entertain the growing hope that they've gotten away with no
soldiers on their trail. This section of the forest seems to have
more light and air than the dense woods they passed through
yesterday. So far, they haven't minded stopping several times
during each day, since Nathan often finds valuable plants they
wish to collect.

They've walked for several hours this morning, and now
the women need to stop for a short break. Nathan soon finds
a place where he is willing to stop, saying he'll allow some
time for them to eat a few bites of food and drink some water.
The man they all call Tooth scouts a safe place for the women
to relieve themselves. Jariel says she doesn't need to go, but
when Shaye comes back, Jariel has changed her mind, so
Shaye simply hands her the knife and points to the selected
tree. The girl should be able to go by herself.

Three of the men are busy with a conversation while the
rest preoccupy themselves with climbing a tall, thorny tree to
obtain some long pods for Nathan.

Just when Jariel is ready to rejoin the group, she realizes she's gotten a pebble wedged in her left sandal. She bends down and pokes a finger between her foot and the sole of the shoe in an attempt to wriggle the stone out without untying the sandal, and is satisfied when it pops out. Before she straightens her stance again, she catches sight of something beyond several ferns and low-hanging branches. A magnificent flower. The color alone makes it a magnet for Jariel and she cannot resist its pull. She picks up a stick on the ground and waves it in front of her to ward off any spiders or other lurking creatures as she crouches low and steps through the foliage to get a closer look.

*Is this a tree or a bush?* she wonders. The top of the trunk is as tall as her shoulders, and the long, branches of the plant grow from the top, extending well beyond her height. Each branch on the plant ends with one gigantic, dark green leaf. Tucked between two of the branches is the flower that captured her attention. The shape of the bloom resembles a large fan that a fine lady might hold in her hand on a warm day. The petals of orange, red and purple are arranged in a flat, half-circle that is more than a foot wide. Now that she's closer, she can see each petal is like a long, inverted claw. She slowly reaches out and touches one petal. She can't help but sigh. The smooth texture of it is like velvety wax—the kind they used to make the candles that sat on the table for special dinners at home. Jariel has never seen anything like this and she wonders, *Does it have any sort of scent?*

Her hand slowly runs down the flower to grasp the thick stem at its base and she stands up on her toes as she slowly pulls it closer. Just before it's close enough for her to take a sniff, strings of clear, thick fluid hidden in the flower drool out and down onto her arm—and the sticky liquid reeks like rotten food! She lets go of the flower and steps back, quickly searching for some place to wipe the nasty stuff off of her skin. Certainly not on her own dress. She'd stink all day, and oh the lecture Shaye would give her!

*I must get it off before they discover what I've done.*

While she's searching, a stinging sensation spreads over her arm and hand. Is it the fluid? When she looks closely she can see a multitude of barely visible, blond-colored ants on her arm and hand. They're tiny and nearly transparent, but apparently capable of delivering powerful bites!  She screams as she uses her other hand to try to rub them off.

It isn't long before Shaye and the men burst through the bushes to find her.  The man they call Mule reaches her first.  He pulls her away from the plant, then opens his bottle of water and pours it over her hands and her arm while he rubs off the ooze and the ants.

Large red welts are already forming and her arm feels like it's on fire.  She quickly asks Shaye, "What are they?  Will I die?  It burns!  It burns!"

"This will hurt, but *not* kill."  Mule says in Genon.  "The flower has [unknown word] water in it.  These ants are small but they have a big bite.  "

Shaye squints at him.  "*What* kind of water?  I don't know that word."

Mule keeps rinsing Jariel's arm.  "Uh.  Bad water.  Sits too long, mixes with sap, and gets . . ." he can't think of another description.  "Uh . . . bad, like something dead.  The water brings insects to the plant, insects bring birds."

Jariel repeatedly looks from her arm to Mule to Shaye while she hops from one foot to another.  "What did he say?"

"He says it's foul water that the plant uses to attract bugs and birds.  He says the bites will hurt, but not kill you."  She sees Jariel's distress, but she can't help but groan.  "You just *had* to wander off.  You just *had* to touch it didn't you?  Have you learned *nothing* yet?  This isn't Aegea.  Everything can't be made clean and safe for you.  This is the wild and you can't touch things or go places without asking."

Even if they can't understand the language, it's easy to see that Jariel is getting quite a scolding.

"She was foolish to do this," Mule tells Shaye.

The others nod in agreement.

The affirmation of the group causes the floodgate holding back Shaye's contempt to spring a leak before she can check it.  "Your parents," she says to Jariel, "should have called you *Corsha*," she says, reaching over to tap the girl's head "for your head is a corsha!"

Jariel knows "corsha" is the name of the gourds that most people on the plateau use for bowls, cups, and spoons.  The gourds have very hard shells but are filled with useless goop that is thrown away.

The Exiles must have knowledge of the corsha gourds as well, for several of the men chuckle and elbow each other.

Jariel's eyes well up.

The amused look on Mule's face evaporates when he sees Jariel's tears. He turns to Shaye and says, "It *was* foolish, but she doesn't know what you know, does she? You brought her, you know of her ignorance . . . you should teach her."

"I didn't *bring* her!" Shaye shouts. Even she is surprised by her own outburst.

Nathan steps through the bushes and looks around. "Why are you all *here*? We must go."

As everyone turns to leave, Shaye leans over and speaks to Jariel in a calm voice. "Sure. You haven't a *spoonful* of mercy in your own soul, but go ahead and make them feel sorry for you."

Nathan calls from the front of the group. "We have far to go if we ever want to reach the boats!"

Another unknown word. Shaye doesn't know what the word "boats" means, but given Nathan's impatience at the moment, she decides not to ask.

### 

By the time they make camp that night, Shaye sits at the fire with the others but she's in no mood to play the role of translator, so she takes a position as far as possible from Jariel, and is content to let Nathan and several of the men attempt to communicate directly with Jariel with limited language and gestures.

### 

The next morning, Shaye gets up early. When Tooth points in the direction where she and Jariel went to relieve themselves the previous night, she nods and takes a knife with her. She walks slowly and realizes, apart from a few times like this, she is almost never alone. How many hours did she spend alone at home, sometimes hungering for the fellowship of others, and now, solitude is a valuable commodity. On the way back she takes her time. She's within sight of the camp when she hears Nathan's voice. At first, she thinks he's talking to her so she stops.

She turns around and hears him say, " . . . Thank you. . . . I know I have no right to ask this, but could you watch behind us so that the women are kept safe?"

She can see neither Nathan nor whomever he is addressing. Embarrassed by the realization that she's eavesdropping, she starts walking again, and almost bumps into Nathan when he steps from behind a tree into her path. Both of them are startled.

"Good morning," he says.

"Good morning."

When they are nearly back at the camp she confesses, "I didn't mean to be listening to you just now. I was walking back to camp."

The old man thinks for a moment, then shrugs. "Well, sometimes I talk to the Maker, sometimes I talk to myself. Sometimes, it's a bit of both."

## CHAPTER 11
## Ty, Basil, Kosh, Old Menoh

"The love of the Maker asks 'What am I willing to give for
you?' The love of man asks 'What are you willing to
give me?'"—*From the Tell of His people*

### In Aegea

Ty McClaren mounts the stairs in the Great House of
Westland with a small oil lamp in his hand.

His shirt is still wet with the tears of Mosha, the cook who
has lived in their home all of his life. Her contagious joy, her
doting love, and her food are part of nearly every childhood
memory—at least all the happy ones. As soon as she saw him
tonight, she collapsed in his arms, sobbing.

> *"Where are our girls? Where are our girls? Tell
> me you will find them! Promise me you will find my
> Shaye and Jariel. Promise me . . ."*
>
> *"I swear to you, Mosha, I will do everything in
> my power to find them."*
>
> *She wailed loudly before she found the voice to
> say, "Please don't think Shaye did this. I <u>know</u> she
> didn't do this. I know she and Jariel didn't get along
> at times, but she is as much a part of this household
> as I am. She would never harm any of you. I know
> she wasn't herself these past few months . . . I've*

*never seen her so sad . . . but she'd never do a thing
like this. . . . Someone has* taken *both of them."*

"*I know, I know,*" he answered as he hugged her.
"*I promise you. Father and I won't stop looking until
we find both of them.*"

Standing at the top of the stairs, he realizes that in the
whole of his life, he's never needed a key for this door before.
How strange to have to unlock a door that was unlocked for
his entire childhood. Mosha's words, "*I know she wasn't
herself these past few months. I've never seen her so sad . . .*"
are still echoing in his mind as he gropes around in his shirt
pocket for the keys and it's almost as if the narrow passageway
is somehow beginning to squeeze in on him.

Once he finds the key, he fumbles with the lock and
wrestles the door open. Grateful to step out into the cool
night air, he blows out the flame on the lamp and sets it down
just beyond the swing of the door. Walking to the waist-high
wall at the edge of the roof, he places both hands on top of it
and inhales deeply, looking up.

It's a beautiful, starry night, like thousands of others he's
seen from this very spot. If he closes his eyes . . . he can
imagine her standing right there next to him and reaching up
as if she could touch one of those stars.

*"If you manage to catch it, are you going to keep
it in your pocket?" he asks. It's a question he
probably asked Shaye thousands of times since they
were children.*

*She doesn't look away from the stars. "Oh no. I
never keep them. It would be a shame if I did that.
And what would people think if all the stars began to
disappear? Panic on the plateau."*

*"I dare say, there would be havoc in the streets.
And if they discovered it was you who'd stolen all
those stars, you might be set before a tribunal."*

"Excuse me," a man's voice says from behind him.

Ty turns to see a soldier, standing in the doorway with
another lamp. "Yes?"

"I was in the tower and I saw someone out here, so I came
over just to check. I didn't know it was you. Sorry to have
bothered you."

"Not a problem," Ty answers. "I'll lock the door again when I leave."

Without another word, the man turns and disappears down the stairwell. Ty looks around and walks to a small alcove in the corner of the roof where his father had builders begin work on another tower but never had them finish it. As a boy, Ty thought of this three-sided niche his as own secret lair, and when he became a teen, he often dragged a blanket up the stairs and slept here in the cold night air.

The last time he was there, he was with Shaye, but, he doesn't recall their passion as he has so many times in recent months. Instead, he recalls the last two times he saw her. The night after their rendezvous on this very spot, she fell and injured herself at Jariel's party. He'd carried her into the house and set her inside with Mosha all in a panic over her injuries.

He'd lingered in the doorway of Shaye's room. The look she gave him in that moment went beyond the pain of her wounds. She looked stricken. The next morning, when his father surprised him with the news that he would be leaving for the Academy a day early, helping to escort all Jariel's party guests back to town, Ty insisted on going to Shaye's door to say goodbye, but his father and Mosha presided over the entire conversation. Again, Shaye said nearly nothing, but looked right into his soul with such sorrow that it was difficult to leave.

During the next weeks at the Academy, he had such a rigorous physical and classroom routine, he barely had time to eat, and would fall into bed at night exhausted. He'd pushed Shaye's look to the back of his mind, telling himself she was just sorry to see him go, upset he had to leave early. He bought her a gift and told himself he would get back to her as soon as he got his first leave. He'd make it up to her . . . he'd reassure her of the deep love he had for her as soon as he saw her again. It wasn't as if he could write to her, since she couldn't read.

Then it came time for his first leave. When his father gave him a chance to meet Sage Dooley, arguably the smartest man alive in the world today, Ty jumped at the chance . . . even though it meant he wouldn't be going home on leave.

*It was all arranged. I wonder what they told Shaye. Did they lead her to believe I would never come back? That I never gave her a second thought once I left home?*

He looks up at the stars. *I have to believe that she is alive. That she's alive and looking at the stars right now.* "Oh, please," he whispers, "Maker of all that is . . . " His eyes burn and his heart feels as if it will melt right out of his chest.

He looks down at his own hands as a rush of guilt comes to him. *I was so angry with Mother over trading her off . . . for treating her like property . . . but what did I do? I got drunk and I took her. I told her that I loved her and I took her—something I knew I shouldn't do—and then I went off to the Academy. And, as far as she knows, I didn't mean a word I said to her and I never looked back.*

"Hey kid."

Ty rakes his sleeve across his face before he turns to face the doorway. It's Basil, an expert tracker whose family has worked for the McClaren family for four generations now. Most Genon workers are indentured servants (who never manage to fully "pay off" what they "owe," and thus spend their whole lives in servitude). But the relationship between Basil's family and Tyrone's is less of a servant / employer relationship and more of a respectful collaboration for the benefit of all who live in Westland. While this is an example of Jubal McClaren's willingness to loosen the chokehold of the military on the Genon who live out in rural areas of Aegea, such collaborations are met with resistance within the tightly knit community of officers who live in town.

From the time he was ten, (much to his mother's horror) Tyrone's father allowed him to tramp through the wilderness on the western plateau, and Basil—three years older than the young McClaren—was given the solemn responsibility of not only teaching him about the land, the animals, the trees, and the water in Aegea, but also protecting him. From the very beginning, Basil wanted to establish his position as the older teacher / boss, so he took to calling Tyrone "kid."

*Would he feel free to call me that anywhere else? Has he ever truly felt like I was his friend?*

Basil stays in the doorway. "We need to talk. Away from here."

The request for conversation is unusual. Although they have been camping, trapping, hunting, and exploring the forests and back corners of Aegea all these years, both men are quiet by nature, so many of the days they've spent in each other's company have gone by without either of them uttering more than a few words—yet both always came away, entirely satisfied that the days were enjoyable.

Ty walks toward the door. "Let's go."

The two men leave the house together and stop only briefly at the back gate of the compound before a soldier permits them to leave. They slip quietly down a mile-long path to a small house that Jubal McClaren allowed Basil's grandfather to build near a pond.

Before Basil can call out to alert the family to their presence, he sees his grandfather, Old Menoh, and his father, Kosh, are already sitting in old wooden chairs by the pond.

As they approach, Kosh and the old man both stand to greet the youngest McClaren.

"My eyes are glad to see you," Old Menoh says, "but you know that my heart is heavy with the news."

Ty nods in acknowledgement. Although he has probably learned more of the taboo Genon language and culture than any other military man of his age, he's only spoken Genon with them during casual conversations that might take place around a fire after a long day, as the four of them sat together. Speaking it now seems dishonest somehow, like a pretense to gain their favor—like false, *I'm-your-brother* flattery. As he stands here with them he realizes that, in his heart, they *have* been like family to him, so he will honor them by just being himself among them. Tonight, he will speak in the language he speaks at home—the official Command Dialect of Aegea. "Thank you. My father sends his greetings to you and asks for all the wisdom and help your family can give us. We don't know whether this is the work of dishonest soldiers alone, or if they were helped by Genon who have left the Way, but he wants you to know he is counting on your skills, your family, and your help—and we will remember it always."

It's a solemn acknowledgement with a promise. The life of Jubal's own daughter is hanging in the balance, and he is stating confidence in Old Menoh's family. Soldiers and Genon have been at odds for five generations—but Jubal McClaren and Old Menoh have formed a bond of trust over a lifetime that both depend upon—a bond that now will span to the next generation.

The old man nods and all of them take it as their cue to sit when he does. The fingernail moon above gives little light to the scene, but Ty knows that Menoh is looking right at him when he says, "We will do whatever we can to find *both* the women."

It is a reference to Shaye as well as Jariel. Subtlety is an absolute *craft* among Genon sages like Old Menoh.

Ty looks at the silhouettes of men he probably understands more than he understands his own father. "I think my father is so worried for Jariel he doesn't know *what* else to believe. But I've told him that I know Shaye is as much a victim in this as my sister is—and my father has appointed me as his personal connection here. I will be his eyes, ears, and mouth in any matter that pertains to this. I will relay my father's orders regarding searches and gather information from the military here. I have his full permission to give you whatever assistance you require. Tell me what you need and what you would like to know. I will do whatever you ask of me to help find them both and bring them home."

Kosh and Basil grunt with approval.

"On that first evening, and the next day" Menoh tells him, "Kosh and Basil made a search of the compound, and then all the grounds that surround the house at Westland. Kosh found a single set of tracks that may have belonged to Shaye. Someone wearing sandals of the right size moved along the fence line and through the orchard just south of Westland. We cannot account for any other servants being there. The footprints lead as far as the road at the back of the orchard. There were also tracks in the orchard from two men in military boots. The person wearing the sandals lingered behind a pile of pruned branches a short distance from where the boot tracks were, then ran separately to the back road.

"Right at the side of the road, the sandal tracks stopped where a wagon was parked. Near that spot were a number of items in bags that seemed to have been thrown there. There were ropes and tools, and supplies that were damaged when they were cast into the bushes. On the road were also fresh tracks of a second wagon. This wagon stopped, then turned and headed back toward Westland. The first wagon went east toward town drawn by two horses with shoes made in town. The wagon heading back toward Westland had wheels made at the Outpost and it was drawn by one horse. That horse was wearing three shoes from town . . . and one shoe forged at the Outpost."

Ty leans forward. "So someone who has access to at least one of Westland's wagons and one of our horses met with another wagon from town on the back road that day?"

"Yes."

"We need to find the horse with one Outpost shoe, the wagon, and the person who drove it."

# CHAPTER 12 Announcement

> "**P**ride is the sieve a man uses to strain the gnats out of a cup of venom before he drinks it. Sometimes wisdom is found in willingness to appear weak or foolish."—*An ancient proverb of His people*

General Jubal McClaren leaves the dining room alone, and gathers his things from the salon on the lowest floor of his apartment, where he spent the night. He won't check on Duana. If she finally managed to fall sleep, he doesn't want to wake her.

His aide, Capt. Joseph Blackwell, is waiting in the front hall. "Maybe we should delay another day or so, and give Menoh's boys and Ty some time to see if they can discover anything more," Seph suggests. "Once everyone knows, you could get buried with false reports, or demands from people who don't have her."

Within an hour of learning about Jariel's disappearance, Jubal sent men to watch Major Lott's son, Gilbert. He wouldn't put it past that young scoundrel to try eloping with Jariel after his false assurances of loving her. After the two consummated their vows, Jubal would have little recourse other than to accept the marriage. Indeed, if he'd caught "Gib" doing anything remotely suspicious these past two days, he'd have locked the young lieutenant in a secret cell where he would been forced to confess. But intelligence yielded no evidence of secret wedding plans or of a wedding night and thus far, Gib continued in his normal daily life, philandering with any female in town who would have him. He'd neither sent nor received any private messages.

As far as Jubal was concerned, Lieutenant Gilbert Lott was a blight in the ranks of officers—but there was no evidence whatsoever that he was mixed up in Jariel's disappearance. If word ever got out that Jubal ordered spying on the Lott family, the boy's entire family would be up in arms.

Compared to the stark alternatives haunting Jubal McClaren now, finding that Jariel had run off to be with Gilbert Lott would be a relief.

In the absence of an answer, Seph asks again, "Are you sure about this, sir?"

Jubal makes a conscious effort to relax his jaw. "I don't think we have any choice. It's been two days now. I'll have to account for it if I continue to keep this secret from the officers. For whatever reason," he closes his eyes and struggles not to think that his daughter—by design or by accident—may be dead. He begins again. "Whatever the reason, we haven't received a second note. If someone was going to make a demand, they would have done it by now. Ty and the others can keep following up on anything they find, but we need more eyes and ears on this, even if some of the officers are hostile to me. The planning meeting for General Fairmont's memorial is an excellent opportunity for a limited disclosure. Everyone already expects all the higher ranking officers to be gathered for a private meeting."

Within minutes, Jubal and Seph walk into the main building at the academy. Jubal's sense of dread grows with every step. While he has his suspicions about who might be involved, he is completely without answers as to how to find his daughter.

Allowing his son, Ty, to travel out to Westland and head up the investigation there was a calculated risk. Duana fears the same people who took Jariel might try to do something to Ty as well—and those fears aren't entirely without foundation. Right now, the list of those whom he trusts absolutely is very small but Old Menoh's family is on that list. He knows Menoh, Kosh, and Basil will fiercely guard his son while they search for every possible clue. And, as he told Duana, if soldiers are behind this—if someone could boldly place a note under Ty's door in the central building of the Academy— would Ty be any safer here?

Ty's friends and the others in the Academy were told that Ty would be absent for a few days while the family sorted out a few of the new arrangements that Jubal's promotion would require.

And for the first time, Jubal will break one of his own rules—he will use signaling for private messages back and forth to Westland.

*If only Duana had been permitted to signal me when this first happened. . . .*

Up until now, he has managed to keep a lid on the news because Westland is isolated on the far end of the plateau and he can control travel coming into the city. Duana and the soldiers who brought her to town are the only persons who've been allowed to travel out of Westland since they discovered Jariel was missing.

But today.

Today.

*Today . . . I will have to let the officers of Aegea, know that Jariel is . . . What is she? A hostage? . . . Dead?*

With every failed search, every passing hour, the chances of her being found alive grow smaller. As much as he dreads disclosure, he knows he needs more help in finding his daughter. The sooner the better.

### ###

The whole assembly stands when General Jubal McClaren enters the tiered assembly room where the business of governing Aegea takes place. Forty-nine of the people are the men who comprise the senior officers of the military, the remaining twenty people are a mix of civilians in high standing and their assistants. There are only three women in the room.

McClaren stands behind the center of the large table in the front of the room, the place reserved for the General, the leader of all Aegea. Former General Bradley Fairmont, hasn't been in this room for nearly a year, so it's both a relief and a jolt to see someone new standing in front of his chair. Because they're here to plan the memorial ceremony for their former leader, the mood is somber.

The new general looks ill-at-ease. While this is understandable, since the heavy burden of office came to him so suddenly, no one expected to see the normally confident McClaren looking so tired and worn.

After a few moments, Jubal motions for everyone to be seated, but he remains standing. Once the room is still, he begins.

"All of you have gathered here today with the expectation of putting together the details for the memorial ceremony for General Fairmont to be held in a few days."

A voice from someone seated at the table to his left interrupts. "Wait!"

This kind of disruption is highly unusual.

Jubal looks at the man, who continues talking. "I think something of grave importance regarding Jubal McClaren needs to be discussed first!" Col. Mosely says and rises to his feet.

No one is entirely shocked by this. While they all hope for a smooth transition, Mosely has long been a bitter opponent of Jubal's. The resentment was stirred to new heights just months ago when McClaren publicly humiliated his rival by entering a quadrant that should have been under Mosely's control, and rounded up a gang of thieves who'd been living in the forest along the main road between Westland and Midtown, boldly robbing travelers for months. What could Mosely say now that wouldn't sound like the talk of an embittered loser? They all focus their attention on him.

"Is it true, Jubal McClaren, that your daughter was kidnapped two days ago?"

A collective gasp seems to suck most of the air out of the room. People begin to murmur, but Mosely keeps talking, raising the volume of his accusations to be heard over the growing din. "And when were you going to share this crucial bit of information with those of us here? Are we not the very ones who should have been called into emergency session and asked for help? Isn't your aspiration to be our leader compromised by this? How do we know what sort of secret deals you were willing to make in order to get your daughter back? I have it on good authority that it's a group of revolutionary Genon who have stolen the girl! The very people with whom you are so friendly! You couldn't even protect your own daughter from them. Are any of our children safe? Are WE safe?"

Nearly everyone rises to their feet. Some talk to people nearby, others are shouting across the room.

Jubal raises both hands and shouts, "I WANT SILENCE IN THIS ROOM!"

Every person but one stops speaking.

"I'm not finished yet!" Mosely says. "I appeal to the Senior Judge Advocate. The future of our entire way of life may be at stake."

Never in his entire life has Jubal thoroughly hated someone. Until now. He makes a conscious effort not to clench his hands before he says, "Whether you like it or not," he motions to two guards in the room, "I'm the senior officer here, I was duly selected General in front of you and other witnesses. I took the oath of office and I am General. If you don't obey my command for silence, I will have you removed from this room, and placed in a cell."

The Senior Judge Advocate, Colin Whitworth, has authority over the tribunal of all Aegea. He has remained seated to Jubal's right, but now rises to his feet. Appointed fifteen years ago by the General Fairmont he's perceived by most to have been loyal to him. Whitworth is the one man in the room who has the means to countermand the orders of a general. All eyes dart between the judge, Jubal, and Col. Mosely.

The judge is quite old—seventy-five. He addresses Mosely first. "Col. Mosely, your outburst was clearly a breach of protocol . . ." he pauses as he glances at Jubal, ". . . but not worthy of arrest—unless you refuse to take your seat."

Mosely sits down and the visibly shaken General of Aegea remains standing. The hush in the room is nearly electric.

Despite his years, the judge is still able to stand erect and his voice remains clear. "All in all, the point Mosely makes, however, is one to be considered. Speak to us now, General McClaren, and we will consider what is to be done." Having said this, Whitworth sits down.

While his pulse is wildly surging, Jubal is somewhat buoyed by the fact that Whitworth—who was there when the old general died, and administered the oath of office—is still referring to him as "General McClaren."

Jubal nods to the judge, then looks out at the people gathered there trying, to connect, not only with those who support him but those who are among his critics. "If I had been permitted to continue, I would have fully informed this body of all the facts concerning my daughter. Yes, it has been two days since she disappeared. But she went missing the same morning that General Fairmont died, on a day when there was much tumult. I was at 'the watch' and I wasn't even aware of my daughter's status until hours later. It's even possible that she was missing for several hours before my wife became aware of it. As soon as she realized Jariel was gone, an informal search of the grounds around Westland was started.

"No one suspected the full scope of it until horsemen from the Signal Corps arrived at Westland to inform the duty officer that the man in the tower there wasn't responding to signals. At that point, it was discovered that the soldier who was supposed to be on duty was *also* gone. Even when I was informed of the situation, I couldn't be sure what had transpired. I had no way of knowing whether my daughter had run away, or eloped . . . or been taken. I had no way of knowing if her disappearance was connected to events in my life or an incident that happened in my home . . . or if all of these things were coincidental. A larger search was launched for my daughter, for the AWOL signalman, and a servant—all of whom had simply vanished." He stops to take a deep breath and a sip of water before he continues. Those seated closest to him can see a tremor in his hand. "Then we found the missing soldier, dead."

Another collective intake of breath echoes around the room before Jubal holds up his hands for order once again.

"Maj. Ratliff can testify that he was duly notified of the death of this man, and the family of the soldier was notified yesterday, although the details surrounding his death were not released, since we ourselves aren't certain if he was participating in a crime or a victim of it.

"Once I became fully aware of these situations, I tried to concentrate all efforts at the west end of the plateau, since the first hours of any search are critical. We were hoping to be able to find my daughter and capture whoever did these things. It wasn't until that night that my son discovered a note someone slipped under the door of his room at the Academy while he was with my wife and me. I brought the note to read it to all of you gathered here today."

Jubal unbuttons one of the buttons of his tunic and extracts a small piece of paper before he reads it aloud.

"'To the McClaren family: We have her. You can waste time looking for her, but you won't succeed. If you know what is good for HER you won't make any announcements to the other officers. We will contact you shortly with our demands.'"

He puts the note back in his tunic and re-buttons it. "Up until this moment I have received no further word, no demands. I don't know if something happened to change their plans."

Jubal looks around the room again trying to make eye contact with as many people as possible. "Let me stop and say something here. It's true that anyone could have taken my daughter . . . or even enticed the signalman to come out of the tower in Westland. It could have been a Genon servant . . . but *one* person couldn't have carried this out alone. Whomever they are—Genons, soldiers, or a combination of both—they had help from this end of the plateau. The chances that a Genon civilian could enter the barracks of the Academy and place a message, under my son's door unnoticed are next to none. It's nearly certain that a soldier delivered the note— and at the direction of a person of rank. This is something that *none* of us would want to believe—but I've had to consider all the possibilities, given what I know."

There are nods and sounds of agreement among the gathering.

Drawing some strength from this, Jubal continues. "The note demanded that we not disclose the fact that Jariel was missing. Knowing her life might be at stake, and now fearing soldiers might somehow be involved, I admit I was careful with the secret for one more day, but I came here today knowing I had to tell all of you what had happened, hoping to lean upon your combined wisdom before launching an all-out search of the entire plateau for my daughter and those who killed one of our own."

"And I submit to all of you," Mosely says as he rises again, "that McClaren is too close to this dire situation to assume command of Aegea. While he has my sympathy, and we should all be willing to assist in the search for his daughter, I propose that the command position be put on hold. I propose that the four colonels, along with this body of officers, guide Aegea until such time as we can select the proper man for General."

After another spate of people standing and shouting, Jubal manages to get everyone to sit down and listen.

"I was duly chosen by General Fairmont before he died because—knowing all of the colonels—he trusted me with the reins of governing Aegea. I was sworn in by Judge Whitworth and have not failed to discharge my duties thus far. I don't believe that it is within the scope of anyone's authority to remove me from my position unless I have failed to fulfill my oaths. Is this so, Judge Whitworth?"

The old man stands once again. "Mosely has raised some serious questions to be considered."

A buzz goes through the room before the judge speaks once again.

"But I say that Jubal McClaren was duly selected, that he took the oath, and that he appears to have operated under the scope of his oath thus far. He is still the General of Aegea."

### 

Within hours, General McClaren signs orders for guards to be posted on all roads and all means of exit from the plateau to the forest to be closed and watched until further notice.

# CHAPTER 13
## The Challenge

"**N**ever underestimate the resolve of a true villain."—*Kyle Dorchester, a General of Aegea in the Fourth Generation for only six years*

General McClaren sits at his new desk in the finely appointed office at headquarters. Shelves behind the desk stand nearly empty, waiting for Jubal's own books and mementos. A deep blue, handwoven rug with bright yellow symbols representing the four different branches of the military—security, signal corps, intelligence, and governance are emblazoned on the rug along with a single star at the center, symbolizing Aegea's general. Mementos of the spacecraft the Aegean C which used to adorn the white walls of the office were removed years ago and taken to the general's house. Only a few small paintings of former generals remain, with the picture of the recently deceased General Fairmont draped with a black sash.

How often, as a boy, did he dream of sitting at this very desk? How many years had he planned to occupy this office? Yet, it's a hollow victory. He's been General of Aegea for four days, and he couldn't feel more alone if he were standing atop one of the ice-capped mountains that look down upon the plateau.

Newly promoted Major Joseph Blackwell taps twice on the door before entering, then closing the door behind himself. Once he's near the desk, he speaks in a low voice.

"Sir," three of Col. Mosely's men are outside. They want to serve an order from the Senior Judge Advocate for all of your communications regarding the disappearance of your daughter. Even the personal messages you got from your wife and sent to her."

Jubal's mouth drops open for a moment before he recovers his dignity and shuts it. "Well," he says, shaking his head, "I've got to give him credit—he never misses a pulse. I suppose he wants to know what we know. He's already tried to plant the notion that a group of Genon did this, so I suppose he wants to see how he can start spinning the details to favor his argument."

Jubal stares at his desk for a moment and taps on the arms of his chair with his fingertips while he ponders it further. *Certainly he could make much of Duana's letters.*

Seph adds to the speculation. "And perhaps, he wants to see what evidence might incriminate him."

Jubal looks at Seph but says nothing. He doesn't need to say anything—they've worked with each other for so many years that Seph knows the look. *You nailed it.*

The commotion and growing volume of a possible altercation just outside Jubal's office door demands investigation. When Jubal opens the door, he sees two of Seph's assistants standing shoulder to shoulder facing three soldiers wearing Col. Mosley's Security Corps insignia. Two of them are prepared to draw swords, the one in the middle is giving an ultimatum.

"You will allow us to locate and impound these documents or you will be remanded to the fort and await a hearing on charges of insubordination, failure to comply with a direct order from the Judge Advocate, obstruction, and contempt."

Jubal steps into the room.

"Stand down. There is no need for swords here. Let me see the order you bear."

The man in the middle of Mosley's group speaks again.

"General McClaren, sir. I have," he yanks the document from Seph's subordinate, "an order from Senior Judge Advocate Whitworth, commanding that your office surrender," he pauses to read from the document verbatim, "'all written communications regarding the disappearance of Jariel McClaren, the murder of Spec. 5 John Grimes, and the disappearance of a suspect by the name of Shaye Penway . . .'"

At the word, "suspect" Jubal and Seph exchange glances.

"'. . . including all personal correspondence between you and your wife and all orders to military personnel in response to these incidents." the soldier hands the document to Jubal. "Any failure to comply may result in your arrest.'"

The general looks over the document and checks the Senior Judge Advocate's signature before responding, "While

I am willing to comply, everyone must be aware of the fact that I'm transitioning from my old office at the Academy to this one. Some of my documents are here, some are there, and some are boxed and in transit. You can wait here while the documents are all located and assembled, but it may take more than a day to do it." He turns to address Seph. "Major Blackwell, you will inform Judge Whitworth of the unavoidable delay . . . *and* of my official request that none of the documents be unsealed before they are delivered directly to him. I also request that at least one captain from each of the other two battalions be sent here as impartial observers of the process, and of the delivery. Certainly we'd all like to avoid the appearance of a conflict of interest that arises if only my men and Mosely's take part in this. Advise Whitworth that I will personally travel with the documents and deliver them to him."

Jubal turns to the soldier who read the order, "Meanwhile, Lieutenant . . ." Jubal eyes the tag on the young man's uniform, "Taylor—you graduated from the Academy . . . was it four years ago?"

The young man's face flushes. "Yes, sir."

"If I recall correctly, you're good with numbers, aren't you?"

"Yes, sir."

"Recent days have been tumultuous for all of us. Col. Mosely undoubtedly told you to expect resistance, so I'll let you off with a warning. In the future, you will give greater attention to how you address senior officers—especially those on my staff." Jubal looks directly into the eyes of each of Mosely's men. "Yes, you have an order to deliver, but you should never threaten violence without cause. If you don't take this warning to heart, all three of you may find *yourselves* in the fort awaiting tribunals."

"Yes, sir."

# CHAPTER 14
# A Reward

For an entire day, at the beginning of each hour, soldiers stand in the Oldtown market, at the crossings of three major roads, and at the gates to read the following proclamation aloud.

A substantial reward is offered to ANY PERSON who willingly provides information resulting in the recovery of Jariel McClaren or Shaye Penway. That reward includes:

Complete cancellation of that person's debt

Private use of 2 acres of arable land for 80 years, transferable to heirs

1 four-room house

Free seeds or seedlings for the first seasonal planting

1 forty-by-twenty foot barn

1 rooster, 5 hens

1 female goat

After the first proclamation is read, a second is also read:

Beginning today, all buildings in Oldtown are hereby subject to a non-damaging search. Only items pertinent to the search for Jariel McClaren and Shaye Penway are subject to confiscation. Evidence or information obtained during searches will not apply toward the reward. Only those who provide information or evidence prior to searches are eligible for the reward.

Interference in the search will result in arrest.

Soldiers engaged in searches are ordered by General McClaren to leave buildings in the same condition in which they were found.

Reports of any damages caused to dwellings
or businesses during a search can be filed at
the office of Homeland Protection near the
fort.

Can the new general be trusted? Jubal McClaren knows
that the residents of Oldtown will be skeptical, but he plans to
make good on every offer. There was an uproar in the Officers
Assembly—complete with challenges from Col. Mosely and his
cohorts—regarding the reward offered, but Jubal hopes that
as word of this opposition leaks out to the public, it will give
him some favor amongst the Genon in Oldtown. In the whole
history of Aegea, no Genon has been openly given the right to
private use of land. In the past four generations, no one has
been offered the cancellation of a service debt. Perhaps the
thought of freedom and land will result in solid clues.

As the first day of search proceeds, the uproar on the
streets requires the presence of more soldiers. Outside
locations being searched, people shout about the indignity of
it all. *"Is such a search being carried on in the homes of the
people in Midtown?"*

When soldiers enter each business and dwelling, they
read the proclamations of General McClaren to the people
inside and offer private consultation with anyone wishing to
offer information.

While the search of Oldtown is taking place, trackers
comb through any uninhabited areas on the plateau where
fresh traces of human movement are found. While there are
no outright searches taking place in Midtown, certain
dwellings are covertly watched.

# CHAPTER 15
## A Piece of the Puzzle

"If you must pick between truth or comfort, pick truth."—*Kol,*
*a gatherer banished to the Poison Forest after the rebellion in the*
*Second Generation*

Sage Dooley avoids sitting upon either of the sofas and
opts for a small chair in the corner. None of the other men
waiting in the room has ever been formally introduced to him,
but they know who he is. He's both a curiosity and a celebrity
of sorts, the resident genius of the plateau. They watch him
with admiration and envy. The vast majority of men who
aren't Genon are in the military. None of the men sitting here
would be allowed to walk around looking as scruffy as Sage
usually does, much less meet with the General in such a
condition.

Like his famous ancestors, he's had greater access to the
combined knowledge stored in the Archives. He's been able to
glean much from what the first generation wrote down when
they came to grips with the thought that they were never
going to be rescued and their combined knowledge would be
lost when their technology died. The engineering specs,
drawings, descriptions, schematics, formulas and recipes were
treated as holy objects at first—now they are hidden away, and
the farther each generation gets from the mindset of those
who first penned the instructions . . . the harder it is to piece
them together into coherent, usable information. Some days,
he worries he's not smart enough to occupy the pedestal he's
been given.

Aware of the stares from the other men in the room, Sage
does what he usually does; he pretends to be preoccupied with
something. When he was younger, he could stand in the
shadow of his father and uncle—heroes both in Agean lore,
men who delivered the goods, who engineered and created the
means to feed and provide for the growing populace of Aegea.
Once they died though . . . the light of all that attention shifted

onto *him*, and most days he isn't sure he *wants* to be in that light, to be responsible, to be the innovator who would help keep the next generation of Aegea alive. Sometimes it's like a weight he's dragging around in his soul. Between that and the pressure to have children—more little geniuses who will "carry on the legacy" . . . well most days he's content to not be seen by *any*one.

He's bored, so he sets the large tube holding drawings and documents on end and spins it on its edge, catching it whenever it wobbles out of control.

"The General will see you now."

He breathes a sigh of relief and rises from his seat, holding the tube. He can almost hear the others in the room thinking, *Perhaps he's come up with some grand new design.*

He nods at the General's aide and says, "Thanks," before he walks through the door to the general's office. Jubal McClaren is standing by the window, reading a document, but looks up as Dooley enters.

"Sage. I was surprised to hear that you wanted to see me." The general extends an open hand to the chair in front of the desk. "Go ahead and sit down. What did you want to show me?"

Dooley glances at the tube and lays it on the desk. "Actually there are a lot of things I'd like to discuss with you at another time. And I brought these designs for a steam powered tractor . . . but that's not really why I came, either."

Jubal sits behind the desk. "Then, why did you want to see me?"

"I'm very sorry about your daughter, sir . . . and I think I may have seen something that day that may be of importance."

Jubal's eyes suddenly come into complete focus on Sage. "What did you see?"

"Well . . . I was running an experiment. I was flying on a kite."

Jubal looks confused. "You mean you were flying a kite?"

"No. I was flying . . . *on* a kite—well, actually, attached to it, but that's not the important part right now. I was out in the country, about nine miles out of town—you know, where the wall is right on the edge of the cliff?"

Jubal nods.

"It was midmorning, on the day you became general. I was several hundred feet up, and I noticed a movement over by the tram station. I looked through my telescope and I saw that at least two people—men in uniforms—were using the tram to send a large crate down into the forest. I'm sorry I didn't say so before now, but at first I didn't know that your daughter was missing. As you know, I lead a sort of isolated life. This morning, when my wife heard what had happened, she realized I may have witnessed something important so she came right to my lab to tell me, and I came right over here. I figured if I was carrying this," he said, picking up the tube, "I could get in to see you without very many questions."

A hint of color comes into the general's ashen face. "Tell me again. Tell me everything you can remember."

"Only what I told you. A movement caught my eye and it took a few moments to train the spyglass on it. I wish I could be more specific, but at the time I didn't know how important it might be and I was bouncing around quite a bit. I *did* notice though, that the crate was one of the big ones—like they load on wagons for a load of tools or farm goods—and it had an insignia on it, but I was too far away to see any details or see if anyone else was in the tram station." Sage leans forward and lowers his voice. "Those crates are easily large enough to hold a couple of people. I'm thinking that if you haven't found them anywhere on the plateau, perhaps that's because they're not here."

Although there's no evidence that Sage was ever loyal to Col. Mosely, the colonel is a distant cousin of Sage's wife.

"Have you told anyone else what you saw?" Jubal asks.

"Tressa is the only one I told, and she came directly to me as soon as she heard." He hesitates a moment. "I realize what you must be thinking. Just know that if *anyone* in my wife's family knows about the use of the tram that day, the information *didn't* come from either of us. I was so preoccupied the day it happened, I didn't even tell my assistant about it. I was the first man to fly in over a hundred years—seeing a tram car was the last thing on my mind when I got down." He shrugs. "I did remember and tell Tressa later that night, but neither of us thought much of it again until she was at a gathering and heard some women talking about what had happened. She instantly sensed that the crate on the tram might have something to do with it." Sage pauses and leans forward. "This is more serious than anything Tressa and I can remember . . . and if I had a family member in this situation, I wouldn't rest until that person was found. I've come here to offer my help. I give you my pledge; whatever I can do for you, I will do it—and no one will hear of this unless you want them to know."

Sage waits while the general stares into the distance.

Finally, Jubal asks, "If we needed it, do you have anything that would aid us in a search of the Poison Forest?"

"I have equipment and weapons that have never been seen outside my lab. They might help trackers and give a tactical advantage in the forest. You say the word and I'll help you outfit them. I'd even be willing to go with them to offer solutions and support if you asked me to."

# CHAPTER 16
## The General's Wife

"**B**lack is the color of mourning because when you are overcome with grief, you see nothing but darkness."— *A proverb of His people*

Duana McClaren opens her eyes. Another day has dawned. Another day. *How many days has it been?* She doesn't know. What woke her up? Was it the sound of horses clopping by on the cobblestones outside, or maybe cadets talking and laughing as they walked below the open window? *It's so much noisier here.* How is it that the entire world can continue, the sun rising and setting, people working, eating, sleeping, talking, laughing, and going on like they always have . . . while her daughter is missing?

Duana sits up and locates the patch of sunlight streaming through the window onto the floor. It's not midday yet. *How will I get through the rest of this day, not knowing where my Jariel is?*

There's a gentle knock on the door.

"Yes?"

It must not be Jubal. He would have opened the door when she answered.

\#\#\#

Outside the door to Duana's bedroom, the new housekeeper waits for an answer. "Madam? It's Belinda. I made you some tea and breakfast."

The general told her not to take the tray up, but to offer the option of coming downstairs first. "Would you like to eat it downstairs?

There is no answer.

"Or should I bring it up to you?"

After another pause, she hears a response from inside the bedroom, "I will come down. In a while."

"Yes, ma'am," Belinda answers before she turns and walks back toward the stairs. Perhaps this is good news that she can share with the general later. *"She came downstairs for breakfast today, sir." The Maker knows that this man could use some heartening news.*

Hastily hired just days ago, Belinda is well aware of the rewards and hazards of her new position as housekeeper for the ruler of Aegea. She's the envy of many of her peers in town . . . but probably looked upon as a bit of a usurper by those who work for the family out in the Westlands. She's already heard about the terrible end to the relationship between Mrs. McClaren and Mosha, the cook who worked for the family nearly all of her life. Word has it that Gen. McClaren found Mosha a new position working for the daughter of the former general, but everyone knows how awful it must be for the woman to move away from all she's known and come back to town to work for someone else. It's like being publicly disgraced.

The Genon of Aegea are in some respects like a single, large organism, an interwoven network of families that watch and discuss the whole of life within their bounds. Belinda has been warned by those in the know: *"Do your job, stay out of the personal lives of the family members. The new general may be a better man than the previous one . . . but Mrs. McClaren will cut you off without a second thought if you displease her. That woman is as cold as a mountaintop. She has no affection for anyone."*

### #

Back in her room, Duana McClaren stares into her closet. Six plain dresses hang on either side of the otherwise empty closet like pall bearers waiting for their woeful task. At home, she has dozens of new frocks for all occasions, and most days she would try on at least three or four of them before making a choice for the day. But these are the dresses she threw into a trunk with some shoes and a couple of shawls. In her haste, she gave little thought to what she packed. Two of the shoes in the trunk didn't even have mates. Duana reaches for the nearest dress, pulls it loose, and drags it back to the bed before she goes to the wash stand on the other side of the room. She pours water in the basin before she cups her hands and leans down to wash her face. She catches sight of herself in the mirror and is amazed at how calm she is regarding her appearance. There are dark circles under her eyes and her uncombed hair falls loosely around her shoulders. She splashes water on her face, dries off with a cloth and looks again. Apart from the water on her hair and robe, she looks the same . . . and she doesn't care.

### 

Even though Duana said she was coming downstairs, Belinda looks surprised to see her employer enter the dining room and sit at the table.

"Good morning, Ma'am. Would you like tea first, or with your breakfast?"

Duana's brow furrows with the effort of the decision. "Um. I think I'd just like the tea first."

Before Belinda leaves to get the tea, she quickly pulls a placemat, a napkin, and a spoon from separate drawers and sets them in front of her.

These aren't Duana's fine linens from home, these are made of the rough utilitarian military issue cloth, requisitioned for Jubal's use when he was in town. Although he likes the status of luxuries at formal occasions at their home in Westland, Jubal always liked the rough-and-ready message that "standard issue" objects gave him while he was in town among cadets and other soldiers.

While she waits, Duana stares at the placemat and the napkin. They are mostly a dull gray with occasional burgundy or brown threads in the weave. Her fingernail scrapes over the cloth and she wonders, *How many threads per inch are these?* She can almost hear a tiny *tick, tick, tick,* as her fingernail slowly scratches across the loose weave. *Jariel would know how many threads were in this just by looking at it. The placemats she made for Westland had at least twice as many threads . . .*

Belinda enters the room with tea on a tray and sees Duana examining the placemat. "I know, Ma'am. Those are coarse, they are. I'm sure you have much finer cloth at home. Soon, you'll be in the general's house and you can send for your own things or have more made."

*This woman talks too much. The servants at home know not to jabber on . . .*

Belinda looks at Duana and stops speaking. After a few uncomfortable moments, she clears her throat and says softly, "I'll check back with you in a few minutes, ma'am, and see if you're ready to eat."

# CHAPTER 17
## Old Menoh's Lament

The old woman moves the rough cloth curtain and looks out. Her husband is still just sitting there on the stool near the pond, staring toward the sunset. The food is almost cold, so she gathers up the broad leaf that holds his dinner and his cup and walks out to him.

Old Menoh doesn't turn to look at her, but as it is with many who've shared so much time in each other's company, he senses her presence.

"Westland seems to be emptying out," he laments aloud. "Our fellowship is shattering and those who should be here are gone or going away."

"Oh?" she says. She puts his cup on a stool to his right and seats herself on the one to his left.

His voice has a distant tone. "I lay on the bed at night, and I feel as if our community is being shaken apart. We're being scattered. First Shaye, then Mosha . . . Ty found out that the girl Chessie who shared a room with Shaye, returned to her family and cannot be found." He remembers one more. "Lemon is gone."

"And after you went to McClaren and stood up for him. I think Mosha was right—that Lemon is a jot in want of a good shaking."

Ignoring Fiona's food and her words, he sighs. "I know that some think that we should rid ourselves of the troubled ones, but doesn't the Maker say that even the parts of our body that need more care or need to be covered are still parts of our body? I cannot but think that we failed them. Westland is starting to feel empty, Fiona. Even the Great House of Westland looks like the skull of some lonely creature that died in the wilderness, with dark, hollow eyes staring out at the world." He stops talking but continues staring into the distance.

She gently places her hand on his sun-hardened cheek and he turns to face her.

"You have not failed," she says. "We will look to see what the Maker does with all these pieces. Perhaps he is allowing this so he can put them together in a different fashion, eh?"

"Time will tell us," he sighs. "Time will tell."

# CHAPTER 18
# Marvel

### In the Great Forest

Jariel shakes her shoulder. "Shaye, Shaye . . . wake up!"

Shaye's first instinct is to hug her pack containing all her possessions tighter. Her eyes open but she's having trouble orienting herself. Part of the problem is that Jariel's face is so close to hers, she can't focus.

"You must have been having a bad dream," Jariel tells her.

Shaye takes a deep breath. "Yes, I think I was."

It's only when Jariel moves away that Shaye remembers where they are.

"What were you dreaming?

Shaye remains completely still as parts of the dream flash by in her mind. It was about death . . . and soldiers with guns . . . searching for them. She was running with a child in her arms . . . and a giant creature was right at her heels. Just before she woke up, to her horror, she realized the child she was holding had no face.

Shaye refocuses on Jariel. "I don't recall what it was about."

"You're able to tell lies quicker these days," Jariel says with a sniff.

Still holding her pack, Shaye sits up and notices several white flowers—undoubtedly tossed into the bed as they slept. Supremely annoyed, she flicks one of them off the bed before looking up at Jariel. In a low but mocking voice she says, "'Mother! Shaye is the one who broke your bottle of perfume. Mother! Shaye put a lizard in my dressing table drawer so she should have to pay for the things it ruined.' Or how about, 'I'm sure Shaye tore open my pillow. Throw her out of the house'." Shaye leans into Jariel's face before saying, "'Mother, I didn't do a thing to Shaye and she attacked me! Trade her off!'" Shaye sits up straight again. "I'm finally learning something from you. Who knows how good I may get at this business of lying?"

She notes the unsettled look on Jariel's face and realizes, *How satisfying this is.*

Jariel scoots away from her accuser. "What are you hiding in that pack? You're even sleeping with it on now."

Shaye reaches around the pack as she ties the knot in the hem of her dress with a jerk of her hands. "I didn't have an entire house full of goods to worry about. I guess I was *lucky* on the day your mother cast me out that I had a moment to pack all my possessions. Too bad I've had to let you wear half of what I own."

At breakfast, the two women sit on opposite sides of the fire. In Genon culture women, especially unmarried ones, usually sit together at meals. Shaye overhears one of the men, David, saying to the quietest of the group, Loash, "I don't know why she brought the girl if she dislikes her so much."

Shaye pretends she didn't hear the remark, but it makes her so angry she feels as if her head may begin to sizzle and fly off her shoulders. This remark is just one of a growing list of things she doesn't like about David. For one thing, he has leapt out from behind trees a couple of times and then laughed when she and Jariel recoiled in fear. And, even though she's made it plain she is *not* amused, he continues to seek attention with antics that are, in her estimation, completely childish.

She decides to ignore David and pay more attention to other things. This morning Enoch, the one they call Tooth, spread out a buffet for them—complete with fruits, starchy cooked roots, a little of the dried meat from someone's pouch, and the usual pile of crawly things. They all note with surprise that Jariel tries a bite of the leathery but spicy dried meat. The stunned expression and flush of her face once the spice detonates in her mouth are unmistakable and all the men chuckle as Jariel pulls in a few deep breaths.

"It's very hot," she manages to squeak out, "but 'him eats good.'"

"Good for you, daughter," Nathan says in her language. "More?"

She quickly shakes her head no, and smiles at all of them as they chuckle some more.

That's when Shaye sees it. Jariel is connecting with them. Shaye's not certain why this is so unbearable to her, but it is. "It's a pity," she says to Jariel, in a sarcastic tone, "that you never bothered to try Genon food before. But then, you so seldom made the effort to have contact with people outside your home."

Jariel's sweet expression evaporates. "I wasn't given the opportunity."

All of the men exchange knowing glances that shame Shaye into silence.

### 

Before the men finish packing up, Mule leaves the camp, then returns. "Shaye, Jariel," he says with a large grin. "Come quickly and see."

The two women, plus Loash, Avallach, and Tooth follow along, weaving between large trees, then pressing through a tangle of brush before they break into a small clearing filled with sunshine, tall grass, and flowering plants.

"Come, come," Mule urges the women with a beckoning gesture.

The other men stand at the edge and watch Mule and the women walk to the middle of the clearing.

Jariel's eyes sweep around the flowered oasis before she looks up at Mule. Morning light silhouettes his head, and shines through the wiry beard hair on either side of his face. A small piece of a leaf or a fruit peel is dangling below his chin and she makes a small gesture as if she is brushing something off of her own face, but he doesn't seem to get the hint. "In your beard," she says in Command Dialect. Eventually, she shrugs, then reaches over and lightly brushes the green flake away.

He considers Jariel's hazel eyes for a moment before he moves away and plucks several brilliant, red flowers. He inspects them before he places one in each of Shaye's hands, then offers to do the same for Jariel. After her disaster with the ants, she's afraid to touch the flowers.

Mule looks at Shaye. "Tell her nothing on the flowers will harm her."

Shaye tells her before she reluctantly takes the flowers.

"Now, both of you—hold the flowers out in front of you, like this," he says extending his hands forward, palms up, "and don't move. Be still, and something marvelous will come."

"Something *what* will come?" Shaye asks.

Mule squints for a moment, trying to think of a different word. "*Hmm*. Uh, something to give wonder . . . and make the heart happy with the Maker."

After Shaye translates, Jariel asks, "It's not some sort of large, hairy bug is it?"

Mule chuckles when Shaye tells him. "No. Hold still and watch."

Both women hold out their flowers and he moves away to sit in the tall grass nearby. As she looks around, Shaye remembers Nathan saying how his mother missed the sunlight. She closes her eyes as she realizes just how much she loves the sunlight as well. *What a gift it is just to stand here and feel the sun, and a breeze on my face.* Her eyes are still closed when she hears a soft, *buzzy* sort of noise and she opens them. There, not two feet away, is a tiny bird of unimaginable, iridescent colors. He moves closer and hovers near her hand, sticking his long, slender beak into one of the flowers she holds. His feathers change hues as the light moves over them—as if there were rainbows hidden in them. His wings move so fast, they are a blur!

"Look look *look*!" Jariel whispers excitedly and Mule motions to her to be quiet.

The little fellow moves away momentarily when she speaks, but then darts back. Within another few moments, five of the little birds are hovering around. Jariel isn't talking but she's nearly hyperventilating with the excitement of this incredible beauty.

Shaye is stunned as well. *Who would ever have believed such splendor existed? And in such small packages! And how can they remain in one place in the middle of the air?*

Mule slowly gets up and stands in front of them. He extracts a small piece of fruit from his bag and bites it in half before holding half in the cupped palm of his right hand. "Watch."

One of the birds lands on his thumb to taste the juice oozing from the fruit.

Jariel and Shaye are awestruck.

"Now," he says softly, "each of you take a half and hold it, like this."

They slowly take the fruit from his hands and stand in wonder as the little bird comes to rest on Jariel's hand and continues sampling the fruit. Another comes near, but the first bird flies at him and pursues him out of sight.

"*Eh eh,*" Mule chuckles softly, "They have all this bounty, but they still fight each other. Like the two of you."

Shaye doesn't translate the remark.

A sharp whistle resounds through the trees before Mule shrugs at the women. "Nathan says we must go now."

"I will remember this all my life," Jariel tells him. "My heart has no words for this joy."

He looks at Shaye, who relays the message.

"Just so," Mule says, nodding. "These things are made so we will *marvel* that the world is beautiful and terrible. We *marvel* at the Maker, and remember with joy that he rejoices over us the same way you have rejoiced over these small birds. Just so."

As they leave the clearing, Shaye remembers a dark little finch with a cream colored belly that lived outside the Great House of Westland.

Mule looks back at Shaye. "*Eh eh.* I see Shaye is sad again. Why did this make you sad?"

She shakes her head. "There is this little bird I fed every day at . . . back on the plateau. He certainly would be envious if he could see the way these birds are dressed!" She sighs before adding, "He will survive without me . . . but I will miss my little friend."

When she realizes Mule is looking at her sadly, she's embarrassed that her emotions are so raw and so visible . . . and by the fact that she appears ungrateful for the spectacle she just witnessed. She gives Mule as much of a smile as she can manage then touches two fingers to her heart, before raising them upward. "But truly, the sight you gave us today did bring me joy. It *is* something to—what is the word?—*mmm*arvel at."

He nods. "Just so."

# CHAPTER 19
# Boats

"**W**hat is faith? Our forefathers believed they could soar above the sky in complete safety. Were they fools? Faith is choosing to trust the One who sees the beginning and the end of the journey."—*A saying of Kya, a Firstlander*

They've spent several more nights in the forest, with air so close and sticky it actually feels like a damp blanket on the skin. Yet Jariel sleeps soundly each night.

On sleepless nights Shaye sometimes watches Jariel's face in the dim light or listens to her breathe, wondering, *How can such a spoiled girl, who rarely ventured out of the house be surrounded by all of this . . . and still sleep at night? She's always been such a miserable thing. Why isn't she still crying for home?*

Every night, the men make a bed in the lowest limbs of a tree for Shaye and Jariel and sleep around the foot of the tree. During the night, when she's holding still, Shaye feels the occasional movement of the baby inside her, and when it happens, she feels a crazy mixture of fascination, love, and terror. In daylight hours, she has to remind herself to refrain from placing her hand on the spot that cradles the little life within her. It's a spot that's now getting larger by the day. Within a few weeks, she figures, even her baggy servant's dress won't hide it. *What will I do then? What will they think of me? I am pregnant because I was a fool . . . and I'm a liar because of my enemy.*

This morning, the baby is quiet but Shaye awakens and waits for Jariel to stir. As soon as the girl's eyes open, Shaye has a comment to make. "When you sleep, you take up the bed like a giant, dead thing. You flop over onto my side and then I can't get you to move," Shaye whispers.

"Maybe you just *think* I'm on your side since you're growing *fat*," Jariel manages to shoot back before they hear Nathan calling them to come and eat.

Shaye *does* feel thicker in every measureable way. Her breasts, hands and feet are swollen and sore. It's as if her body is trying to outgrow her skin and it's all she can do to clamber down the tree without help. She pulls the opening of her pack closed and adjusts the strap so it's comfortable in the front.

"I could carry that for you," David offers.

"This is all I have," she says without looking directly at him. "I hope you can understand that I want to keep it close."

Jariel begins her climb down, so he turns to help her and Shaye quickly moves away. On her way to the small campfire, she watches where to put each foot, avoiding areas where the mist rising from the forest floor obscures her view. *Another day. Another steamy day in this moldy, musty-smelling jungle lies ahead.* If she allows her mind to dwell on the odor much longer, she knows she will have dry heaves.

So much has happened, she can't seem to get a handle on any of it. But, at least thus far, she's managed to anticipate the questions they would ask Jariel and waylay any slip-ups during questioning.

*"When they ask you about your 'real' family, just say you don't know. Tell them you made different kinds of cloth for the family that raised you."*

So far, no one seems suspicious. Although she should be breathing a sigh of relief over this, she can't bring herself to relax.

It's not long before the men start to pack up, and Nathan gives directions for the day while Jariel munches on the last of the fruit. As Shaye finishes up a few bites of her own food, she ponders other unresolved issues. A few days ago, she saw the warrior again. She was last in line as the main group walked and, sensing rather than hearing something, she whirled around, thinking David was sneaking up to scare her. But it wasn't David. It was the warrior, maybe thirty feet away. *So he isn't an illusion, he's a real man . . . isn't he?* When their eyes met, he stood still for just a moment, then veered into the brush and was gone. And, last night when everyone was sleeping, she awoke, terrified when she heard strange whooping and howling noises nearby. Then she heard his voice whispering from above, "Don't be afraid, Shaye. They are noisy, but they are silly creatures . . . just talking to one another. I'm watching over you. As long as I'm with you, I will see no harm comes to either of you."

Eventually the animals woke everyone—even Jariel. Mule stood at the bottom of the tree and told them that the animals were much smaller than they sounded and wouldn't hurt them.

Shaye remains awake after that, speculating, *Who is he? Am I the only one who sees or hears him? How does he know my name? Am I going mad? Am I becoming like Beth's mother-in-law? By all accounts, the woman was always a little stupid in the head . . . but by the time she was old, she didn't recognize her surroundings and spent her days talking to people who weren't there.* Shaye takes a deep breath. Between the heat, the noise, and wondering over the mystery, she stays awake for yet another night. *Maybe the lack of sleep is making me crazy . . .*

It's fully daylight now and Shaye doesn't know if she'll have the energy to keep walking today. Once the sun climbs above the dense canopy of trees, both the temperature and humidity climb in the shadowy land beneath.

On the Aegean Plateau, the high altitude made for moderate days—*much* cooler than here—with nights that were sometimes even chilly. *In Aegea, one could feel a breeze, smell clean air. Here, there is no relief, no airflow, no cooling sensation from evaporating sweat, no way to stay dry—especially when one is either walking through showers of rain, or rising mists, or squishing through warm, muddy little streams.*

Suffering with the oppressive heat, with mosquito bites, and now with rashes that simmer in the salt of her own sweat under her filthy, damp clothes, Shaye understands why the soldiers called this place "the Poison Forest." *How do people live down here? How much further will we travel before we arrive . . . wherever it is we're going?*

She finds she can understand more and more of the language the men speak each day and each night, Nathan is willing to tutor her about words and concepts all but lost in Aegea. Last night, he told her more about his father and the Exile's first trip through the forest.

"My father's first wife, Eva, and their only child died of a fever six years after the crash. His second wife, my mother, died in the Great Forest several months after the Exile. By then, they all knew we could no longer stay near Aegea—even if they longed to go back and see their families. That was when my father spoke to the others of something he saw from the sky when they were coming down. He believed that the Maker had shown it to him for a purpose."

Shaye listened with eager fascination. This was as exciting as the stories from Aunt Pearl, plus she had the added enjoyment of watching the animation in Nathan's eyes, and the wag of his long beard as he talked.

He saw her obvious interest and nodded his head. "Yes. My father was on that machine that flew through the air. And when he looked out the window, he saw a place that, later, he knew they could live if the Maker would guide them through the forest. Several times a day, he would climb tall trees to see which direction to go and we kept walking. Some became afraid that he was mistaken and stopped travelling with us— but most of the Exiles stayed together until we got to our homeplace."

"What happened to the ones who stayed behind?"

"We sent people back to them to lead them—and some couldn't be found, some had already died, but ten were still alive and they came out to the homeplace." Nathan waves a hand at the trees above them. "This forest was a mighty work of the Maker. It is too much for humans—even for Genon."

"You don't live in the forest? Where *do* you live? Is it another place like the plateau? What's it like?"

He winked and smiled. "That is the most wonderful surprise. I will not tell of it now. You will see it soon enough for yourself," he said. He wanted to resume the story of his father, so he just picked up where he was before Shaye interrupted him.

"Not long after we got to our homeplace, my father took a third wife. She died twenty years later, after giving him two more sons and a daughter. By then my father was very old and people thought it would be better if he didn't try to marry again. Still, he lived long enough to stay with me and my wife three years before he finally went to be with the Maker."

"So you have a wife."

"Oh yes," he said. "Peony. She is named after a flower in the other world, and she is *my* flower in this one."

Shaye smiled. "She is waiting for your return?"

"Most certainly. She didn't really want me to go," he said, shrugging, "but I am a man like my father who must do things at times. I felt compelled to come on this trip—for several reasons. One is that the next generation must learn the ways of the forest so our people don't forget how to travel and survive here when we need to. There are many valuable plants that only grow here—and fewer of us who know where to find them, how to harvest them while leaving some to grow for the future. The apothecary there will pay well for the plants we've gotten on this trip. The second reason is that I had a small hope in my heart that the Maker might provide our community with more people," he said smiling. "And three . . . " his voice trailed off. "Well two reasons is good enough, eh?"

"Do you have children?" she asked.

"We had two sons and a daughter. One son and our daughter still live, but they have no desire to know of the forest. Our other son died as a child."

The old man's face turned somber and he stopped talking. He sat, staring into the distance for a long while and Shaye didn't think it was appropriate to talk, so she just sat there, too.

### 

Jariel continues to recover from the spider bite she got during her first conscious moments in the forest, but in the daytime, she suffers with most of the same torments as Shaye. Plus she is weak, which means that she's not able to keep up. Often they must slow down to carry her or slow down to walk at her pace. The Genon culture doesn't favor coddling people, so mostly they just slow down and let her walk.

There is no one other than Shaye she can really talk to, but during most daylight hours, Shaye keeps her distance, which gives Jariel plenty of time to think about her situation.

Each night, Shaye goes to bed exhausted, yet sleep often eludes her as she ponders the weight of all her decisions . . . and all the lies she's told.

Today, Jariel is walking at the back of the line, but she's feeling stronger, so she speeds up and closes the distance between herself and Shaye. They are many miles from Aegea now, and as far as they know, no soldiers have followed them, so there isn't a need to hide their trail like there was in the beginning.

"You seem to be continuing in the same dark mood you've had in the past months," Jariel observes. "Why is that?"

Shaye's eyes dart to the men just ahead of them and she starts to say something, but then stops.

Jariel tries another question. "You're not happy to find the Exiles aren't a fable?"

"You know *nothing* of me."

"I don't want to argue. I didn't mean it the way you think. I just meant you always look so . . . sad, or upset . . . or something. I'd think you'd be more accepting of this situation, more pleased than I."

Although she's annoyed, she can't help but ask, "Why aren't *you* more distressed? Why aren't *you* still crying to go home? Don't you care that . . ." she looks about cautiously before she continues, ". . . your people probably think you are dead? Don't you think about *their* sorrow? You almost never left your house, you barely ate food at home . . . and yet now you seem satisfied to trample around in this place and eat most of the food they bring you. . . . I am *certain* that I don't understand you."

It's the closest thing to honest communication they've had since they were five years old and it's not comfortable for either of them.

"You're right, you don't know me," Jariel says. "At least you got to enjoy the company of Mosha and Beth and others there. You were able to walk about outside and even to travel to town sometimes. . . . Do you think I stayed at home, that I had no friends because I wanted it that way? Did it ever occur to you that my seclusion wasn't by my own choice? And now, who besides my parents would miss me? Ty and Mosha," she says with a shrug. "And maybe Gib."

"*Who?*" Shaye asks.

"Gib. Gilbert Lott," Jariel says with a sigh. "A sol—" she looks around, "A young man who was going to court me. He was the one who spent so much time with me the night of my—the night of that party."

"UGH! That *pig?*"

Jariel stops walking. "He's *not* a pig and he cares . . . cared for me."

Shaye halts as well and scoffs, "He cared for you about as much as any other woman who could draw a breath.   You should have seen him sniffing around every nearby female whenever you weren't looking and lamenting how it was his *duty* to be seen with you, to kiss you."

The last night she was at Westland, Jariel and her mother had a terrible argument. Her mother's words start to replay in her mind.

Jariel's face flushes. "You apologize for saying that!"

Shaye shrugs. "I could, but it would still be *true!*"

The sudden rise in the volume of their conversation causes the men in front of them to stop and turn. The two women glower at each other for a few seconds, then begin walking again.

After a long silence, Jariel says, "I'm out in the wild world and no one knows I'm alive." Her voice starts to quaver when she says, "And, if what you say is true . . . perhaps no one even *cares.* And, even if I could get away somehow, I wouldn't last an hour in this wilderness.   What's the use of longing to go back?"

Shaye sighs. "What I said . . . it was not meant as an insult to you, it was about the kind of man that Gilbert is. Genon have men like this, too."

Jariel tries to gather the right words together.  They step under a branch that's leaning across the path before she says, "Where I am right now is overwhelming . . . yet I'm not sure I ever had any more power over my circumstances at home." Jariel ponders it a moment. "And this place," she says taking in the view around them, "is more beautiful and powerful than anything I've known before. . . . I can see why they call it the

Great Forest. It's fearsome, yet filled with colors and smells and tastes and sounds one could never imagine . . . it's overflowing with things I never would have been *allowed* to experience, things that are," she tries to repeat the word Mule said in the clearing with the tiny birds, "*Mar-ve-lous.*"

Shaye nods.

"I'd like to think," she continues, "that Mosha and Ty and my parents will miss me, will mourn me . . . but maybe they'll just accept that I'm gone. Ty will probably marry Linsey and have children and a life of his own . . . and life on the plateau will go on as it always has."

Shaye stops walking. "I need to relieve myself."

"Should I go with—"

"No. I need some privacy."

Jariel thinks for a moment. "Sure."

Shaye looks ahead and calls to the last man in the line in front of them. "Hello! Can we stop?"

The youngest of the men, David, calls to the others, then turns and walks toward them. When he gets close enough, Shaye says something to him and he hands her his knife before she walks away from the path.

After several minutes, Jariel starts to worry. Should she find a way to tell David to look for Shaye? She's about to do so when she catches a glimpse of the girl walking back toward them.

Shaye wipes her face as she draws near. "I don't know what is growing over there," she says to David, "but it is harsh to my eyes and nose. We should move on." She says the same thing to Jariel and wipes her nose again.

Jariel doesn't need any more convincing. "Maybe we should move on quickly."

David remains behind to walk with the two women, but after multiple unsuccessful attempts to engage Shaye in conversation, he begins pointing to different things and telling Jariel what they are. She gladly participates in the communication, trying to repeat the simple words he conveys, like, "tree," "leaf," and "fern." Once they've covered the simple description of most of the visible objects several times, David attempts to teach her other useful terms.

He puts his hand on his own chest. "David, *man.*"

"Man," she repeats.

He motions his chin towards her. "Jariel, *woman*."

"Woman."

He points to the features on his face. "Eyes."

She echoes, "Eyes."

"Ears."

"Ears."

"Nose."

"Nose."

"Mouth."

"Mouth."

"Chin."

"Chin."

He puts his hand on his chest again. "David . . ." he says and tilts his head to the side as if he's asking her a question on a test.

"Wait, wait," she says, holding her hand up. "I know this. Wait. David is *man* . . .?"

"Yes!" he nods and smiles. "And what is this?" he says, pointing to a tree.

She squints with the effort. "*Ummm* . . . " She finally shrugs and says, "I can't remember."

"Tree."

She taps herself on the head. "Oh I knew that! Yes. *Tree*."

Shaye picks up her pace until the sound of their banter becomes an indistinct chatter that she can ignore and she moves along, trusting that the men ahead of her know where they are going, numbly putting one foot in front of the other.

An hour later, though, she's stirred from her oblivion by a smell. The very air around them has changed. She's wondering what this new scent is when she hears shouts and whistles ahead. David and Jariel hurry to catch up.

*Obviously,* Shaye realizes, *they must no longer fear being followed.* Someone hacked a path through the dense brush. Shaye and the others squeeze through the compact, green hallway single file before stepping into blinding light. The noonday sun is not only shining down all around them but reflecting up off of . . . water.

Once she's able to open her eyes beyond a tight squint, Shaye sees that they're standing on the bank of a large body of water which appears to be hedged in by jungle on all sides. Neither Shaye nor Jariel has ever seen this much water gathered in one spot before . . . and Shaye is puzzled by evidence of a strong current in it when a branch and several leaves swiftly float by.

Old man Nathan approaches them with a spring in his step. He's apparently very happy to be here.

"Look, my daughters," he says in Genon, raising both hands into the air. "We have come to the great river . . ."

For a moment, Shaye is astounded. How can it be a *river* when she can see the ends of it all round?  Nathan is still speaking.

". . . and it will carry us very close to our homeplace."

Once the full meaning of his words soaks in, Shaye can hardly breathe at the thought of it. "We *cannot*," she sputters, "we don't know how to . . . what is the *word?* We cannot go in the water!  We will *surely* perish!"

Nathan leans toward her. "You think we mean for you to 'swim'?" he asks before he gives her a wink and a grin.

Shaye looks like she might faint, but he throws back his head and laughs.

Jariel can only witness the fact that Nathan is excitedly talking about something, and the normally fearless Shaye looks terrified. "*What?* What is the matter?" she asks.

Shaye puts her hand on Jariel's arm. "Wait.  Wait a moment," she says, while she keeps her eyes on Nathan, who is speaking again.

"No one expects someone from Aegea to know how to *swim*," he says. "We have *boats*!  See?" He pokes his chin in the direction of three long, wooden vessels beside a cruder, smaller one carved from a single log. "We will sit in these and they will carry us very far with little effort.  Do not worry, daughter."

Shaye swallows hard. *So this is what he meant when he said "boats."*  She looks at Jariel, and, if she didn't feel so scared, seeing the girl in the sunlight with her tangled hair and her muddy face, wearing that soggy bag of a dress would be comical.  But she's too frightened to enjoy the spectacle. She takes in a gulp of air. "They want us to get into those . . ." she looks at Nathan as she indicates the watercraft.

He nods and says the word. "Boats."

Shaye starts again. "He says we are going to travel in those things—called '*boats*'—and ride on the water."

Jariel gasps. She holds onto Shaye and blurts out, "But the water will pull us down and we will *die*! Remember the son of Clement? He fell into the big pond at Westland, and it took him down and he *died*!"

While the rest of the men watch the drama between Shaye and Jariel, Mule, walks over to one of the boats and steps into it.

"Look!" he calls out to them, then whistles loudly.

Shaye and Jariel turn to see him standing in the boat, bouncing up and down, keeping balance by waving his arms. While they watch, he sits down on one of the shelves in the boat and shrugs his shoulders with his hands spread wide. "See?" he says in Genon. "The boat travels on the water like a cart goes over a road."

Shaye translates. "He says, the boat goes on the water like a cart goes over a road." After a few moments, she remembers something. "Also . . . I must say that my Great Aunt Pearl told me how people in the world before Aegea would make boxes to travel on the water. She must have been talking about boats. She said that some of the boxes were so big that many hundreds of people could ride on them all at once."

Jariel shakes her head as her brows assume a skeptical pose. "How *could* that be true? Where would one find trees large enough to make it? And everyone knows that there was no other world."

Shaye understands the cynicism. When she heard Pearl speak of men building boxes that could ride on the water, the concept almost made her dizzy. She realizes it's one thing to think of Pearl as a teller of truth, to *acknowledge* her stories about boats . . . it's another thing altogether to *trust* that she herself can sit in a boat and ride on water.

Jariel and Nathan watch Shaye's face as she weighs all these ideas. "Jariel," she finally says, "I believe my Aunt Pearl spoke the truth—she said her grandfather told her of this and that many of the Firstlanders wrote about such things in the Archives. Aunt Pearl had no way of knowing these things from personal *experience*—yet she believed her grandfather and those who wrote down their experiences. They said there were boats . . . and here are boats. They said that people rode in them over great distances."

After some of Nathan's cajoling and many promises that the water wouldn't pull the boats down and kill them all, Shaye is willing to be brave and try it, but Jariel is still terrified.

"What if there is an accident and the water pulls the boats down? We will die."

Shaye translates before Mule reaches into one of the boats and retrieves a length of rope. He steps close to Jariel and looks her in the eyes before he ties one end of it loosely around his midsection. Still holding her gaze, he asks Shaye to translate, "Tell her to put her arms up." When Jariel does so, he ties the other end around her waist with a secure knot, leaving less than five foot of rope between them. "Our lives are bound together now. See?" he says, clasping his hand on the rope. "If the boat fails, my fate and yours are the same. Even if you cannot hold onto me, I will swim to the land, and you will be drawn there with me. You will live."

"This is good thinking," Ben says as he retrieves another rope. He ties one end of it to his waist, and manages a smile as he steps close to Shaye. "Arms up?"

She says nothing and raises her arms while he ties the other end around her.

Several of the other men protest. "*Eh eh! Eh eh!*"

They fall silent when Nathan gives them a stern look and says, "You know Mule and Ben are the strongest swimmers here. Come, we must be going."

The women, Mule, Ben and Nathan step into one of the three long boats. The rest of the men load the gear plus their pouches and baskets of plants onto the other two long boats, and they all launch out into the river. Jariel keeps a white-knuckled grip on both sides of the craft as they push off and begin to paddle along with the current. Shaye, Ben, Mule, Jariel, and Nathan sit in single file in the same boat, with Shaye in the nose of the craft. At Nathan's direction, several men in one of the other boats paddle faster and, much to Shaye's surprise, disappear to the left. When the remaining two boats reach the same spot in the river, Shaye can see the trees open in that direction and that the river flows on, snaking its way forward.

Once they're around the corner, the river narrows and the two boats no longer travel side by side. The boat with women in it takes the lead.

Shaye's eyes are drinking in the scenery when Ben leans close to her right shoulder as he paddles, and he speaks to her in a gentle voice. "This place is beautiful is it not? The people of Aegea couldn't conjure up such a sight."

She doesn't know what to say, so she just nods her head.

"I can imagine," he continues, "the most beautiful thing they had in Aegea was you—and now the light of your eyes is gone from their world. I should feel sorry for them, but I don't."

She wants to move away from his breath on her neck, but doesn't want to offend him. He's being kind at the moment, but he's a fierce sort of man. She wants neither to entice *nor* to offend him so she leans away ever-so-slightly and then holds still.

He keeps speaking to her. "I can see you are also a modest woman, an upright woman. A true gift for our people."

Shaye's eyes close. If she could "swim," she'd consider jumping out of the boat. She wants him to stop talking, to move away from her.

Nathan's voice rings out from the back of the boat. "Benjamin, I can't hear you. You must speak louder for me."

Ben straightens up his posture and speaks up. "I was saying that anyone could see Shaye has the beauty of our people, that she is an upright woman."

Nathan's head bobs up and down. "It's true. So we must respect her. You wouldn't want the young men to see you leaning upon the sister and think ill of her, would you?"

"You are right, Nathan."

"Just so," the old man says.

###

After the first hour, Jariel relaxes somewhat as she watches the unfolding beauty all around her. The myriad greens of the jungle, patches of clouds, flowering plants floating along the river bank, and the brilliant blue of the sky are all mirrored in the water. Large white birds with their long legs lagging behind them fly overhead or sometimes stand with crooked necks, wading along the shore, catching shiny creatures in the water. They have entered yet another new world, filled with sights, sounds, smells, and textures. Like the widow tree, these things are frightening yet beautiful. No one living in Aegea has ever seen such sights.

The river picks up speed and all of the men in the boats keep paddling, so they're moving along at quite a clip. Shaye keeps trying to slowly inch away from Ben and once she realizes there is sufficient rope to do so, she slides off her seat into the nose of the boat. The rope pulls taught for just a moment when she curls up so she scoots back toward him with her feet under the plank she used as a seat. She pulls the skirt of her dress over her legs and tries to find a comfortable position, with her head just on the edge of the boat so she can look out at the water and the jungle gliding by. She's made every effort to keep her hands off her belly, but in this position she can fold in one of her arms and cradle it without drawing attention to the little bulge growing there. The child is dancing inside her and Shaye closes her eyes. For a few moments, the sorrow lifts and she allows herself to be fully aware of this growing life. *Hello little one! I wonder, what would they all think if they knew about you? My baby!* But the thought of the scowls she'll soon get pops her little bubble of happiness. *Chessie was right. It cannot remain a secret much longer. Even Jariel has noticed that I'm expanding. What will I tell them? That a colonel's son said he loved me, so I just gave him my sacred self? That I couldn't manage to be the strong woman my mother was? That I threw away my future for a few minutes in his arms? There certainly will be no more talk of me being an upright woman once they know. And what will become of my child? Will she be as despised in the "homeplace" as I was in Aegea? Everything I ever thought of myself, everything I ever wanted is upside down.*

She can see Ben is watching her, and she doesn't want to look back at him, so she closes her eyes and curls up just a little more, resting her head inside the boat. The sun is warm, and strands of her hair are shifting around in the breeze, softly dancing on the skin of her face. She can hear the sound of the water rolling past the hull of the boat along with the rhythmic *plunks* of the paddles breaking its surface. She's so exhausted, it isn't long before she falls asleep.

While Shaye is curled up in the front of the boat, Jariel keeps pointing to things and asking for someone to name them. Each time, she tries to repeat what they tell her, and this pleases Nathan.

"What are *those*?" she asks excitedly when she sees one of the large wading birds downing a fish. "The creatures from the water, what are they?"

"Fish," Nathan says.

"Fish," she repeats. "Fish. *Fish*." Now she turns to look at Nathan. "Fish *live* in the water or hide there?"

Translator Shaye is unavailable. He opens his mouth to speak several times, but stops each time. He finally settles for, "Fish *live* in water."

Rarely in her life has Jariel spent much time outside. Certainly, she hasn't spent more than an hour in full daylight on any day since she was a small child.

Nathan notices her skin is turning dark pink, "*Eh eh*. You is very . . . white." Then he leans forward and speaks in Genon. Mule agrees with whatever he said and repeats it to Ben, who also nods.

Within another half hour, they hear whistles and see the lead boat is pulled up on the shore where the men have started a fire. Two of them, Philip and Jude, are rinsing off in the water as the group with the women makes for shore.

Ben laughs and shouts to the bathers, "Perhaps we should always bring women on our trips if it means you will mind your own smell!"

Ben's voice startles Shaye awake. *What was he saying? Something about a smell.* And she realizes there IS a horrible smell. It's not the smell of a man, it's similar to the smell she first noticed when they neared the river, only this odor is much more intense. She sits up and looks around just as the boat bumps on the shallow bottom along the shore. The men in the other boat jump into the water and wade toward the beach, dragging the small craft until the keel is as near to the shoreline as they can get it, then they help do the same with Shaye's boat. After that, lines are tied to the prow of each one with the other end tied to a stake firmly embedded in the shore.

As usual, eager men reach out to help the women.

"Don't suffocate them! Let them decide if they want your help," Nathan advises again.

Jariel lets Mule and David assist her, and has both feet on solid ground before she unties herself from the rope. Shaye unties herself from Ben, grabs the side of the boat, and tries to get out by herself, but soon she realizes that everywhere she puts her weight or leans that the boat tips, she finally opts for some assistance from Ben—who has already stared down any competitors for her hand.

Several of the men complain to Nathan that it's "unfair" for Mule and Ben to be the ones who were allowed to be "tied to the women."

Nathan quickly holds up a hand to silence the whining. "Mule and Ben are the oldest and they are the strongest swimmers. *It's only rope*, it means *nothing*."

Once the controversy is settled again, Shaye looks at Jariel and has to pull her lips in to keep from smiling. In addition to all the other visuals that were going on earlier, the girl is now well on her way to a sunburn—something that rarely happens in the families of soldiers.

The men rolled a log into the shade of several large trees and built a fire nearby. They motion for the women and Nathan to come and sit upon on the log, but Shaye stands at a distance repulsed by the smell of whatever it is they are cooking. Jariel is fascinated, by it.

"Fish?" she asks the old man.

He laughs and nods. "Yes. Fish. Good for birds, good for people." He takes his place on the log and extends his hand to the rest of it, welcoming the women to sit there.

Shaye realizes that *this* is the source of the smell and she fears that the reek of the cooking creatures may make her throw up. "I think I shall stand," she says. "My legs need to be straight for a while."

Nathan nods before he looks around the group and says in Genon, "Well then, we thank the Maker for safe journey, and for His gracious gift of fish today."

The men nod in agreement before one of them holds out a fish on a stick to the old man. He breaks off a chunk from the side of the fish and plops it on a broad leaf before he peels back its skin. Jariel leans closer and Shaye stands on her toes to see it. Neither of the women have ever seen meat this white before. Not even the breast meat of a sooshi hen is this white. It looks nearly as white as the ice on top of mountains! Nathan squeezes some juice from a small green fruit onto the fish, rubs a slice of a small orange-colored pepper on it, then leans toward Jariel, offering the leaf. "Him eat good!" he says in her language.

Much to Shaye's amazement, Jariel pinches off a bit of the fish, gives it one last whiff, then puts it in her mouth. She rolls it around on her tongue for a moment, then exhales several times as the heat of the pepper zings her mouth. She finishes chewing the meat and swallows it. It's flaky, moist, and succulent. She's never tasted anything like it before. "*Mmmm! Fish!*" she says, and the men all smile.

Shaye's mouth drops open at the idea of seeing picky Miss Jariel eating spicy Genon cooking.

Nathan looks at Shaye. "Tell your sister to break off only small pieces. The bones of fish are very small and sharp as needles!"

The fire is hot and it isn't long before Jariel moves further from it, saying she's feeling "a bit baked" already. She scoots further down the log.

Nathan points his chin at the open spot on the log, "Why don't you sit while you eat?" he asks Shaye. "Then you can move about before we get back in the boats." He watches her reluctantly move to the spot Jariel vacated and sit.

She tries to nonchalantly breathe through her mouth as she accepts a segment of fish. Oddly enough, after she swallows a few bites of it, she doesn't feel *as* nauseated—but she doesn't dare eat more of it. "May I have some of that?" she says, eyeing several fruits piled on the ground.

The moment the words are out of her mouth, the two men closest to the stack reach for them. Philip is faster, and offers, "I can cut it for you."

She accepts half of it and stands—not far from Nathan, but upwind of the scent of the fish. While she's chewing on the fruit, her focus drifts over the water and comes to rest on the boats pulled into the shore.

"Why did you leave the little boat behind?" She suddenly asks. "If we were followed, couldn't someone find it?"

All the men look at Nathan.

She can see a complex range of expressions fliting across his face, and she realizes she should have kept silent about the boat.

Finally, the old man just shrugs.

Everyone looks back at Shaye, but she asks no further questions so the men go back to talking and eating.

Mule leaves the fireside with a machete and hacks fringe-like branches off a few of the nearby trees. Within no time, he and Ben strip off the individual fingers of the fringe and begin weaving them together in a circular pattern. This fascinates Jariel who asks to sit with them and watch.

Shaye looks at Nathan. "My aunt told me about boats, and sw-sw . . ." she makes a paddling motion with her hands.

"Swimming," he answers, smiling.

"Swwwimming and," she motions to the bones on the leaf he's holding.

"Fish."

"Yes, and fish, in the time before."

"What family is your aunt in?"

Shaye shakes her head. "No. She is my father's aunt. She wasn't born Genon—but she is a Genon of heart. She became a 'chaplain,' a woman who follows the Maker and helps His people. She also lost much because of her faith."

He nods. "Yes. I believe one can be a Genon in their heart . . . It seems as if your mother was a woman after the Maker's own heart—to influence others to follow at such great cost. Does your aunt still live?"

Shaye nods, but looks down. "My aunt is very old, and I fear that when they tell her I am gone, it will be one of too many sorrows she has faced in recent years. But I worry most for Mosha—the woman who raised me when my mother died. I am like her child," her voice begins to thicken and her chin quivers, "and I fear the sorrow of this may be too much for her." Shaye stops talking, knowing if she says another word about Mosha she will break down.

"I see your heart is very heavy," Nathan says. "Don't worry—the Maker has a way of working things out for good, even when it doesn't look like it could ever be so. My parents and I were left to die in the Great Forest, and my mother *did* die . . . but in that time of so much sorrow, the Maker reminded my father of something he saw many years before that, as the flying machine was falling toward the ground." The old man points up to the sky. "He saw it from way up there. Our homeplace. It is a good place and you will be welcome there. You will be free, child. *Free.* All because my father was set on a sorrowful path." He then nods to Jariel as he says, "Tell your sister what I said."

She calls Jariel over and begins to relay the information to her. When Shaye gets to the part about being free, she can't resist adding a comment of her own. "I will be free. I will be where no one can cast me off or trade me like I was household goods."

Jariel's focus darts around as she processes Nathan's words. "He believes that there really *was* another world, and that his grandfather was brought from there to the plateau . . . and eventually cast out with the Exiles . . . so that he could lead them?"

Shaye's shoulders slump when she realizes her barb missed its mark. Nathan asks what Jariel said, and once Shaye relays it, he nods and says, "Just so. Now tell her the rest."

After she hears Nathan's thoughts on the redemption of the Exile's sorrow, Jariel says, "So . . . regardless of the *intent* of others, Nathan believes his Maker used it to save them."

"Yes. Just so."

"And therefore," Jariel contemplates aloud, ". . . the Maker used it to save *us*—to save you and me. . . . And that even *our* presence here could be part of a larger design?"

Shaye feels entrapped by Jariel's logic. She hates it, but must admit that it is true nonetheless. She nods once, and looks down.

Shaye's growing silence and her posture say that she doesn't want to talk anymore, so Nathan starts a quiet conversation with one of the men near him and Jariel uses the opportunity to move back to where Mule and Ben are still engaging in their weaving project.

Walking to a shady area, Shaye stares at the river that will bear her away from everyone she loves.

Within twenty minutes Jariel dons a beautiful, broad-brimmed hat, and Ben is nearly finished making one for Shaye. By the time the group packs up to leave, both women have their special headgear on and Jariel thanks both men for teaching her another weaving skill.

Before they board the boats again, Nathan tells the women to reapply mud to their exposed skin. The mud here isn't the red soil of the forest below the plateau, it is tan in color, and Shaye realizes that the water here isn't as dark as the water was at the beginning of their journey, probably due to the color of the soil.

Jariel balks at first. "Must we? We have hats now, and I'll hide my hands in the folds of my dress."

Nathan has the gist before any translation and replies, "Yes, the hat stops sun from above, but light also shines on water and flies back up. Hats can't stop the light from the water. See?" he asks, stepping into the water and holding his hand out with his palm facing downward. "There is shadow here, but see the light dancing here as well?"

After Shaye translates, Jariel nods.

"That light will still burn you."

The women reapply the mud to their faces and arms—and the men put some on their shoulders and faces.

When they get back into the boat, Shaye perches on her seat in the nose again and watches as trees and plants she's never seen before slide by on the shore.

A hint of a smile comes to her face. *This is all so beautiful.* Before she realizes it, she's caught up in the desire to share it. *Wouldn't Ty love this? The plants, the trees, and all this water . . . all this wilderness to explore. He and Basil would wander here with such joy. He would—*Shaye stops, mid thought and slowly slides off her seat. She curls up in the nose of the boat again and covers her head and face with her newly made hat, trying to concentrate on the sounds of the river, the conversations of the men—anything to pull her mind away from the stark realization of her loneliness.

With every turn in the river, Jariel breathlessly points to new sights. All around her is a world bursting with new input for her senses. And, after more than a decade in seclusion, she's surrounded by men who seem to want her attention. To her fellow travelers, her over-the-top responses to everything are a source of amusement.

### 

The river widens again and slows down. When the boats turn a corner, a large, cream-colored sandbar comes into view.   Standing all around it are possibly a hundred tall, brilliant pink-orange birds with stick-like legs, long looping necks, and huge, bendy beaks! *Never* before has Jariel seen such a color . . . or creatures so comical.

"Look!" she calls out, startling several of the birds.

The men smile at her outburst.

Shaye awakens at Jariel's shout, bolting upright, totally unprepared for the sight of these birds. *Who could imagine such things?* Tears sting her eyes and she looks back at Nathan, who leans to one side of the boat to see her.

He laughs with delight and winks at her.   "Didn't I tell you?" he says, beard wagging in the breeze.   "The world has much more than we can know."

The youngest man, David, dives into the water—and to the breathless amazement of the women, he swims! The other men turn the boats and paddle back around against the current.   Dozens of birds take to the air to escape when David approaches the shallow water of the sandbar and stands up. Once he's there, he steps around, then stoops down a couple of times to collect items before diving back into the water and swimming for the boat where the women sit.   As soon as he grabs the side of the boat and pulls his chin over the edge, the whole vessel tilts in his direction.   Jariel immediately throws her arms around Mule, who gives David a triumphant smile.

Then David's other hand appears over the edge of the boat, holding two brilliantly colored feathers.   His reward is the gush of gratitude he gets from Jariel when she sees the feathers.   He speaks to Nathan who gives him a bit of a scolding, but then translates.   "He say, one feather is for you and one is for you sister."

Jariel pulls one of the feathers from his hand before David drops back into the water, makes two sidestrokes to the nose of the boat, then hands Shaye the other feather. Overwhelmed, she nods at him and says a quiet, "You honor me."

Jariel runs her fingers down either side of the smooth, wild-colored feather, perhaps thinking of what she might do with it.   Shaye, on the other hand, already knows what she will do with her feather.   She will roll it up in the cloth where she keeps all of her precious objects: her mother's earrings, the captain's bars from her father's uniform, one of his buttons, and the little bag of small treasures from the other world that Pearl gave to her.

### 

An hour later, Jariel's lips are burning.  Reflections off the water, while almost hypnotic, are hurting her eyes and burning her lips.  Earlier, she'd made the mistake of trying to lick her lips, and the taste of the mud was terrible!  Then she tried holding her lips in, but as soon as she wasn't consciously doing it, she'd stop and they would continue baking.

She plucks up her courage and actually leans to her right to dip her hand into the river.  Even though the water isn't cold like the water from the mountain streams of Aegea, it's refreshing to her skin.  She leans to the opposite side and places her other hand in the river, dipping out some of the liquid to apply to her lips.

*A month ago, who would have thought I'd be riding on a "boat," down a river, through the Poison Forest—going someplace that no one from my family has ever been?  And yet it's real and I'm here.  This is what it's like to be truly alive in the world, and to face everything square on.*

She dips her hand in the water once more and the water feels so nice, she lets it linger there, but the voice of Nathan breaks into her musing.

"*Eh eh!*" he says, lifting her hand out of the water with his paddle.

She looks back at him and he points to several creatures basking in the afternoon sun on the right bank of the river.  The animals are dark and shaped like the lizard that Beth took out of her dressing table drawer one day.  Only these creatures are gigantic—longer than a man is tall—with long ridges of bumps down their backs, and she can see they have many jagged teeth.  Two of the animals slink into the water in the direction of the boats and disappear beneath the surface.

She jolts when Nathan taps her on the shoulder to draw her focus back to his face.  He nods in the direction of the creatures, then points to his own temple, saying, "Him think *you* eat good.  All people stay in the boat here.  Keep hand and foot inside."

She nods and notices that Ben and Mule have set spears and a machete nearby in case a need arises. She pulls a fold in the skirt of her dress and hides her wet hands in it. The men in the boats keep paddling and the boats slide downriver.

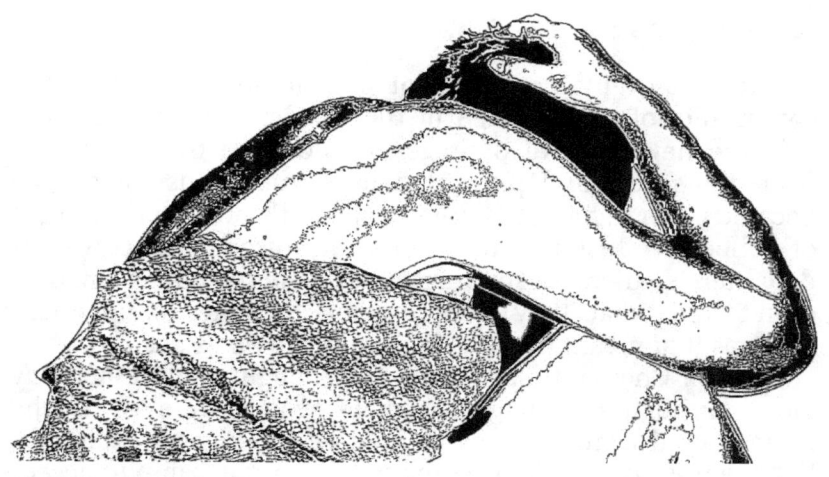

# CHAPTER 20
# Wild Women

"So often we assume things about others or ourselves. We make rash vows. We think we know who the heroes and cowards will be, who will be resolute or unable. But only the Maker knows the entirety of the matter. We ourselves don't know until the opportunity is at the gate."—*A saying of Kya, a prophet of His people among the Firstlanders*

### In Aegea

The woman can only see through one eye, but she dips the corner of a cloth in the water and then carefully wipes her face with it. Although the bleeding has stopped, the pain has not. Last night's beating was the worst she's ever gotten.

In the distance, she can hear shouts of men and screams from women . . . but it's only slightly louder than normal, so she doesn't give it much consideration.

Living "wild" in the forest situated to the north of the road that runs between Midtown and the Outpost wasn't at all what Chessie imagined it would be like. There are no rules or laws here that define what you *can't* do. That sounded so appealing at first. Disappearing from sight just one day after joining her family wasn't that difficult. Her cousin probably didn't even notice she was gone until meal time.

Recent events caused a lot of fear and tension in the community of wild women in the woods. They'd been told that the new General of Aegea would have them removed from the forest and punish their clientele. Just before he became general, hadn't McClaren cleared a neighboring forest of robbers? Just two days after the disappearance of his daughter, soldiers swept through the camp, but when they didn't find what they were looking for, they simply left. Perhaps that meant that business could go on as usual.

When Chessie first arrived, she thought finding her way alone through the tangled ancient woods to a place she remembered from years ago would be the biggest challenge, but she was wrong. Getting the women of the camp to accept her into the "clan" was death-defying. Because there are no rules here.

In order to be accepted, Chessie needed to prove her willingness to be loyal. The initiation involved multiple beatings, followed by the leader of the group chopping off her long hair with a knife. During her first days in the clan, Chessie's was told she must clean up after the other women, scrub their clothes and bedding on the rocks at the little stream nearby, and haul large jars of water to the encampment. They barely fed her and told her they would kill her and her family if she tried to leave.

Once the threat of a raid had passed, soldiers and workers once again drifted into the camp bringing food, meechi juice, and other goods in exchange for spending time with the wild women. Chessie, the newest member of the clan, was forced to go with the men who were sick or whose idea of a good time was to beat up a woman. Kneeling down in the mud on the bank of the little stream, she realizes that with one small nudge, she could plunge into the blackness of death. *Who would ever know? Who would even care?*

Before she joined them, she thought the wild women of the woods had the freedom to do whatsoever they wanted. The reality was that most of them were defenseless against people who had no boundaries. They were a community of desperate people, willing to plumb the depths of Chessie's capacity for humiliation and pain in order to help sustain their tenuous life in the wild.

She looks up from the stream just as a soldier and a Genon man come through the trees. They're looking straight at her and moving quickly in her direction. She wants to run, but knows that with her injuries, she can't get far enough fast enough. Instead, she assumes a fetal position, and covers her head. She can hear the rustling of their footfalls in the grass as they approach.

They stop several feet away and one of them asks, "Are you Chessie? Did you work in Westland before?"

She raises her head and opens the uninjured eye to look at them. Seeing their shock, she's suddenly aware of how she must look. Worse still, she realizes that these men actually *do* know her from her life before she was here. One of them is Basil, the grandson of Old Menoh, and the other one is Tyrone McClaren.

The shouting in the camp rises measurably.

"Are you here to arrest me?" Chessie asks. To her own surprise, she's actually hoping they *will* haul her away from this place.

"They have orders to arrest everyone in the camp," Tyrone says, "but, technically, you're not in the camp right now. *Are* you Chessie, the woman who worked at Westland?"

She looks down at the dirty rag, in her hands. "Yes."

"What are you *doing* here?" Basil blurts out in Genon. "You traded your sacred self for *this*? Why would you—"

Tyrone interrupts him. "If you come with me, I am authorized to offer you protection from the prosecution that the people in the camp will face. Do you want to come with me right now to safety, or do you want to stay here and be arrested?"

She can't bring herself to look up again, and she starts to shiver. "What do you want from me?"

Ty kneels down so he is face to face with her. "I give you my word, if you come with us, no harm will come to you. We will take you to a place of safety and food. I need to ask you some questions, and once you answer them, we will deliver you anywhere in Aegea you wish to go. I can take you back to your family or find temporary shelter for you in town until you have work."

Her whole face begins to hurt from the involuntary spasms of sobbing. She covers her mouth and looks at them as she nods. She cannot speak, but eventually holds out her hand and Ty helps her up.

### 

She just keeps chewing and swallowing the food. Two hours ago, she didn't know if she would live another day. Now, Chessie is sitting at a table—of all places, in the dining room reserved for high-ranking officers at the inn of the Outpost—and she is eating a second plate of food. She's used to having all her food piled on her flatbread and eating it with her fingers, so she ignores the fork and the spoon on either side of her plate. Her free hand moves to touch the soft napkin resting near her plate. The only thing that's softer than the napkin is the dress she's wearing. The dress has seen a lot of use and is probably something one of the girls in the home has outgrown, but it's clean and in better shape than anything she's worn for a long time. Two of the women here helped scrub her skin and comb her matted hair, and when they handed the dress to her, she just held it for a full minute before she put it on.

She's so full she feels like she could pop, but keeps looking at her plate, only allowing herself to occasionally look at the décor on the table and walls. This room is separate from the part of the inn where the caretakers live—and while its ornamentation is simple, it's pleasant, even by military standards. The walls are paneled and the table has a smooth shine. The main "feature" of the room is that it's up a flight of stairs where people of rank can enjoy a bit of privacy and cool breezes coming through the large windows. She looks out one of the windows at the opposite end of the room and sees a column of smoke rising in the distance. She wonders, *Is it the camp in the woods?*

Ty turns around to see what has captured her attention. After watching it for a few seconds he says, "They had orders to take everyone from that place to the fort. Now they're burning the shacks. No one will be allowed to go back there."

When he turns around again to face her, she's looking at her plate again.

The stunned stares she's gotten from everyone are so painful, she can't bring herself to meet his gaze but eventually her curiosity wins over her shame and she asks him a question.

"Did my family ever try to find out what happened to me?"

"No."

"Then why did you come looking for me?"

"You were one of the people who was at Westland that day."

She doesn't have to ask him what day he means. She says nothing so he continues talking.

"When I asked around at Westland just two days later, soldiers said you'd been questioned, but nobody seemed to know where you were. When we tracked your relatives down and asked them about you, they only knew you were 'gone.' It took a while, but we eventually found someone who could tell us where you might have gone."

He watches her bruised fingers as she uses the last bite of bread to sop up all the remaining gravy on her plate. She carefully works the bread into her swollen mouth, eventually managing to chew and swallow it.

"Would you like more?  You can have as much as you want."

She continues looking at her plate. "No.  I'm full."

"More water?  Juice?"

She shakes her head.

With deliberate calm, he asks, "Do you know what happened to Shaye and my sister?"

Her posture shrinks a little. "No."

"I *promise* you, no one is accusing you of anything. I just need to know.  Did you see either of them?  Did you see anything odd that day? Anyone out of place?  Do you have *any* idea who took them or where they might be?"

She glances up at him and weighs the idea of contriving some sort of story, of misleading him in order to gain an advantage. "I already told the soldiers who questioned me.  I wasn't working in the Great House that day so I have no idea where anyone would have taken Miss Jariel. As for Shaye . . ." Chessie says, looking into her lap, ". . . she and I weren't friends, so we didn't talk much.  I was out of the room the night before . . . and I didn't see her that day either."

"Where were you that morning?"

She folds her arms and straightens her back.

He immediately softens his tone.  "I just want to find my sister and Shaye.  *Please* tell me, where were you?"

She chances another look at him. "I was in the barn. Up in the place where they put the hay. I was with someone."

"Did you see or hear anything unusual?"

She rolls her eyes. "What do you think? We were sort of busy." She chances a longer gaze at him and is surprised that he doesn't look angry or embarrassed.

"So why," he asks, "did you take off after you were questioned? Why did you disappear?"

If she'd never joined the wild women, the old Chessie would have tried to give him some sort of coy answer. She might even have flirted with him or offered to give herself to him. She dares to look up at him again and when his head moves to one side, she catches sight of herself in a large metal tray that's hanging from one of its handles on the wall behind him. Even in the less than perfect reflection it provides . . . she's hideous. Her eyes come back to him. Two and a half hours ago she was hiding in the woods wearing dirty rags after being badly beaten. Now, she's clean, dressed, fed, and so far as she can tell, safe.

"I come from *gleaners*," she tells him. "My kind tend to be the first under suspicion and the last to be believed. My kind are also the first to be squeezed out of a living situation— I figured it was time to go, and I hoped I could find a better situation elsewhere," she answers.

He's confused. "How could you think that place in the woods would be *better* than working at Westland . . . or working *anywhere* for that matter?"

When she shrugs, she can feel every bruise on her shoulders and her neck. "I didn't plan on it being like that," she says, in a shaky voice. "I thought I'd be free. Free from the endless hours of working for your family, free from the bad looks I got from people like Basil's mother every day. Free to just enjoy myself and live where people don't judge you. I thought I could just . . . I don't know . . . have a few drinks whenever I wanted, have fun with men whenever I wanted. Like living in a party."

He cannot think of a response, and his silence feels like judgement to her.

"I told you, I didn't plan on it being like that."

"Then why did you stay there? You wouldn't go back to those people *now*, would you?"

She lets out a sarcastic, "*Ha!* What else am I good for? Who would have me now? Who would let me work for them? Does it make you feel better to help me for one day? *You* don't have to worry about how you'll live, where you'll sleep, what you'll eat, what you'll wear, or if anyone will ever want to marry you—you never did. All you had to do was be born on the right side of a sheet. As long as you're a lawful heir, you'll get everything you ever want." She points to herself. "I'm from a family of mixed-blood, a family of gleaners. *My own family didn't even come looking for me!* Why would they? There wasn't much to glean out of the crops this year and I'm just another person to feed." She thought she was all cried out, but her eyes burn with more tears and she covers her face. "There's no hope for someone like me."

Ty sits in silence for a while before he says, "I . . . I don't *want* what you said to be true . . . but I know for the most part, it is. Even if I were General, I couldn't change everything that makes it so . . . but I will do what I can to see that you get a chance for something better."

Her expression hardens. "In exchange for what?"

He holds up a hand as he shakes his head. "I asked you to tell me what you knew about that day, and I'm hoping you told me the truth. What I offer now is simply because I think you should get a chance at something better. I've already spoken to the family that runs the Outpost here. One of their daughters is getting married and moving away within a few days. That will leave them shorthanded. They will need some help with the livestock and with the plants they grow, so if you're willing to work as hard as anyone else here, they'll give you a small room of your own on the other side of the yard and all of your meals. If you are willing to learn the jobs that they need done and you don't make trouble, the arrangement can become a steady one and you can have a small share of what you help them produce."

He can see she's actually thinking about what he's saying. After a pause, he adds, "This means work and rules . . . but it also means safety, food, shelter, and maybe something more. They know you're injured, so you can have a day of rest, and several days of light work . . . but then you'll be expected to pick up your fair share of the labor. If you agree to this, you can stay. Otherwise I can look for a job for you in town or we can find your family and take you to them."

Both of them look at the doorway when they hear people coming up the stairs. He pushes his chair back and stands up before he speaks to Lu, the second daughter of the family that runs the inn. "Could you see if we can get Chessie at least one change of clothes?" She nods and leaves the doorway. Next he speaks to Basil. "Ask Johnathan to hook a fresh horse up to the wagon. We'll be ready to go soon."

Finally, he looks back at Chessie. "You can stay here, out of sight for a few weeks, and help out while you think about it. Do you *want* to do that? Tell me what you want to do."

She is anxious about her choice, but finally answers, "I will . . . try to stay here."

Ty nods. "I'll be back this way in a few weeks and we can see if it's working out."

He starts to leave the room but turns around when one last question occurs to him. He turns to ask, "Did anyone *else* enter or leave the barn that morning for any reason while you were there? It doesn't matter how insignificant or normal it seemed at the time."

She shakes her head *no*, but then stops to think about it. "Well . . . no one but Lemon. He works out in the stables and barns now—since your father cast him out of the house. He brought a wagon back just before I left."

"Was there anything in the wagon?"

"Nothing but one of those crates that they use."

"How many horses were pulling the wagon?"

She closes her eyes to picture it. "I think . . . only one."

### ###

Once he's downstairs, Ty looks around the room and realizes there is nothing to write with and nothing to write *upon*. Few Genon know how to read or write, so there would be little reason to keep any paper, parchment, ink, or pens about. He lifts his knife out of a sheath on his belt and pulls out his shirt tail. Holding the hem of it with one hand, he uses the sharp blade to slice off a piece of the shirt. He scans the room again until he sees a small bowl of dark berries.

"May I?" he asks, as he reaches for the bowl?

Lu is puzzled, but she nods.

He lifts one of the berries out of the bowl, then squashes it on a cutting tile on top of the counter. He places the strip of his shirt on the counter, then dips his ring in the dark juice. After stamping the cloth with his ring, he looks at the imprint and seems pleased with the result.

Handing the cloth to Lu, he says, "When you get to Westland, have Ski give this to Monique, Basil's mother—she recognizes my mark. Tell her that she is to make arrangements for your work and meals, and she'll see that you and Ski get moved into a good place to live."

She blushes and says, "Thank you. Thank you for doing this."

"Nonsense," he answers. "Basil told me that you and Ski have been sweethearts for quite a while and that Ski has been feverishly trying to work some sort of trade or deal so that the two of you could be married. I'm just helping to make it happen sooner."

A few minutes later when he's alone with Lu's parents, Lilly and Jon, he finishes the private talk they began earlier.

"I must be on my way," he tells them, "but I gave Chessie the offer I spoke to you about and she's decided she'd like to try and stay on here." He rubs his chin as he looks at the couple. "We can all see that she's been treated very roughly, and you may have heard rumors about her. All I'm asking is that you treat her with the same respect I've seen you give to everyone else, and that you show her how to do the work that will be expected of her. If she makes trouble or she decides that she wants to leave, send word of it to me and I'll come and take her away. Keep track of your expenses, and if they exceed what I gave you, I'll repay you when I return in a few weeks."

John and Lilly both nod before she says, "Shaye is a distant cousin of my family and a dear friend to our youngest daughter. Have you learned anything? Is there yet hope?"

She sees a spark of something in his eyes but she cannot tell if it's something hopeful or something dreadful.

He clears his throat and says, "Right now, we're just following every trail we find."

# CHAPTER 21
## Lemon

"Fear doesn't lead you away from danger or trouble, but rather, drives you to them."—*from the Soldier's Manual in General Fairmont's collection of ancient books*

Once again, he's passed out at the small table where he sits nearly every night, so he's oblivious when someone puts a hand on his shoulder and calls his name.

"Lem!" the man repeats, and then shakes him.

Lemon jolts and falls off his stool, banging his chin on the table in the process, but he doesn't feel any pain.

"C'mon, Lem," the man says, before hauling him up onto his feet and placing one of Lemon's arms over his shoulder. "Let's take you home."

Inebriated, Lemon responds, "But I don't want to go anywhere." and then tries to crane his neck far enough away from the other man to focus on his face. It doesn't help so he asks, "Do I know you?" He squeezes his eyes shut and then opens them, extra wide, in a continuing effort to look at the person walking him toward the door. "Hey. You're not the person . . . you're not who you think . . . you're not who I think . . ." He stops for a moment to consider his words before he finally says. "I don't know you, do I?"

A few of the patrons look up as the stranger keeps walking Lemon out of the tavern. "Of course you know me."

"Well . . . okay then."

More patrons come through the door. The stranger lets them enter and then takes advantage of the open door to pull Lemon outside into the chilly night air.

Once they've moved out of the light shining through the open windows, Lemon's legs suddenly become rigid and he digs in to resist any further movement away from his favorite stool. "Hey. Wait a minute. I DO know you!"

"I *told* you that you did," the other man says and attempts to get him walking again.

He takes a step back. "You're Old Menoh's grandson. You're Basil."

"Yes. I know that."

Lemon yanks out of the man's grasp only to fall on his backside. He can barely see Basil's silhouette, but he points at it and says, "I'm not going anywhere with you."

Another figure joins Basil, and his voice is familiar as well. "Yes you are. You're coming with us right now. And you are going to sober up and answer some questions."

"I don't work for your family. You can't make me do anything."

"Wanna bet?" Ty asks before they drag him several feet and hoist him into the back of a wagon. "I have all authority given to me regarding the disappearance of my sister and Shaye. Your life is in *my* hands now, Lemon."

Basil is already up in the back of the wagon tying a gag over Lemon's mouth before Ty climbs up. They quickly tie his hands and feet. Ty clambers over the top of something to get by Basil and the trussed up Lemon, then shouts to the horses before the buckboard lurches forward and begins pounding over the cobblestones at a rapid pace. Even in his inebriated state, Lemon's mind is beginning to fill with thoughts of what they may be planning to do to him.

Within minutes, Ty turns the wagon, and they enter a small barn. Once they're inside, the wagon stops and Basil lights a small lamp, then jumps down to close the barn door. Ty sweeps over the seat and back into the rear of the wagon, then pulls Lemon's face within inches of his own. "Do you have anything to tell us, Lemon?"

Lemon's eyes remain defiant and he shakes his head no.

"I guess you're in for a little trip, then. Surely you're familiar with this method of transporting people, aren't you?"

The lamplight allows him to see the other object in the wagon with them. It's a large cargo crate with a hasp on it.

"Open the box, Basil," Ty says.

Lemon begins to struggle against his bonds, but they heft him up and drop him into the crate.

Ty's voice is shaking with emotion. "We're going to take you for a ride and I want you to think about how it feels to be taken against your will and thrown into a box, not knowing where you're going or what will happen to you."

### 

Lemon awakens in the box. How long has he been in here? Moments? Hours? The thumping pain in his head is growing and the movement of the wagon only makes it worse. It must be daylight now, for he can see a tiny shaft of light coming around the edge of the box lid . . . and he's getting quite warm. He tries to prepare himself to resist telling what he knows, but as the alcohol leaves his system, fear takes over. The wagon isn't moving on cobblestones anymore. Could they be on the perimeter road that runs alongside the wall? Might they take him up there to dangle him over the edge of the wall? If he breathes a single word of what he has done in order to save his own skin, the people who coerced him to participate in the kidnapping will certainly kill him in some horrible fashion. *Wasn't that inevitable?*

The wagon slows to a stop and he hears voices. First Ty, then Basil . . . and another man.

The wagon resumes movement, but the ground is uneven. He can hear Basil urging the horses to move forward and every part of the wagon creaks over the terrain. Lemon's heart pounds wildly as he bounces around in the crate.

The wagon slows and there's a low, grinding noise as the driver pulls on the brake.

They've stopped.

The wagon leans to one side, then the other.

Muffled voices.

The voices stop.

Lemon can hear his own ragged breathing . . . and a low rumble.

Then silence for several minutes.

The wagon creaks and leans again.

Someone slides the bolt out of the hasp.

The box opens.

Blinding light.

A voice.

He *knows* this voice.

"Lemon! Lemon! Son, what have you done?"

He squints as hard as he can and opens his eyes just a sliver. It's Old Menoh, leaning forward into the crate, placing one hand on his shoulder then using a knife to cut his bonds. "Sit up. Sit up, son, and talk to me."

His head feels as if someone were pelting it with large rocks, and his legs are cramping from being folded up in the box. He pulls the gag loose from his mouth and manages to push up on his left arm to look around. At first, he thinks it's just a residual of the drink, but then he realizes there really *is* a roaring noise nearby. They're near the watermill of Westland, at the bottom of the great waterfall. No one besides the old man is in sight.

"Lemon. Look at me."

He concentrates upon the old man again.

"Come out of the wagon and sit with me. There isn't much time. You must tell me what you've done."

Menoh helps Lemon clamber out of the box, then off the wagon before they walk a short distance. The strip of cloth they used to gag him hangs from his neck, swaying back and forth like a bell as he lumbers along. After a short distance, the old man sits on the ground and Lemon clumsily follows suit.

The roaring of the water is almost more than he can bear. "My head," he finally says as he presses his fingertips just above his eyes and rubs.

"There is no cure for that, Lemon. And there is no getting away from what you've done. You *must* speak to me."

"Where are the others?"

"Look at me, Lemon. I begged for this time with you, but it won't last long. Tyrone and Basil are here—Jubal McClaren himself will be here soon and I won't stand in his way. Not this time. You've done this terrible thing to all of us! *Nothing* can justify it."

Lemon's head is spinning. This is the truth that he has wanted to drown every single waking moment since the day it happened. He pitches forward onto his hands and knees as waves of nausea seize his body. Even when he's heaved up the small amount of liquid in his stomach, his body continues to spasm until he feels as if he will break in half. Finally, it subsides and he leans back on his folded legs, completely spent. "My life is over. No matter what happens now, the others will find me and kill me in some terrible way."

"Only the Maker knows for sure how and when you will die. What you must decide is, whenever that is, do you want to go with the truth of this terrible thing still locked away inside you? Do you want to carry your blackened heart with you to stand before the Maker . . . or do you want the power of all the untruths to be broken here, today, and to live whatever is left to you with a clean heart?"

Lemon crawls over to Menoh and bows with his face to the ground. "I'm sorry! *I'm so sorry!* I swear I didn't know she was in there! I was told to drive the wagon with a box in it over to a place along the perimeter road. When I got there, they opened the box and pulled out a large sack—like the ones they use for hogs. They slung the sack over into another box on another wagon and closed the lid. I thought then that it might be a body—but I swear I didn't realize it was *her* until later when I heard she was missing and they started questioning everyone. I was up to my neck in it by then and given the history with me and McClaren, I knew no one would believe that I didn't know it was her."

Pain is etched on the old man's face. "So . . . you think she was dead?"

Lemon sits up on his knees again and wipes all the tears, snot, and spit off his face with his hands. "Yes. . . . Well, I don't know. The sack was limp. And there was a bad stench."

Menoh can barely say it. "What did it smell like?"

Lemon tries to concentrate all his will on the memory. "I don't know what it was. I've never smelled it before. It made me feel . . . dizzy."

"Was there a second sack?"

"No."

"Was the box where they threw the sack empty?"

"No. They threw her on top of other things in the box."

"Where did they go with it?"

"I don't know where they went. I had to get back to Westland before the wagon was missed."

"Did you ever see Shaye?"

"I never saw her that day."

"Is that all you know? Who are the people who made you do this? Who were the men in the other wagon?"

# CHAPTER 22
# Solid Proof

"We chased them into the Poison Forest and did not let them return. We chased all of those who would strike down the order of our civilization—and therefore life itself. We chased them without pity, and their names will not be found in the record of the Second Generation."—*Captain Martin Jared, a keeper of the history of Aegea in the Second Generation*

## In Aegea

Ty McClaren paces back and forth on the roof of the general's office building while he waits. Since it's three stories up, all of Oldtown and much of the eastern end of Aegea can be seen from here. Rather than sit on one of the chairs under a covered area, Basil sits on the balcony wall and cleans his fingernails with a small knife.

The first ransom note said the people who had Jariel would be following up with their demands, but a second note never arrived. Whether that's due to the disclosure Jubal made or to other snags in the kidnapper's plans is unknown.

Three days have passed since they questioned Lemon. Until today, Ty knows of no progress in the effort to find his sister and Shaye. Until today. This afternoon, Ty received word that he should bring Basil and meet his father here. He can't stop pacing. *There must be news.*

General Jubal McClaren steps through the door alone and walks to a table in the covered portion of the roof. He places his leather satchel on a small table and opens it while Basil and Ty draw near.

"I sent two trackers down to the forest the day after we talked to Lemon," the general tells them. "Asher and another man they call 'Stack'—he's you're cousin, isn't he, Basil?"

Basil nods, then looks at Ty and reassures him, "Stack is good. Maybe the best tracker in the Great Forest."

"Yesterday, they found a trail," Jubal tells them. "It's not a direction gatherers usually take, so they followed it—and found an open cargo box with my insignia on it. I guess whoever hatched this plot figured that my insignia on the box would keep nearly anyone in Aegea from demanding to search it."

"Sure," Ty says. "Who would dare?"

"Near the box was one of the large, cloth sacks we use to hold livestock and food. Inside the box were machetes, and the remnants of bags of food, ravaged by forest animals. The fact that there were provisions in the box suggests they planned on staying in the forest—for several days at least. *If* they had a place where they planned to stay, we haven't found it yet, but the fact that weapons and bags of food were still in the crate tells us the men never had the opportunity to use them." Jubal stops for a moment, knowing each new piece of information will become more difficult to receive.

"At various distances from the box, they found partial skeletons of three men in torn uniforms. All of them were missing some limbs, one of them was missing his head. All of the bones were picked nearly clean by various animals and insects. Each of the skeletons was on the ground, and looked as if the man was moving away from the crate. There were large marks on the two skulls we found and on other bones . . . Stack says a Chemosh took them down."

Ty is completely motionless and Jubal can see the color draining from his face.

"They also found a leg bone about a hundred yards from the box, that didn't belong to the skeletons we found—but Stack and Asher agreed that the bone is too big and too long to have belonged to either of the women. It means there were more than three men. We may never find the rest of the man, but we can be sure he's dead."

Jubal reaches into his satchel and pulls out a rag. "This was also on the ground beside the box. Smell it."

Basil picks it up and smells it, then frowns. "I don't know this smell. It's not a natural thing."

Ty holds the rag to his face. The scent is faint, but it does jog a memory. "I've smelled something like this before."

Jubal looks grim, but he nods.

Ty sniffs it again. "Remember when Edward broke his leg? They used something like this to make him sleep—so he would hold still. They said it was a rediscovery—from the Archives. I remember I had to leave the room because it made me feel sick. It made Edward sick, too. After he woke up, he was nauseated for—" Ty clenches the rag in his fist when he recalls what Lemon said when they interrogated him. "Remember what Lemon said? He said the sack they threw in the box had a bad smell he hadn't smelled before. Maybe this was what he was talking about."

Jubal nods. "Precisely. It puts people to sleep." He takes a deep breath before he pulls the next thing from the bag. It's a piece of fine cloth. Father and son look at it and then each other before Jubal speaks, his voice is thick with emotion. "This has to be Jariel's."

"Have you shown this to mother?" Ty asks.

"No. I haven't had the heart. You know what she's been like since this happened."

Ty stares at the cloth as if it was the corpse of his sister.

Jubal reaches into the bag again. "I almost don't have the heart to show this to *you*," he says. When he takes his hand out of the satchel, he's holding what appears to be dark thread looped into a bundle, tied with a bit of string. He sets the bundle on the table and says, "They found these snagged on the wood inside the box and bundled them up to bring them to me."

After Ty picks up the bundle he realizes it isn't thread. It's long strands of black hair. He drops the bundle onto the floor and the only word he can manage is, "Shaye."

"Son," McClaren says, in a clear voice, "these things could mean our worst fears are true . . . but there are still two things that give me hope."

"What are they?"

"First, Stack and Asher found no other traces of Shaye or Jariel. It's as if they floated out of the box and disappeared. Second," Jubal says, extracting a broken arrow and an arrowhead from his bag, "They found this arrow lodged *way* up in a tree. They broke it and had to dig the arrowhead out of the tree, but here are the pieces of it."

Ty sees a look of surprise on Basil's face, so he asks, "*What?*"

"That arrowhead is stone. Maybe one of us would make something like this if we were trapped in the forest and ran out of arrows but . . ." Basil picks up the back end of the arrow and rolls it between his fingers, "the shaft of the arrow . . . it's made from a different kind of wood than we have in Aegea . . . it's even different from any wood I've seen in the Great Forest." He runs a finger along one of the feathers at the base of the arrow. "And the feathers in the fletching . . . are from birds I don't know."

Jubal nods. "No one from Aegea made that arrow."

The two young men just stare at him.

"Who do you think made it?" Ty wonders aloud.

Basil answers him. "Exiles."

# CHAPTER 23
## Pearl

"Secret, humble prayers are the ones that have the shortest path to the Maker's ear."—*From the Tell of His people*

The old woman awakens, then slowly closes her eyes before she hears it again. A soft tapping sound on the shutters outside her window. She looks at the candle on the small table and sees it's nearly spent. It must be the middle of the night.

There it is again.

*Tap, tap*, and this time, a soft voice asking, "Chaplain?"

She struggles to rise out of the sagging brown chair, then stiffly makes her way to the window, wrapping a shawl around her shoulders. "If you're up to some sort of mischief," she says without opening the shutters, "I'm not in the mood. Don't trifle with me."

"No Ma'am," a male voice says in Genon. "I need to speak with you. About Shaye."

The hand holding the folds of her shawl clenches closer to her chest. "Go to the door."

She grabs the candle on the shelf, then the walking stick next to her chair, before making her way to the door as fast as she can.

*Could it be a joke? A ruse for a robbery?* She'll take the risk. She opens the door to see two men standing on the steps. "Who are you?" she asks, and moves the candle closer to them.

The one closest to the door is Genon, probably in his mid-twenties, the other is wearing an old cloak with a hood.

"My name is Basil, and we need to speak to you. I know it's late . . . but may we come in?"

She hesitates.

His companion raises his face so the candle light reveals his features. *Definitely not Genon,* she tells herself, and then notices the blond-red hair framing his face. Only one other person she can think of has hair this color.

"You are her great aunt, are you not?" Basil says. "Please, let us in."

Pearl backs up, "Come in and close the door behind you," she says before making her way back to the living room.

"We knocked on the door but you must not have heard us. We apologize for the late hour but we wanted to be sure we could speak to you privately."

She gets out an oil lamp and lights it before she sits in her chair again. "There are two small chairs in the kitchen," she says, pointing at a doorway behind her. "Go and fetch them."

Ty removes his cloak and looks around the tiny room, crammed with stacks of books and baskets of small objects. When Basil returns with the chairs, there's barely enough space on the floor to put them and once they're seated, the three of them are so close to one another, their knees are nearly touching.

Pearl searches their eyes for any hint of deception. "You said this was about Shaye."

"Yes," Ty says. "Basil already introduced himself, and I am Tyrone McClaren."

"Just so," Pearl says with small shrug. "Who else would have that hair?"

Ty leans forward and says, "I've been told it's likely that you know more about information in the Archives than anyone alive in Aegea, and I'm hoping you have information that will help us in our search for Shaye."

"I will do anything you need to help find Shaye . . . but how would the information in the Archives help?"

"We have reason to believe that the reason we haven't been able to find Shaye and my sister is that they are not in Aegea," Ty tells her. "We believe Shaye and my sister were taken to a place not known in this generation. Perhaps a place beyond the great dangers of the forest where people could settle in safety. If this is true and *if* mention of such a place was made in the Archives, there is some hope that they are still alive and we might be able to find them."

At this, the old woman raises her hands upward. "Oh, Maker of all that is . . . Thank you. You have answered my prayer," she says, her voice beginning to quake with emotion, "that I would not pass from this world without seeing your goodness and mercy in Shaye's life. Please, let it be so." She lowers her head. A silence grows . . . and with it, a sense of peace.

Ty closes his eyes and bows his head as well as Basil and the three of them keep this soundless communion until Pearl puts her hands on theirs and asks, "How could this have come about? Who in this day and age would know that much about what's beyond the forest?"

"We're not sure how it happened or why, but we think they may be with descendants of the Exiles. *If* that is so, we need to ask you about any early maps that Firstlanders may have drawn or things the Genon knew about the forest on a larger scale."

Pearl takes several large breaths with her hand clenched over her heart, then shakes her head. "Between the purging of information and the careless handling of documents, some of the records are gone forever. . . . But I did see and read many things about the early days."

Ty scoots his chair a little closer. "Did you ever see any maps of the regions beyond Aegea? Did you ever see speculations about what might be beyond the forest? My father has always believed the Exiles lived on but the forest is vast and, without some idea of where they are . . . we may never discover them."

The old woman closes her eyes, then leans her head back on her chair while she concentrates. The two young men watch as her hands move ever so slightly—as if she is walking about the Archives in her mind. Her right hand flattens and moves as if it's gliding over the surface of something.

Her eyes open and she says, "Yes. There was a map drawn by one of the cartographers—maybe a year after the crash. She interviewed people as to what they saw from the craft while it was coming down, and worked with one of the engineers to calculate distances based on the possible height and the direction the craft was going when each landmark was seen. Some of the accounts were too varied to make any sense of them . . . but she did draw a map from the common threads in the descriptions."

"Do you know if it still exists?'

She frowns. "Not likely. Many of the early documents were mishandled by the people in the third generation, then damaged by water and mold. It was greatly faded when I saw it." She stops talking while she tries to remember, then nods. "It did show an ocean."

"A *what?*" Ty asks.

She looks at him and thinks, *I had to teach Shaye that word, too.* "An ocean. *O-shun.* It's a great body of water—one you could travel on for days before you reached the other side. Salt water. The map showed one beyond the forest. In the world before, many people lived by the ocean." She focuses on the memory of the map, then points forward. "To the North. I couldn't tell you how far away. Guessing by the scale of the map . . . it was a long way. . . . Wait!" She closes her eyes and squints as if to see it more clearly. "There was a river. A long one—to the Northeast of here . . . and it led to the ocean." She opens her eyes and peers into Ty's. She intends to say something else, but she forgets it when he returns her gaze. *There is so much intensity in these eyes,* she tells herself. *Is he just using the angle of finding Shaye in order to get my cooperation in finding his sister . . . or is there more in his heart?*

As if he's echoing the words in her thoughts, Ty asks, "Is there more?"

She leans back, as her wrinkled hands caress the worn leather on the arms of her chair. "Yes. There were interviews with Firstlanders regarding the crash."

"Military, professionals, or Genon?" Ty asks.

"People from all groups." Her face becomes somber and she looks from Ty to Basil. "Most Genon can't read or write now, but in the first two generations they did—mostly in their own language and some in Command Dialect. I've read some of the Genon writings. But diseases from the Poison Forest, then insects and blights sweeping the crops made focusing energy on anything not pertinent to daily survival seem trivial. And then, after they banished the rebels in the Second Generation, the knowledge of the old world and the speculations of the Firstlanders became fading memories, best handled by a few who could decide what was important to remember.

She shakes her head. "In recent times, we had the purging of information that didn't support the military view, so that means many of the early writings are probably lost. Even if some of those documents still exist, I'm not sure anyone working in the Archives today has the ability to find or to accurately translate the ones written in Genon. The military mind," she says with a wry smile, "has trouble understanding the Genon view of life or the world."

Ty leans closer to her. "But the records and maps regarding what Firstlanders saw, if they still existed, where would someone need to look?"

# CHAPTER 24
# A Look Back Through Time

Jubal sits at his desk and carefully unties the leather binding that holds the first year's record. This book was probably intended for use as a diary, but became an official record book once the accident occurred and other logs could not be accessed.

Jubal opens the book and reads words written more than a century ago. The sheets of paper in this first log, are of even thickness and uniform size but they have come loose from the binding. The pages are brittle and show signs of water damage at some point during their history. He must be very careful handling them or they might break into small flakes. Although dim, the writing on the pages is still legible.

Before the writer finished the pages in this book, everyone realized they would need more paper—a lot of it if they wanted to store all that future generations might need to know. But the Firstlanders had little experience with *using* paper when they arrived here, much less making it. Prior to the crash, nearly all information was stored in the machines they called computers. In the first years of the settlement, they had to experiment with how to make paper, so several of the logs after this one are in even worse shape. The manufacture of ink was another significant hurdle in the beginning, and several of the inks considered "permanent" by the Firstlanders faded considerably within the first decade. There are several volumes from first decade of the settlement that pose significant challenges to anyone trying to read them.

Jubal doesn't want to open the shutters on the window for more light, so he lights a second lamp and sets it near the first one on the desk. He begins reading the concise even script of Aegea's first record keeper.

MISSION Log of B-X-9, the *Aegean C*
Begun on November 24, 2044,

Captain Arthur Penway, 2nd Jump Battalion

## SUMMARY

It has been 97 days since the Aegean C crashed. We've managed to rig up some solar power, but we don't have enough for all of our tech gear, so non-essential functions will have to go low tech. Since this is the first attempt to record events on paper, what follows in the next few pages is a summary of what has happened thus far.

On August 19, 2044, just after leaving the Earth's atmosphere, our B-X-9 spacecraft suffered multiple catastrophic failures and crash landed here with 1,903 souls onboard. The aircraft commander, Major Rice, managed to land us on a large shelf that sticks out from the side of a mountain in a long range of mountains. All of the cockpit crew were killed in the crash. Most of the B-X-9 remained relatively intact and skidded to a stop on the northeastern end. Our first hours after the crash were spent getting people and then livestock out of the wreckage along with any weapons we could carry. That first night, we found places to take cover and tried to care for the wounded.

Our original mission was to relocate a group of 1,434 Genon—the "terraformers"—along with their livestock, supplies, and equipment to the settlement of New Hope. Also aboard were 218 scientists and techs, most of whom would remain with the settlement for at least 2 years to record and analyze the methods that have made the Genon so successful in taming new ground. And lastly, there were 251 members of the Second Jump Battalion. Our task was to assist the techs and scientists in the unloading and setup, and remain until it was determined that no significant security threats to the new settlement were present.

## CASUALTIES

We lost 201 people in the crash, mostly Genon passengers but soldiers as well. In the days that followed we lost another 43 who were critically injured in the crash (among them, 5 small children). A separate list with the names of all casualties is being maintained for the records.

On August 24, 2044, we buried the first of the casualties in a common grave before the bodies became a health hazard. The gravesite is east of the wreckage of the B-X-9, on the eastern end of the plateau. To serve as a kind of memorial or headstone at the gravesite, a group of men hauled a chunk of the nose of the craft where the name, Aegean C, was, to preside at the eastern end of the gravesite. We've continued to bury people there.

Two doctors survived the crash, but we lost nearly a third of our medical supplies. Medical records will be kept by the medical officer in charge of the infirmary, Capt. Sandra Voss. Luckily, we were able to save most of the livestock, and a lot of the other supplies and equipment. Lt. Kevin Tolliver is charged with keeping inventories.

MISSION STATUS

We still have no contact with the outside world, no communication through satellites or any other method. There are still no signs that anyone knows we're here and nothing is coming through on the com—not in any language, not on any frequency.

Although there are no indications of an imminent threat by hostile forces, we don't know what brought the Aegean C down. We've remained vigilant, since we have no way of detecting attacks from long range. Another source of concern is the fact that we've sustained multiple attacks by indigenous creatures. So far, they've killed 9 people, 1 cow, and 5 goats. These creatures are like massive panthers—at least three times the size of anything any of us has ever seen before—and without our weapons, we'd be no match for them.

Jump Squadron Commander, Major Roland has energies focused on survival—both short and long term—as we wait for rescue. Looking at some of the long-term prospects, the Genon have begun planting food crops and setting up shelters for the people and livestock.

Thankfully, one of the Genon found a spring of fresh water not far from the wreckage so all of the housing is being built there. We've set up a perimeter around the camp so we can defend the people and animals at night. We have a limited supply of ammo, so orders are to shoot only if there is a deadly threat.

Three of our translators were killed in the crash, and our electronic translators are failing, so communicating with the Genon has been frustrating at times. We've had a number of problems with them—mostly stemming from the fact that they're used to being autonomous. It's true that the military presence on the mission was supposed to be for a limited duration, and that once the settlement was established, unless there were large security concerns, we'd return home. But currently, there are no means for us to leave and there *are* significant security threats. For now, the key to our survival is in unified effort directed through the command of a senior officer. Major Roland is well within his bounds to stay in charge of all these efforts until we're rescued.

A number of professionals among the civilian crew have been a b g help. Hal Dobbins and his daughter Janna helped us make a small power station using solar collectors we pulled out of the wreckage and will help us salvage as much of our tech as they can. Meanwhile we have power for medical needs, for lights, and signaling.

LOCATION

The temperature goes down to about 50 degrees during the right, but it warms up into the low 70s during the day. We are hedged in on one side by ice-capped mountains that exceed our capacity to cross without oxygen, and on the other three sides, the plateau steeply drops off. In some places, there is a sheer drop of thousands of feet. At the bottom of the mountain range, all we can see is a vast jungle, stretching all the way to the horizon in all directions. Both our climate and the jungle below us lead us to conclude that we must be near the equator of the planet.

The plateau itself is two and a half miles wide at its widest, and nearly thirty miles long.

When the spacecraft was on its way down, a few of us could see a coastline and a large expanse of water through the tiny windows, most likely to our north—but we have no idea how far away this coastline might be from our present location.

Jubal stops and reads the sentence aloud, his heart pounding. "When the spacecraft was on its way down, a few of us could see a coastline and a large expanse of water through the tiny windows, most likely to our north—but we have no idea how far this coastline might be from our present location."

The ray of hope it gives him is small, considering the sentence after it:

Given the timing of when the people saw it during the descent, our estimate is that it's hundreds of miles away at best.

SPECULATIONS

None of us recognizes the constellations in the sky. The planet has only one moon that appears larger in the sky than the moon of earth and it has different markings than our moon—but our scientists say this could be due to temporal displacement. Our scientists here are starting to speculate about our circumstances. Several think we may have somehow slipstreamed to another planet. Most, however, think it isn't a case of *where* we are, but *when* we are.

Jubal carefully closes the book and stows it, then goes to his door to summon his aide.

# CHAPTER 25
## Last Night in the Wilderness

*"If you could rule it all tomorrow . . . would you rule with fairness or demand revenge for what His own have suffered? When would it ever be enough? Would you then become the very thing you hated?"*—Pearl Ruth Penway Curtis, a chaplain for His People.

Shaye and Jariel have both lost track of how many days they've been travelling, but tonight, according to Nathan, will be their last night in the wilderness. Tomorrow afternoon, they will arrive "where Genon walk free—homeplace." Other than that, Nathan has been careful about details of their destination. It's as if he's allowing them to both mourn what they've left behind and adjust to the idea of life in new surroundings with new sights, smells, and tastes. Or perhaps, he didn't want to share too much until he was certain they wouldn't be recaptured by soldiers and asked for details about their destination. Of supreme importance to the Exiles is the concept of protecting homeplace.

The scent of the evening meal drifts away on a tropical breeze and they can hear the sound of the river moving by. When they all gather by the fire there is a solemn expectancy, and everyone looks at Nathan.

"Everyone must listen—even the men," he says, "for this is probably my last journey into the Great Forest. You must learn what I have to say so that you can say it in the future when you find others to bring home." He points his chin in the direction of the women and says, "Shaye and Jariel must listen because it's about a new life for them. Shaye, be sure to translate all that I say to your sister."

The old man sweeps his hand toward the river. "This long journey has prepared you for a new life. Tomorrow we will take the time to wash in the river that brought us here, then set out for a short ride in the boats, before we stop along the opposite shore. We will then walk to the place where our people live." He momentarily digresses with a few details of the Exiles' original journey. "This won't be the path our people took when I was a boy. We continued on the river that first time and found rough waters. After that we discovered that the place where the water took us wasn't the most suitable place to live. But within several weeks, we found the place where we made the settlement. Later, we realized we could take a shortway through some hills back to the river—"

Shaye stops translating, and waves at Nathan. He stops talking and looks at her. She asks, "Hills? What are 'hills'?

He smiles. "Hills are like small mountains. Once we made our settlement, we found we could go over these hills to get back to this river. It's what we call a 'shortway'—a path that made the travel shorter. We will leave the boats behind and take the shortway home . . . and when you see what we have, your hearts may melt. Just like the forest and the river, this place has beauty you haven't seen, colors you don't know, food you've never eaten—and it will be *your* new home."

Nathan waits for Shaye to finish translating this part before speaking again. "Tomorrow can be a rebirth for you. You were born into a life of captivity and oppression . . . you will have come through wilderness and water. And when you cross over those hills, you will leave all that is behind you," he says, as he makes the motion of throwing something over his shoulder, then lifts both of his hands with open arms, "and find a new life is before you. You are free to enter into the fellowship of our people. It will be like coming into a family. It is a place of hard work, yes, but also of joys . . . and of *expectations.*

"The Genon in Aegea have no voice, but after you enter the fellowship of our lives together, you will be *expected* to listen and to speak, to receive something *from* our fellowship and to bring something *to* it. Learning to be free *and* wise is difficult. It will be a time of *un*learning, especially for the sister Shaye brought," he says nodding to indicate Jariel.

Shaye continues to translate.

He rises and walks over to the women before he squats down, and reaches out weathered hands to grasp theirs. "Perhaps you have great sorrows or tales of terrible abuse at the hands of the military. I know that you may have been forced to live with hardship and given no dignity. . . ."

As Shaye translates this part, her eyes burn and tears flow down her face.

Nathan squeezes her hand before he continues, "But I would *beg* you, dear children, to leave as much of that as you can behind you. When you come to our homeplace you will meet some of our people who have never let go of the pain they suffered, and you will see others who carry the offenses they learned from their parents or grandparents," he says, glancing at the young men.

"Five generations ago, the Genon people who volunteered to become settlers in a new place had the expectation of walking in what our people knew as 'shared life,' in *mutuality*—as was the purpose of the Maker. It was the way my father and the others planned to live when they stepped onto the flying machine that fell to the ground in Aegea. The military was supposed to leave our people in the new settlement here and go back to where they came from . . . but something happened and they crashed their machine. After that, because they had the weapons, they came to think that this entitled them to rule over us.

"But my father and others remembered how it was *supposed* to be and they reminded our people—and that was their crime. For that crime, they were exiled. I don't know how much of this our sister Jariel knows since she has been sheltered from our people, but this is the truth. It's a sad and terrible truth, but real freedom always starts with truth." He puts his hand on his chest and says, "But I tell you with sorrow in my heart that some who come to live with us are still not free. They have chosen to carry the captivity of Aegea with them. It's as if they are dead and their hearts are far from us. They are ghosts who haunt the streets of Aegea, still bound to enemies who cannot see or hear them. They are yet slaves who allow their hatred of Aegea to play a part in all they think or do."

Shaye chances a glance at Ben, Philip, Jude and Loash who were the first of the group to encounter her and Jariel. "So . . . these people would still wish to harm the people of Aegea—the soldiers and their families—if they could?"

Nathan studies her a moment. "I see you are shaken by this, Shaye, but it certainly won't apply in your case or that of your sister. People will understand that your father did right by your mother that he took on our ways and paid for it. As for Jariel, she had no choice about being the daughter of a second woman. Many of our people are the children or grandchildren of second women. Your lives are merely examples of the way of oppression in Aegea."

Shaye translates with tears running down her face.

Nathan says, "But hatred is not our way. The Maker warns us all about the poison of bitterness. I hope you will watch those who have chosen it and see how they destroy every today by reliving a terrible yesterday. It solves nothing. I told you that real freedom always *starts* with truth—but the *path* of freedom is forgiveness. . . . To walk in bitterness is to walk in captivity. *Choose* freedom. Choose joy."

The old man falls silent with only the crackling of the fire and the sounds of the forest filling the air.

Sitting on the other side of the fire, Mule shifts around uncomfortably. Eventually, he looks directly at the women, then at Nathan. "Are you going to explain about the shortage?"

Shaye can tell by Nathan's expression that this topic isn't something he planned to address.

He sighs with resignation before he says, "I suppose they should know."

He moves to sit on the log near them and begins. "More than half of the first Exiles were men. Along the way, we lost two women, one of them being my mother." Nathan pauses, as if the loss needs a moment of reverence, then resumes speaking. "Over time, we were blessed and girls were born to our families so the disproportion grew smaller again and we were content to stay far from the Great Forest near Aegea."

"But after that generation, a greater number of sons were born, and we realized that we would need more people if we were to continue on. So, on occasion, we would go back to the Great Forest near Aegea, and if we saw a Genon and had the opportunity, we would invite them to join us. We heard that many Genon women in Aegea were forced into hard or shameful lives, so we were glad to offer freedom to them, and they were glad to take it. Over the next two generations, ten men and nearly thirty women joined us, one at a time. But perhaps the military suspected something—especially toward the end when two women joined us on one trip. They were nearly the last to come to homeplace. We knew it was a risk, but these were sisters and they both wanted to come. Not long after that, the military stopped women from coming to the forest, and more soldiers went with the gatherers when they went there. So we stopped going."

"I know of this," Shaye interjects. "My mother was nearly the last woman to be a gatherer. She told me of the two sisters who were never found. And she saw an Exile once, but it was only for a moment and they didn't speak. She said he made the sign for the vow not to tell just moments before several soldiers appeared and told her it was time to leave." As Shaye says it, she gets chills. One of the soldiers was probably her father. If he and the others hadn't arrived at that very moment, her mother might have been asked to become an Exile, and Shaye can't help but wonder, *If Mother would have had the time to consider an offer, would she have gone? If she'd agreed to leave before soldiers arrived . . . would the man have killed the soldiers? Would I even exist? How different might her life have been without my father and me? Would she have lived into old age?*

Jariel doesn't like being kept out of the conversation, so she places a hand on Shaye's arm and gives it a small shake to remind her that she needs to keep translating.

"The soldiers may have thought the people were dying," Nathan says, "when the situation was that many of them left and joined the Exiles."

"Just so," Shaye answers him. "They told everyone it was too dangerous for women to work in the Great Forest anymore. But some of our people still believed that the Exiles might be living on in the forest. I know I myself always hoped the missing people were with the Exiles," Shaye tells him.

"Really?" Phillip, the man sitting next to Jariel asks. "Do you think some of His people in Aegea would still come to live with us if they could? Would other women want to come?" All of the men lean forward for the answer.

This is a new concept. She needs to ponder it, but Jariel gives her arm another shake, so she tries to briefly tell the girl what's been said.

Jariel is so caught up, that she says, "Wait. You mean, the Genon in Aegea *know* there are Exiles still living? How is it that my—"

Shaye's eyes widen and Jariel stops herself mid-sentence, then rephrases her question. "How is it that people like the family I grew up with didn't know this? Why didn't I ever hear about this?"

Shaye fights the urge to be irritated. "It wasn't something everyone 'knew,' it was something *some* of us *hoped.* It was a dream—to believe Genon weren't being traded like property, to believe they were out in the forest, walking free. Even among those who believed, I don't think anyone thought that the Exiles lived this far away."

She's been speaking in Command Dialect to Jariel, so now all of the *men* are still waiting for her response. She begins by trying to recap what she and Jariel just said. Her brain and her tongue feel worn out. She takes a deep breath before saying to the men, "About others of our people in Aegea wanting to join you . . . I don't know. I would think some, maybe many of them would be interested . . . but I cannot speak for them."

Nathan clears his throat. He wants to finish what he was saying, so they all quiet down.

"We stopped coming to the forest about a decade ago. Besides myself, Ben and Mule are the only ones here who have travelled so close to Aegea before. But, nearly two years ago, a big storm came . . . and we thought it had passed, but when a group of the mothers and young women went with small children to bathe and wash clothes in the river near the settlement, a great rush of water came down abruptly . . . and washed them away. Eighteen of our young women with eleven of the small children from our village were swept away and killed. Losing them was a great loss for all of us, and we have been in mourning for them since then. Many began to wonder if our people would just fade from existence."

"But then," He says, tapping his temple with a finger, "I began to think, it has been years since we visited the Great Forest near Aegea. Perhaps we should take the chance of going to look. I thought about it for many months and then talked with others in the community. It seemed to be a good idea to most of them, and it looks as if," he smiles and uses a sweeping gesture to indicate the women, "the Maker smiled upon our journey." Having finished his tale, he crosses his arms in satisfaction.

Shaye translates his final words, then looks around at the group. The men are all looking at them with such expectancy. It's as if each man's heart has been laid completely bare, as if he wants the women to see his bids for attention along the way as more than simple lust. Shaye now has a greater understanding of all that she's seen and heard among them— and she feels the weight of their hope.

After she translates to Jariel, she cannot look directly at any of them, especially not Ben. She glances at Nathan and then looks down, and says, "I know I am not worthy of the honor you have paid me, my brothers."

Jariel doesn't say a word.

After a long silence, Nathan looks at all the men, then at the two women and says, "Certainly we have come a long way and we are all tired. We will let you rest now."

Everyone stands as the women walk to their bed. A silence remains upon them all as they each find a place to rest.

Shaye feels so frightened and raw, she cannot bear the thought of being alone with Jariel. Not right now. She slows her walk and lets Jariel begin the short climb up to the bed in the tree, then walks in the opposite direction for about thirty feet to be closer to the river bank. She steps out from under the trees and waits. Her eyes need to readjust to the darkness. She can't see the water gliding by, but soon, little reflections of light sparkle here and there. She looks up into the clear night, and for the first time since she left Aegea, she can see the stars.

All of the *"If only . . ."* regrets piled upon her heart over the past months begin to assert themselves again and she knows she must silence them or break into a million pieces. She lowers her head and slowly raises a hand to the Maker, unable to voice her sorrow.

### ###

When Jariel crawls up into the bed, she realizes that Shaye isn't behind her. She lays down, but her thoughts are in a jumble . . .

While they sat by the fire this evening, she was grateful that it was dark and that she was sunburned. She hoped they wouldn't see her face burning with fear and humiliation. Never before had she given much thought to how the Genon might feel about their status . . . or how much hatred it engendered. *What would they do to me if they knew the truth? What will Shaye do to me now that she is in a position to exact revenge?*

As Shaye relayed Nathan's information earlier tonight, it felt as if ground was disappearing out from under her feet. Her mother had told her that the story of a flying machine crashing in Aegea was a myth concocted by Genon who wanted to usurp the rightful place of the military. She was told that there was no "other world," and that the rebels of the Second Generation deserved to be sent into the forest where they all died. Until the day she woke up in the forest, she had no real reason to doubt it. Her heart races as she reconsiders all these things. *If there was no view from a flying machine, how did Nathan's father know the way to the homeplace? If there was no other world, how did Shaye's aunt know about boats? And, if the Genon version of events is true . . .*

### ###

Shaye stands near the river in silence for several minutes before she steps back under the cover of the trees and goes to her bed.

Jariel is awake but doesn't move or make a sound for several minutes while the camp falls silent, then she whispers, "Shaye? Are you awake? Shaye?"

Shaye doesn't turn toward her, but she whispers back, "What do you want?"

"What do you think it will be like there? Are you afraid?"

"I believe these are good men. If they heed the words of Nathan, they will mature into honorable men."

Jariel scoots a little closer so her faint whisper can be heard. "What if they don't listen to Nathan?"

Shaye rolls over and says, "I'm less afraid of them than some of the men at ho . . . in Aegea."

"So . . . you miss Aegea?"

"Why would I miss anything but Mosha, my aunt, and a few friends?" Shaye snaps. What else would there be to miss?"

"You won't miss your life there?"

"What are you getting at? What sort of life did *I* have? Certainly not one filled with lazy days, and parties, and fine dresses. I wish you were still there and not here where I must live a lie to keep you safe."

"Don't be so angry, Shaye. I miss my family, but, believe it or not, I don't miss my life there. I didn't plan all this either. I knew in my heart that my mother shouldn't trade you off . . . but I was just so angry with you that day. I'm sorry I didn't say something to keep her from doing it. I know you won't believe me, but I'm sorry."

"You're just 'sorry' because you are afraid—well don't have any fear on my account. I have no intention of telling them about you." Shaye turns her back to Jariel in hopes it will end the conversation.

Eventually, Jariel can tell that Shaye has fallen asleep. For the next few hours, she listens to the sound of the river and the animals in the trees. It's the first time in the whole trip, she's not tired. Before she falls asleep she whispers, "Perhaps you don't remember, but we used to be friends when we were little. We played hopscotch on the terrace behind the house and helped Mosha make things to eat. Your mother would take you and me and Ty with her on the wagon sometimes to get plants and we would hide from Ty and make him find us. . . . When I wasn't allowed to spend time downstairs with you or Mosha anymore, I missed you. And, believe it or not, I envied you for being able to spend all that time with Mosha."

# CHAPTER 26
## Last Look . . .

"There is much you've never seen before. The Maker was very busy. You will see. The world has much more than we know."—*Nathan*

They are almost to the top of the last hill, and Nathan marches forward, leaning with all the elderly determination he possesses, taking small continuous strides, encouraging them with the idea that they will see some "marvelous" things when they get to the top of the path.

Yesterday, Shaye rinsed out a dress for herself and told Jariel to do the same. Although stained, these frocks will serve for the last part of the journey.

This morning, the two women were shown to a small, rock-enclosed pool at the side of the river where each of them could privately bathe before the final trek to homeplace. Shaye's hair still feels damp and greasy, but she feels so much cleaner than she was when she woke up this morning, she doesn't care.

David and several of the younger men ran ahead of them early this morning to deliver some of the baskets of goods harvested from the forest and to share the good news of the trip.

"There it is," Nathan calls out. "We're nearly there."

Indeed, the top of the hill is in view. Before they started this last, long climb, both Shaye and Jariel needed a rest. Nathan told them, it is not only the last, it's the tallest one, so it will offer them a "marvelous" view. He must be looking forward to it, for he presses on with continuous small strides that leave them behind.

Shaye has noticed several new kinds of trees here. Less formidable than the trees in the Great Forest, they are shorter, and allow more light and air beneath. She's already picked her favorite kind. These trees have dark, smooth bark and broad, flat canopies that bow in the wind like ladies in fancy gowns being introduced to new beaus. As if their grace wasn't sufficient, each leaf of the tree is as small as one of her fingernails—and thousands of them quiver and flutter like fringe in the wind while fire-colored flowers glow from the tops of branches. Here and there, long, flat seed pods dangle down like swords on a soldier's belt. Could anything be more perfect? Several times on the way up the path, she stops just to admire another specimen and only continues on when the others call to her.

Nathan stands in an open area just before the crest of the hill and waits for them. When they arrive, he gestures with his hand, and tells them. "Turn now and look, daughters. See your journey behind you."

The trees in this spot were cut away long ago, allowing anyone standing here a clear view. When the women turn, stretching out below them is a view of the entirety of the land they have traversed. They can see the ribbon of the river here and there, and a wide swath of green jungle. Last of all, in the hazy distance, is a range of mountains with white caps.

"Look right there," he says, pointing. "See the tallest one? The one just to the right of it—that's where Aegea is. Take your last look, my daughters and I pray you will say goodbye before you turn again toward homeplace."

Shaye steps to the side to put some space between herself and the others. She needs to feel as if she's alone as she strains all of her will to see the mountain better. But it's only a purple-blue bump amongst many obscure bumps against a vast sky. She dares not count up all the sorrows and losses that led her to this view. It's as if the vast space between where she's standing and the mountain couldn't hold all the grief in her heart. She takes slow, deep breaths before she carefully works her hand under her pack to cradle the little bump on her belly. *All that I've left behind must be dead to me now. Those I love in Aegea will never know that I am here. I cannot go back. I am lost to them and they are lost to me forever. I must make a life here with my child. I will not let grief take me into death as it did Nathan's mother . . . as it eventually took my mother. I will cast aside this pain and I will love you, my child, with all that I am.*

The men mill around on the path, impatient to press on, but Nathan holds up his hands and says to them, "Give them some time. You can go on ahead if you want to get home sooner."

They wait.

After several minutes, as an act of her will, Shaye turns away from her last look upon Aegea and starts walking. Once Shaye moves, Jariel takes that as her cue to wipe her face and walk away as well.

Within another few paces, a strong breeze swooping over the top of the hill hits them with the smell of something new: salt air. Then they make the crest and see it for the first time.

It's something that both women know they'll remember all the days of their lives. They stare, breathless, as they take it in. Swaying, brilliant green foliage with bright sparks of color sweeps all the way to the foot of the hill, and beyond it, sparkling turquoise water stretching out to darker blues that reach beyond the horizon. The soft hiss of the surf is in the wind.

"Did I not tell you?" Nathan whispers to them.

The infiniteness of the water makes Shaye feel as if she's falling from a great height. She steadies herself by holding onto Jariel's arm before she manages to say, "It's the ocean."

"Yes!" Nathan says.

"*What?*" Jariel asks.

"The *ocean.*"

"It is the ocean," Nathan affirms in Command Dialect.

Jariel is transfixed. *Who could imagine such a color?* Finally, she manages to look at Shaye and ask, "We've never seen anything like this. How do you know what it is?"

"My Aunt Pearl told me about the ocean. Her grandfather told her about riding in boats and how the water was full of creatures that move through it, like birds glide through the sky, how these creatures *breathe* water just like we breathe air."

"Oh, my. Fish?"

"Fish . . . and other creatures."

"Oh, my."

Shaye catches sight of a boy running up the path toward them. As soon as he sees the travelers, he stops and waves, then disappears back down the path, laughing all the way.

"I suspect," Nathan says with a chuckle, "by the time we reach the bottom, the whole village may be waiting for you. It's been years since anyone new came to our homeplace."

For the next twenty minutes, they snake their way down the hill. Along the way, the path turns into a hard-packed road where carts can travel to terraced gardens and pens with animals. In some of the gardens, older children are guiding the work of younger siblings. When the travelers pass by, some of the children run to the edge of the road to wave or stare, but are quickly shepherded back to their tasks. During the entire trek downward, though, it's the water that holds most of the women's attention.

At the bottom of the hill there are fewer and fewer trees, but tall green grasses line the road, waving in the wind as if to greet them. At times, the grass is so tall it blocks their view of the sea. When they make the final turn in the road and pass the last tall stand of grass, small homes made of wood and stone come into view, several of them are two stories tall. Directly ahead of them, a large crowd of people clogs the road. David, Tooth, and Philip stand in the forefront, smiling proudly.

*Imagine that,* Shaye tells herself. *A whole village of Genon people! People free to come and go as they please, to build homes, to keep what they earn. What would our people in Aegea think if they could see this?* As the distance between travelers and village folk narrows, she assesses the people. Most of them have Genon features, but she's relieved to see about a third of them look like they have other ancestry.

Jariel stays close behind Shaye as they approach.

There is a stark difference between the vivid hues of the landscape and the drab clothing so many of the people are wearing. Even the buildings here are sun-bleached shades of gray or beige.

A growing number of people continue to jam into the space between the buildings until David and Philip step out and begin closing the distance to the travelers. Once they do so, the whole crowd surges forward, enveloping the women. It becomes a reverse parade of sorts where the main attraction becomes stationary and the spectators move by.

Some offer words of welcome as they pass, some offer to carry the baggage. Shaye says a polite "no" to each request and continues to hug her bag tightly. Some of the people inspect them closely, peering into their eyes, touching their hair, and asking questions. "Are you hungry?" "Aren't you tired?" "What do you need?"

Jariel holds a frozen stance, as if she were an animal about to be slaughtered.

Nathan voices a continuing string of gentle admonitions to the crowd. "Now don't poke at the women. . . . She doesn't understand you. . . . Be polite."

A toddler with a mass of tangled brown curls and startling blue eyes pops through the stream of observers and latches onto Jariel's leg. She doesn't know what to do, so she continues to stand still, hoping the little boy's mother, whoever she is, will come and retrieve him.

"He likes you right away," a middle-aged man with sun-crinkled skin says to her.

She doesn't understand, but she glances at him. He's nodding and smiling, so she smiles back nervously.

Three young men who look enough alike to be brothers push their way into the viewing line, walking around Shaye and Jariel slowly eyeing them up and down as if they were entirely naked.

The largest of the three has a scar on his left cheek, and he's clearly in rebellion to Genon traditions because he's clean-shaven. He leans in toward Shaye and says, "After you've seen all the other [unknown words], you'll want to find me."

Shaye gives him a fierce look and says, "You are a jot in want of a good shaking!"

He steps back, opens his arms, and says, "Is that an offer? You can shake me if you'd like."

She's insulted, disgusted, and horrified all at once. "*Never!*"

He roars with laughter before he leans even closer than he was before. "Never is a long time. They call me Flint," he says, before he moves on to harass Jariel in a similar fashion. She has no idea what he's saying but she gathers from Shaye's response, he must be saying something offensive. She turns her face away from him, and he laughs at her as well.

Mule, Ben, and David push toward the interloper, "*Eh, eh!*"

Nathan gets close to the man first, raising his voice with a rebuke. "Francis you are a scandal! Stop with your rude self. You will give the women a bad impression of all of us. Away with you!"

Francis backs up, winks at Shaye, then slowly turns and swaggers his way back through the wall of people, his two companions in tow.

Shaye's relief at his departure is short-lived. It isn't long before she notices a porch on the second floor of one of the houses to her left, where six women of various ages stand with arms folded, scowling—almost as if she and Jariel had committed some foul crime.

The toddler clinging onto Jariel's leg starts to wail when someone steps on his foot. Not knowing what else to do, she takes him up into her arms. He smells of urine and he's dressed in rough cloth, but she tries not to make an unpleasant face. Onlookers continue pressing in, peering into her eyes, touching her hair, and saying things she can't understand. "Shaye, I'm frightened," she calls out. "What am I supposed to do?"

Before Shaye can answer, Ben and Mule take up posts on either side of the women to force a larger perimeter around them in a crowd of people that now must number in the hundreds.

Mule smacks the hand of one man touching Shaye's hair. "This is no market! Behave yourself!"

An old woman pops through the throng, heading straight for Nathan. He opens his arms wide to her and the two share a sweet embrace before he inches her closer to the women. "Peony," he says with a smile, "this is Shaye, and this is Jariel."

"Well," Peony says, over the sounds of the passing crowd, "this is a *good* thing. I admit it." She gives her husband a kiss on the cheek and then shows a smile that's missing as many teeth as his. "I was worried for you . . . but this is a *good* thing." She hugs each of the women, saying, "Welcome."

"What do I do with the boy?" Jariel asks Shaye.

Once Shaye relays the question, several passersby open up their arms to him. The child chooses an older man and allows the transfer of custody, but Jariel still feels somewhat responsible for him.

"Is that okay?" she leans forward to ask Shaye. "Where's his mother?"

Nathan tells Shaye, "His mother was taken in the flood. His cousins take care of him now."

Shaye passes on the information just as the breeze picks up and the air becomes noticeably cooler.

"We should move along quickly, since rain is coming." Nathan says. "We will go to my sister's house. She has plenty of room, and you can stay there for now."

Before Shaye can register shock at the thought of being left with a stranger or ask any questions, the old man moves up behind Mule to tell him where they'll be going. The men start opening a way through the gathering of curious well-wishers. It isn't long before the first large drops of rain begin pelting heads, shoulders, and thatched roofs. Within moments, the shower intensifies and the onlookers rush to find cover on either side of the furrowed dirt road, but many of them continue to watch from the comfort of a doorway, a window, or an overhanging roof.

Hugging her pack closely to keep it dry, Shaye struggles to maintain the hurried pace and not turn an ankle, choosing where to put each foot in a growing maze of mud puddles of unknown depth. She glances back long enough to see David helping Jariel navigate through the downpour.

On one of the narrower streets, a jumble of shabbier buildings reminds Shaye of Oldtown, but after a few turns, the road broadens. On either side, one and two story buildings reflect greater care and craftsmanship. Along one street, the small homes have gardens.

*All of this belongs to Genon people,* Shaye marvels.

They're all drenched by the time they stop in front of a home at the corner where two roads meet. Nathan helps Peony up onto the narrow porch before he taps on the door. Within moments, a sour-looking old woman opens it. Her face softens briefly at the sight of her brother and she embraces him before he and Peony step across the threshold into the home.

"As you see," he tells his sister, "we've returned. Have you heard the news?"

"Yes. Just a few minutes ago," the old woman responds, "Ruby told me . . . but you've been away for so long, I didn't think I would see you till tomorrow."

Nathan looks back through the doorway at Jariel and Shaye. "When I woke up this morning, I was thinking . . . you have this home, you have bedding and you probably still have the clothing . . ." he stops to clear his throat, "and here I have two young women who have escaped their bonds and travelled so far to be with our people. And I thought, as an elder, you would want to be the example of hospitality to them."

The old woman turns a stern gaze upon her brother, then squints at the newcomers. "You thought that, did you?"

Outside, the intensity of the rain doubles, pelting them like an onslaught of cold needles. The puddles in the road quickly merge into a large splattering pond before Nathan gestures with his hand, beckoning Shaye and Jariel to step up onto the porch.

David takes Jariel's hand and guides her up the two steps to stand under the protection of the narrow thatched overhang, then he turns to offer Shaye his hand. But when she tries to move, Shaye realizes one of her feet is stuck in the mud. She looks down and flexes her foot. Its ankle deep, but she hopes to loosen the suction without breaking the binding on her sandal. Once she notices Ben moving in to offer more assistance, she's more determined to extricate herself quickly. She hauls on her foot and there's a momentary feeling of progress just before the strap of her sandal snaps. Shaye's foot pops out of the mud with a comical sucking sound and she loses her equilibrium. Her arms flail around in giant, jerky circles and Ben makes an attempt at grabbing one of them, but only succeeds in snagging her pack while she plops backward into the mud.

She's heartily embarrassed. Embarrassed, and surprised that no one is laughing. That's when she realizes that the rain has revealed one of her secrets.

The force of the downpour suddenly slows, just in time for Jariel to shout, "*Shaye! Are you pregnant?*"

Water runs off the ends of Ben's hair, his nose, and his beard as he stands in the rain, like an open-mouthed statue with his gaze frozen on Shaye's belly.

After a momentary hesitation, Mule moves closer, clasps her arm, and helps her up.

Ben takes a step back, then realizes he's still got Shaye's pack. She reaches out for it, but he holds onto it.

"What was it I told you?" he asks. "That I could see you were 'a modest woman, an upright woman, a true gift for our people'? I believed you were a frightened refugee, clinging onto her pack because it was all she had left. Were you *laughing* at me?"

Shaye doesn't answer.

"Benjamin . . ." Mule says, putting a hand on his friend's shoulder. Ben jerks away. "Don't try to defend her, Samuel. I am such a fool!" He hands her the pack before he turns and walks away.

"Wait!" Mule calls out, but his friend keeps walking.

Shaye holds the wet bundle in front of herself while she watches Ben stride away in the rain. Once he rounds a corner, she stops watching and allows Mule to help her step up onto the porch where a wide-eyed Jariel cannot take her eyes off Shaye's midsection. After enduring the stare for several more moments, Shaye's anger boils over, "*Stop looking at me!*"

Jariel tries to comply, but she can't keep herself from glancing at the bulge that's only halfway hidden behind Shaye's pack. Mule stands on the porch with them, not saying a word. David, Tooth, and the other men join them under the thatched roof, all of them purposely staring out at the street and equally mute.

Nathan doesn't look entirely surprised, but after a momentary pause, he manages to slide this new wrinkle into the discussion with his sister.

"Well! Now it looks as if you will have *three* guests," he says spreading his hands and shrugging. "But I'm certain," he adds, "that they will be no trouble to you."

Before the old woman can mount any sort of argument, he starts the introductions. "Willow, this is Shaye, who can speak much of our language, so she will understand anything you say in simple terms. And this," he says, poking his chin in the other girl's direction . . . is Jariel."

Even though she knows Shaye is furious, Jariel cowers just behind her. When she hears Nathan say her name, she lowers her head in a little bowing gesture.

"We have taught her maybe . . . twenty words in our language," Nathan tells his sister. "You will need Shaye to translate anything important."

Willow looks around Shaye to give Jariel a visual inspection. "My. She looks so thin. Did you not feed her?"

Jariel keeps her focus riveted on the rough-hewn planks under her feet.

Nathan shrugs again. "Certainly, she needs more food and some care. But you should have seen her when we first met her there in the forest. She was already starved, and if not for us, she would have died from a spider bite. She was sick for days, but she is on the mend now." Nathan continues with the introductions. "Shaye, this is my sister, the youngest child of my father. Her name is Willow."

Shaye chances a glance into Willow's stern face before she joins Jariel in staring at the floor. They both shiver while the drips from their dresses make splash patterns in the layers of dust and accumulate into muddy puddles in the low warps of the wood. All they hear is the rain while Willow pauses to gather her thoughts.

It's a surprise when the old woman suddenly steps aside, and motions to the door. "Come inside daughters, and we will see if we can find dry things for you to wear."

They wring out the accumulation of water in the hems of their dresses before they pass through the narrow entrance to the house. The air inside is stale and hot. A lone candle on the table is the only light in the room, but as her eyes adjust, Shaye can make out two other doorways; one at the back of the room, the other to her right.

"You should go home to your families now," Nathan says to the men still standing outside the door. One by one, Mule, Tooth, Philip, Jude, Matthew. John, Loash, David, and Avallach each stand in the doorway to say farewell to Shaye and Jariel, then, just like young cadets who've been dismissed, they sprint off through the rain to reconnect with friends and family.

While Nathan and his wife speak to Willow, Shaye stares out the doorway at the pouring rain. *The journey has ended,* she tells herself, *and perhaps, all of them regret bringing us here.*

As quickly as it started, the rain stops. Dark clouds scoot away, and late afternoon sunbeams lean into the entryway. Shimmering puddles out on the street reflect into the home, creating dancing patterns on the ceiling and far wall of the room.

Nathan takes advantage of a lull in conversation to squeeze past his sister and open the shutters on one of the windows. More light reveals a tidy room with simple furniture and few decorations. Four chairs huddle like companions around a small, square table where the flickering candle is now all but invisible in the bright light of day.

Willow gives Nathan a scolding look, but he ignores it. "We will let people know that you've taken in Shaye and Jariel," he says, "so they will know where to bring everything."

"As if you would have to make any sort of announcement," Willow scoffs.

Her point is quickly proven. When the rain stops, people begin to gather around Willow's home. When the doorway fills up, others congregate around the open window. Unconcerned about any impropriety, they stare into the home, ready to hear and repeat whatever conversation takes place. Shaye notes that more than half of those gathered are men of varying ages, at least half a dozen of them are carrying white flowers.

One middle-aged woman catches a glimpse of Shaye's bulge and she elbows the man next to her "*Eh eh!*" she says, poking her chin in Shaye's direction. "That one brought a baby with her!"

More people jostle up to the doorway and the window to see the belly, before a chorus of *"Eh eh!"* followed by excited chatter that rolls through the gathering.

Her fury at Jariel now smothered in her own shame, Shaye lowers her gaze, certain she can feel the pulse of her wildly beating heart all the way to her toes.

Jariel can tell by the stares, the animated responses, and the expression on Shaye's face that the current focus of conversation must be Shaye's condition.

Unruffled, Nathan raises his voice, to include everyone in the conversation. "Yes, these are the newest editions to our homeplace. He puts his hand on the shoulder of one, then the other, saying, "This is Shaye. This is Jariel. I hope you will help Willow make them feel welcome here. There will be plenty of time for them to get to know each of you—and as they acclimate to their new lives of freedom, I'm sure you can play a part in teaching them about our lives here. I hope you will remember that for all who have come here—there was a sense of joy, a sense of sorrow, and the need of a little space to consider it all. Please show Shaye and Jariel consideration— especially Jariel who does not know our language. I know you have many questions and will want to introduce yourselves, but I'm sure you must understand how weary all of us are. Perhaps tomorrow, we can have a gathering to properly welcome them." Nathan stops to clear his throat before making his last point. "As for immediate needs, some of you may have items that you could bring—since these poor women have walked so far and have next to nothing with them."

Another cool wind sweeps through the street before Nathan turns to Shaye and Willow, "And now, I'm sure you will understand if Peony and I go home before the next shower starts."

Shaye grabs Nathan's hand with a look of panic in her eyes.

He leans close to her and whispers. "Don't be afraid. You aren't the first woman to show up at homeplace carrying a child. And you will soon discover that Willow is a good woman with kindness in her heart." He looks into her eyes and shakes her hand for emphasis as he says, "You don't know it yet, but you have come at a *good* time daughter. The rainy season has just begun," he says with a smile, "and that's a good time for growing all sorts of things."

Nathan's wife Peony hugs Shaye and then Jariel. When she hugs Jariel she again speaks one of the few words she knows in Command Dialect: "Welcome."

Just as Peony says the word, someone appears in the nearby window and passes through some bread. Then a child sets a small bowl of fruit on the window sill.

Willow says a soft, "Thank you," to each of them before she takes the items and sets them on the table.

A bundle of dried, salted fish is passed up through the crowd before a man hands it to Peony, who sets it near the other items on the table.

"See?" Nathan says to the gathering. "Already, you are showing them what good neighbors do."

Before he leaves, Nathan hugs his sister. "We will go now," he says. "I'm certain this will be a blessing to you and to them. They have suffered many days and nights so it is good for them to have a home here for a while. Perhaps, your burden will begin to lift, too."

Peony embraces Willow before Nathan takes her hand and then waves to the young women. "We will see you tomorrow, daughters!"

With that, the couple squeezes through the people in the doorway.

Willow steps close to Shaye and Jariel and sizes them up again before she says. "I'm certain I have dresses in the other room that both of you can wear." She opens the door at the back of the room. "Some were . . . some are meant to fit a woman expecting. Get the candle from the table and come this way."

Shaye takes the candle and they follow Willow into the room. It's a small space with one shuttered window at the far end. On one side of the room is a bed and a small table with an oil lamp, on the opposite wall, is a tall cabinet. Two sleeping mats are rolled and stacked beside the cabinet. The old woman tells Shaye to light the lamp near the bed.

Normally, the heat in the room would be unbearable, but the young women are wet and cold, so for the moment, it's a welcome warmth to both of them. Willow opens the doors to the cabinet and shows them six shelves with stacks of neatly folded clothing. Nearly all of the clothing is faded, like the villagers were wearing, but a few garments in each stack have bright colors in them.

"Most of these are for daily wear—for working," Willow tells them, before she points to a stack in the upper right quadrant of the cabinet. "These might be a bit [unknown word] for—Jareed?"

"I'm sorry, the clothes may be *what*?" Shaye asks.

Willow thinks for a moment. "Large. They may be large for her, but they will do. Is her name Jareed?"

"No, ma'am. Her name is Jariel. *Jair*-ee-el." Shaye says, then she points to the stack of clothes and tells Jariel she can select something to wear.

"Thank you," Jariel tells her.

Willow stretches out her hand toward a stack on the upper left side of the cabinet, but then withdraws it before she touches the cloth. "And those," she says, "will do well for you. Forgive me, but will you say *your* name again?"

"Shaye."

"*Shhhay*."

"Yes, ma'am."

The old woman points to two stacks in the middle section of the cabinet. "And here are cloths you can use for towels," she says. "Bring out your wet clothes and we will hang them up so they will dry. They will smell sour soon if we don't hang them. Later this week we can wash all the clothing," she says before she leaves the room.

Shaye rests her wet bag on the floor, next to a wall, then removes her remaining shoe. Before she sets it next to her bag, she studies it. *I got this last year. Soon, I won't have many items from Westland.*

When Shaye straightens up and stretches a bit, Jariel takes the opportunity to steal another look at the budding tummy, then bites her lip to keep from asking any of a dozen questions that are now dancing around in her head.

As both women begin to examine their choice of clothing the silence in the room becomes tangible.

"Even though these are old and faded," Jariel says nervously, "the cloth in some of them is nice. This one," she says, extracting a dress with a faded floral pattern, "must have been pretty when it was new. It's *still* somewhat pretty. . . . Whoever made it had some skill. I wonder who originally wore the dress. Was it Willow's dress? What will she think when she sees me walking around in her old dress?" Jariel eyes Shaye's stack before she says, "And look at *this* one. Blue! I wonder how they came by the color . . . it's so pretty— almost the same color as Ty's eyes, don't you think?"

Shaye already had her hand on the folded edge of it. She nods, then selects another dress.

They change clothes and both of them are grateful to feel something warm, soft and *dry* on their skin. The sensation is so relaxing that Shaye suddenly realizes how tired she is.

Before they exit the room, Jariel asks, "Do you think we are safe now?"

"I think we are. No one in Aegea even knows this place exists. The *chemosh* killed the men who took us into the forest, and like Nathan says, if more of them come looking for the box, they will think the beast killed us as well."

"Do you think we will *ever* be able to go home?"

They've had this conversation several times, but Shaye is relieved to talk about this, rather than the obvious questions Jariel could ask right now. She takes a deep breath and reflects on what to say. "I know it's frightening to consider it, but the people who took you obviously had something terrible in mind. Although we don't know *why* they took you, I cannot imagine they had any thought of ever giving you back to your family. I would have shared your fate had the *chemosh* not killed them. I believe the only reason we're alive is that the Exiles saved us—and given that we were imprisoned in a box, it never occurred to Nathan and the others to offer to take us back to our captors. We must remember also that the law of Aegea says that Exiles are to be killed on sight. Even if they wished to take you back, they would have to risk death yet another time to do it. They have treated us with respect . . . and it seems you will be free to live in ways you could never have imagined in Aegea. Other than sparing your family the grief of thinking they'd lost you . . . what is it you would go back for?"

Jariel looks at Shaye's stomach and pokes her chin in that direction. "Have *you* no reason or desire to go back to someone?"

Shaye sits on the bed and sighs. "My child will be born here—and grow up *free*. This is nearly the most any Genon woman could hope for. I will become part of the fellowship that Nathan speaks of and make a life here. To be in a place with such great beauty, among my own people, to be free. . . . In time, it will be a joy to me. I hope it will be the same for you as well."

###

Over the next few hours, a continuous flow of people come by the house bringing food and other useful items. Shaye and Jariel sit in the chairs near the table as visitors introduce themselves. Jariel isn't sure that she'll recognize half of them when she sees them again, but she tries to commit as much as she can to memory.

Evening comes and a cool breezes float through the house, bearing the scent of some sweet flower. Shaye closes her eyes and pulls the shawl Willow brought her closer. *Ahhh. Perhaps the stifling days of the forest are forever behind us. No more sweltering nights . . . or days when the air is so thick you could slice it. This is good.* For the first time in many months, something inside Shaye unwinds. A glimmer of the Maker's love appears in her heart, and it spills over into a silent prayer. *Thank you. Thank you for bringing us through all those dangers to this place of beauty, this place of safety and comfort. I'm sorry for the mistakes I've made, and I want to turn and talk to you again . . .*

The flow of visitors slows as the world outside darkens, and when Willow sees the girls are starting to nod off in their chairs, she closes up the house.

The sound of the latch as she closes one of the shutters stirs the girls.

"The bed in the back room is mine," Willow tells Shaye. "You each can have one of the mats in there to use. We'll all sleep in there."

While she's translating, Shaye's eyes gravitate to the door on the other side of the room and she begins to notice that nothing is near it. Not a single piece of furniture is close to it, no lamp or decoration shares the wall where the closed door stands like a solitary sentinel, guarding a forbidden space.

Willow notices the look, but offers no explanation.

Upon further reflection, Shaye decides the closed door isn't ominous . . . *Nathan certainly wouldn't have taken such care with us to leave us someplace where we are unsafe . . . but it is a mystery. Perhaps when we get to know Willow better . . .*

The combination of exhaustion, a stomach full of food, and the cool night air work together to make Shaye so sleepy she can barely navigate. With a word of thanks and a "goodnight," Shaye wanders back into the room with a candle, dons one of the long night gowns Willow offered, then curls up on one of the mats with a blanket. Jariel isn't far behind.

For the first time in many months, Shaye sleeps soundly all night.

# CHAPTER 27
## Homeplace

The bright light of the moon overhead lights the small space. *Has he fallen asleep?* Rising panic replaces the overwhelming passion she felt an hour ago. She moves slowly out of his embrace, but he stirs and pulls her back in.

*He's awake.* He moves his head and she can see his face, but not the clear blue of his eyes. "Stargazer Shaye . . . stay with me," he says.

"I must go."

"Please. Stay with me."

A suffocating sense of fear continues to grow. "I should not have come here," she says, pulling away. "I should—"

He gently places his fingertips on her mouth to silence her before he reminds her, "I love you with all my heart."

She shifts out of his grasp and sits up. "What will happen to us?"

He sits up, facing her. "I promise you, we'll work this out." He reaches over to stroke her long, black hair. "I'll be home on leave in a few weeks and we'll work it out somehow."

Her heart latches on to the casual tone of his words. *Work **it** out . . . **somehow**? Work* *what out? Secret meetings on the roof? Her mind begins to race. What have I done, **what have I done**?*

*She leans away from him and begins winding her hair into its customary knot at a frantic speed. "Mosha might look for me and see that I'm not in my room."*

*The knot of hair unrolls, spilling down her back when he takes her hands. He kisses the palm of her left hand, then places it over his heart. "I must go to the Academy but I'll be back at the first opportunity—when I get my first leave. You'll barely have time to miss me. I promise . . ."*

Shaye awakens and looks around. *Where am I? In a room . . . in the house of Willow . . . in the homeplace of the Genon.* She glances around. *And I am alone.*

### ###

In the front room of Willow's house, Jariel sits at the table. Earlier, the old woman said something about Shaye—undoubtedly that they would give up waiting for the girl to wake up and eat breakfast—because she then shrugged and started cooking. Jariel ate two helpings of nearly everything Willow served up.

Without Shaye, conversation is limited to Jariel pointing to different things in the room and repeating what Willow tells her. So far, she's learned the name of several common items (*chair, window, table, bread, eggs*) and attempted to learn the names of several new things she'd never seen before: *coconut, hibiscus*—and an odd bird that Willow had to shoo away from the porch. It was quite large, and all too willing to help itself to items that people left by the door of the house. Jariel hopes she can remember the name of the bird so she can tell Shaye: *seagull*. There were other words she's already forgotten and will need to hear many more times, but she thinks it's a good beginning.

The room feels warm, so Jariel points to the shutters on the window and asks, "Can I open these?" When she adds the motion of pretending to push them open, Willow understands and nods.

White flowers, piled upon the sill during the night, are swept to the ground by the shutters. She leans out to grab several of them and shows them to Willow.

"*Eh,eh!*" the old woman says.

Jariel starts to ask why, but then realizes, once again that they don't speak the same language. She holds the handful of blossoms up, inhaling the fragrance and sighs with delight. *This is what I smelled last night. The tree or bush where they grow must be nearby.*

Willow takes the flowers and places them in a small bowl of water, while she quietly mutters to herself.

With all three windows open now, a cross breeze floats through the front of the house, billowing one of the gauzey old curtains into the room, and the hem of it nearly brushes the table. Jariel catches the curtain and walks back to the wall with it to tie it to the side. The fabric slides through her hand and she holds it up for inspection. One of her brows arches up as she concentrates on it. "I wonder what kind of fiber this is?"

A movement out in the street catches her eye and she turns to watch a dark-haired woman in a baggy brown dress walking by. In her right hand, the woman has a bunch of long, curved yellow fruit. Nestled between her left elbow and her hip is a baby that's old enough to sit upright. Three children of varying size follow behind—a boy, a girl, and another boy. They turn the corner and step up onto the covered walk in front of Willow's house, intently gazing at the items others have left there. When the woman notices the open window, she stops her search and smiles in at Willow before she says something and holds up the bundle of yellow fruit.

The hard line of Willow's mouth softens slightly before she nods.

When the woman sets the fruit on the window sill, the baby starts grabbing at it and making a grunting noise. She pulls off one of the fruits and hands it to the baby before the little girl tries to reach the bundle. Mother pulls off another fruit and places it in the girl's hand, then looks at Willow again, smiles, and shrugs.

Willow says something in Genon and nods again, before the mother and the children start searching through the items on the porch.

Jariel silently moves closer to a window in the front of the home just in time to see the mother point to a bulging cloth sack and say something to the oldest child, who picks it up. Meanwhile the little girl has managed to peel the fruit her mother handed to her, but before she can get a bite of it, her younger brother breaks off half of it and begins to eat it. She starts to howl. Mother takes the remaining half and gives it to the baby, then gives the baby's unpeeled fruit to the girl . . . who starts to peel it before her older brother grabs the whole thing. The howling begins again before the exasperated mother looks at Willow.

Willow nods again.

The mom pulls another fruit off the bunch and hands it to her daughter, then waves at Jariel and Willow before she walks away with the bag she got off the porch.

Jariel is dying to ask, *What was that all about?*

Willow understands the expression on her face and holds up one hand and shakes her head as if to say, *don't ask*. When Jariel picks up what's left of the bundle of fruit on the sill to look at it, the old woman beckons her to bring her the fruit, so she does.

Willow pulls one fruit off the bundle and holds it up. "Banana."

"Bah—*what*?"

"Ba-na-na."

"Banana."

"Yes," Willow says as she peels it, then hands it to Jariel.

The door at the back of the room opens and a red-nosed, sheepish looking Shaye emerges.

"Good morning. Did you get a good rest?" Willow asks her.

Shaye studies the old woman's face. Although the frown lines are deep, in her eyes there is a soft glow. Perhaps the glow is a reflection of the kindness that Nathan said they'd come to know. "Good morning. Yes, thank you."

Jariel looks up and smiles. "I'm glad you're up, Shaye." It's not a falsehood. Shaye is the one familiar thing in this new world, and the only one with whom she can communicate.

"Are you hungry?" Willow asks her. "We saved some breakfast for you. You'll need to eat more in the coming days—for the baby. Do you get the nausea?"

It's the first time Shaye has been able to actually discuss her condition with someone. She's had so many questions she's had to hold in her heart rather than ask someone and reveal her condition. "Sometimes. It's mostly certain smells that bother me. Why is that?"

"It's natural—many women have it. It will probably stop happening soon. Any smells bother you in particular?"

Shaye wrinkles up her nose and looks at the bundle of dried fish hanging on a string in the corner.

"Ah," Willow says, lifting the string off the hook. "No fish for Shaye then. We'll bless a neighbor with them, eh?"

The old woman places the offending creatures in a window that's downwind of Shaye, who gives her a grateful smile.

Someone at the door calls out, "Willow?" the Old woman goes to the door, then steps outside as she speaks to another woman.

When Shaye was standing, her bump wasn't visible, but when she pulls out one of the chairs near the table and sits down, the drape of her gown reveals it.

As an act of her will, Jariel *doesn't* look at it. Instead, she tries a bite of the fruit she's holding. "This is pretty good. Mild flavor, sweet and starchy. You should try it." She breaks off a piece of it and gives it to Shaye before she tells her, "They call it banana."

Shaye sniffs it, then tries it, and nods her head with approval.

Jariel scoots her chair closer and hands her another chunk of the fruit. "We haven't had any time to speak alone since . . . yesterday. I didn't sleep very well last night and I think it's because I needed to say I'm sorry. . . . I didn't mean to yell it out like that or to stare. I wasn't trying to humiliate you or anything, I was just shocked. Please believe me—I'm truly, truly sorry."

A sad look comes to Shayes face as her hand slides down to caress her bump. "I knew it wouldn't be a secret for much longer. Even if I hadn't lost my pack while my dress was all wet . . . it would have been a week or so at most. She's growing really fast now."

Jariel's eyes open wider and she dares to look. "*She*? You know it's a *girl*?"

"Well, no. I guess I just hope that."

"How long before she's born?"

Shaye's face flushes. "I don't know much about having babies. Beth is the only friend I've had who had a baby while I knew her . . . and she would have had her second one by now." Shaye thinks for a moment. "About three months."

Willow walks back into the house, arms full of items left in front of the home, and says. "It's settled. Tonight, after the workday is over, the community will come together to celebrate your arrival. You can help with preparations later," she says, setting the load on the table, "but first, you can go and spend a little while on the beach. The sun is stronger here than in Aegea, so it's best you go in the morning and come back before midday."

"What's a beach?" Shaye asks.

Willow's eyebrows arch up. She's never had to explain it before. "It's where the ocean meets the land." The old woman heads for the door again. "I'll collect the rest of the things out here, you two go and change clothes."

Jariel heard the word "ocean" so her face is lit with expectancy before Shaye translates, then they both grin.

"My friend Iris will take you," the old woman says. "She and her sister are from Aegea. They were gatherers many years ago, and I think they were the last people to come to homeplace from there."

Shaye sits upright. "Really? Perhaps she knew my mother. Is she here yet?"

"No, but she will be soon. The two of you need to go get ready. And remember to take your hats when you go."

Before they can leave the room, a woman appears in one of the windows, asking, "Can I trade this for *this*?"

As soon as Willow goes outside to talk to her, Jariel whispers to Shaye. "It's that woman again."

The two of them tiptoe to another window.

Shaye can see that the woman has an item in a sack and apparently wants to trade it for a bundle of cloth that someone left on the porch. She has a baby and three young children with her.

Willow picks up the bundle and hands it to the woman in exchange for whatever is in the sack before Jariel says a quiet "*Hmph.*" and heads to the bedroom.

Before the woman leaves, Willow says, "Oh wait. Could you do me a favor? One of the girls is expecting a baby and the smell of these fish is too much for her right now. Would you be kind enough to take them?"

The lady gladly takes the fish and hands the bundle to the oldest boy, who immediately starts to gnaw on one of them.

Just watching the boy munching on the creature, Shaye's nose wrinkles up again. Soon the lady and her children begin walking down the street.

When she gets to the bedroom, Shaye asks Jariel, "What was so interesting about that? They were just making a trade. People do that everywhere. Even in Aegea."

"She was here first thing this morning with the bananas," Jariel says in a low voice. "She traded them for whatever was in that sack. This time, the sack looks like it's half empty, and now she's trading it for the cloth."

Shaye makes a face. "And the fish. So?"

"Well, she was just . . . *odd*. And I could tell there was a history of some sort there. Willow gave me a look that said so."

"How would you understand anything about people? By your own admission, you've been inside your house most of your life."

"You're right," Jariel answers in a somber voice, ". . . but I've spent a lot of time watching the world through my window . . . watching people work and laugh and share life with one another. You can know things about people, just by observing them."

Willow calls through the door to them. "Hurry up or you won't have much time to spend there."

Shaye smiles, before she becomes somber again. "About the woman taking us to see the ocean—she and her sister came here from Aegea. That means she speaks Command Dialect—*and* she knew people there. She may have known my mother . . . she may even have known your father. Please be *careful* about what you say."

### 

Jariel squeals when the leading edge of a wave splashes up on her foot. "Come and feel it, Shaye! It's *warm!*"

Shaye remains firmly seated ten feet above the waterline, thankful that Jariel is occupied with the water. It makes for less worry about what the girl might say in front of the woman who brought them."

"Iris," she asks, "why is the water doing that? It looks as if it's trying to lick up the dirt."

The woman scoops some of the beach into her hand and chuckles as it sifts through her fingers. "Sand. It's called sand. And the water lapping like that is called *waves*. See how the waves roll in toward the shore? They never stop. Night and day, the waves keep coming like that. And it has cycles—certain times of the day the waves come further up the beach, other times, they diminish—but they never stop entirely. It didn't seem at all natural to me when I first came here. I was here nearly a year before I would set a foot in that water." She laughs. "I love it now."

Shaye surmises that Iris is probably in her late fifties, but the woman's tall, slender frame still moves gracefully when she walks, and her smile reveals a full set of white teeth. There are numerous streaks of silver-gray in her long hair, which she doesn't wear in the customary bun. On the walk to the beach, Iris told them that she and her sister both married after arriving at homeplace, but she was too old to bear children. She also said that before she left Aegea, she only saw Shaye's mother on several occasions, but knew Shaye's grandfather. So far, she hasn't asked Shaye any personal questions. Perhaps she, too, felt raw and fearful of rejection when she first arrived.

A wave shoots by Jariel, splashes up to her knees, and Shaye quickly scoots backwards when it nearly touches her feet. "Why does it 'wave'? What causes it to do that?"

"I don't know," Iris tells her, "but you can ask one of the men that goes out in boats. Maybe they have learned why."

Shaye holds onto her stomach as if she's protecting her child from something. "They go out into the *ocean*? Are they not afraid they will disappear, or get lost and never find their way back?"

"The ocean can be very dangerous at times . . . but we get many useful things from it and the men who go out there have been doing it for generations now."

Meanwhile, Jariel has become fascinated by her footprints in the wet sand. She bends down and begins to play with it. "This has such a strange texture!" She takes a handful over to Shaye and Iris. "Look what it does when it's wet! I've never seen dirt like this before."

"It's called *sand*," Iris tells her. "The children from the village come here on rest days and they make all sorts of shapes with it."

Jariel walks back to the water and rinses her hands.

"I'm *so glad* you are staying with Willow," Iris says. "How is she?"

"She is a serious sort of person, but she's been kind to us."

Iris draws lines in the sand with her fingers. "We had nearly despaired about her. So many bad things, so much sorrow."

"What do you mean?" Shaye asks her.

Iris looks up in surprise. "Nathan didn't tell you?"

"Tell us what?" She motions to Jariel. "Come here, Iris has something to tell us."

Jariel sits in the sand facing them.

"Do you know about the flood that killed the women and children?" Iris asks?

"Nathan told us there was a flood nearly two years ago that killed many of the young women and their children. That's all we know."

Iris shakes her head. "Willow's daughter and both of her grandchildren were taken. And her daughter was expecting another child."

"How *terrible!*" Shaye gasps. "How could anyone endure such a loss?" When Shaye looks down at the dress she's wearing, a thought suddenly comes to her. "Jariel! These must be her *daughter's* clothes!"

Jariel sucks in a deep breath. "Oh, my! Poor Willow!"

### 

An hour later, the two newcomers believe they can remember the way home, so Iris lets Shaye and Jariel walk back without her. Since everyone will probably know where Willow lives, it's not like they could get lost for very long.

Even though Iris stressed to them that their presence has brought more life to Willow than anyone has seen in nearly two years, the walk back to the old woman's house is somber compared to the trek down to the beach earlier. As they meander up through the village, the people they pass greet them. It's not the mayhem they experienced yesterday, but the two newcomers are still of great interest to villagers and everyone says, "Good morning," to them. Shaye teaches Jariel how to say it in Genon (because it would be impolite to not return the greeting).

At one point, Jariel is lagging behind when a man approaches and hands her a white flower. She's heard Shaye use the standard phrase for *thank you* enough times to use it in response: "You honor me."

The man smiles broadly before Shaye walks back to where they are standing and says something to him. The smile fades and he bobs his head in acknowledgement before he turns to walk away.

"What did you say to him?" Jariel asks in an annoyed tone. "He was just trying to be nice. I hope you didn't insult him."

Shaye steps back and folds her arms, conveying her own irritation. "Among Genon, this is a custom. The man gives the woman a white flower to say he wants an opportunity to court her. You don't even know this man and he looked fifteen years older than you. Do you plan on courting him?"

Jariel thinks about all the flowers that were in the "nest" each morning when they were in the forest, and the piles of them that fell off the window sills this morning. Her voice has lost its fire when she answers a meek, "Oh. Well, no."

"I didn't think so. I told him that you don't yet understand our ways or customs yet and that, to you, it was just the gift of a pretty flower. If you want me to call him back and tell him I was wrong, I can."

Jariel drops the flower. "No. I'm sorry."

"Don't rush into things you don't understand. And don't be so quick to assume the worst about me."

The two women walk on, only feet apart, greeting all who greet them, but maintaining icy silence toward one another. They are nearly home when a man approaches Shaye to offer her a flower. She nods politely and clasps her hands under her stomach, before Jariel hears her say, "You honor me," and something more in a polite voice—and she doesn't accept the flower.

Jariel waits a while before she speaks. "May I ask what you said to him?"

The effort of walking uphill has allowed some of Shaye's steam to evaporate. "I said he honors me, but it will be a *long time* before I ever *consider* courting anyone."

Jariel bites her lip as she glances at Shaye's stomach. "Oh."

When they arrive at the house, people are still bringing food and other goods to set on the porch, and Willow is busy with preparations for what will be a feast in their honor.

They both look at her with new understanding; then, nod at each other.

"Here," Jariel offers, "let us help you."

# CHAPTER 28
## The Feast

"True community is not the result of efficient organization nor is it found in a place—it's a sacred, living being."
*From the Tell of His people*

All along the street where Willow lives, people bring wooden tables and chairs out of their homes to place them on porches or even in the street itself. A growing multitude of torches on poles glow against the darkening sky and warm lamplight spills from windows of the houses, illuminating the growing feast. People young and old begin to walk all along the route, testing food set out on tables, exchanging the latest news. As more people arrive with food, the smell of spices, cooked meats, and baked goods fills the air. Music from a stringed instrument, a flute, and a timbrel wafts between the houses, and everywhere there is laughter. Many of the women are wearing ribbons in their hair and clothing with more colors than the drab working garb of daily life.

While Willow takes a short rest, Shaye and Jariel stand with Nathan and Peony on the porch of the home and gaze in amazement.

"It' like a festival they would have in Aegea. Only this is less planned out, more like dining with lots of friends." Jariel says.

"Yes," Shaye answers. "It's wonderful,"

"In another day or two," Nathan tells her, "you and Jariel will be finding work—but tonight is your night to begin experiencing what our shared life is like. Walk about! You are free to sample anything people brought. There are usually smaller common meals like this in neighborhoods once a week . . . but this is a *special* occasion and I'm sure most of the village will come."

Nathan's wife Peony doesn't speak much, but there is a happy glow about her that Shaye finds endearing.

Iris arrives on the porch with her sister and once she's near enough, she speaks the language of Aegea to the guests of honor. "Shaye and Jariel, this is my sister, Coriander—we call her Cori."

Cori looks very much like her sister, with long slender limbs and but less silver in her hair. "Nice to meet you, Cori. We very much enjoyed going to see the ocean with Iris today."

"Yes!" Jariel chimes in.

"Oh," Cori laughs, "I'm surprised you were able to get her away from it. Once she learned to swim, we couldn't keep her away."

Almost simultaneously Shaye and Jariel say, "You can *swim?*"

Iris nods.

"Will you *teach* me?" Jariel asks.

"Yes. Perhaps we can even convince Shaye to try it someday, eh?"

While Iris is talking to Peony and Willow in Genon, Cori looks at Jariel and says, "I'm not as good remembering how to speak in Command Dialect as Iris, but I think more will come back to me as we talk. Would the two of you like to walk with Iris and me?"

They can't convince Willow to walk with them, so Nathan and Peony stay behind to keep her company on the porch.

While they walk, Shaye is careful where she steps. She has no shoes on and several passing showers during the day have left puddles in the street. Her heart skips a beat when she hears Cori say to Jariel, "So tell me about your family."

"I don't have much to tell." Jariel says. "The home where I worked was also where I lived and I stayed indoors, away from people, most of the time—so I don't know many people. I'd much rather talk about the journey and this place. I've seen more to wonder at in the past few weeks than in my entire life before that."

Shaye turns to look at Jariel with an approving smile.

As they walk along, they stop to sample some of the pulled meat on one of the tables. It's savory and Shaye takes a second, small helping. While she's chewing, she sees two women glaring down at her from the porch of the next house. It only takes her a moment to remember they were in the displeased group staring down at her during her first entrance into homeplace. Cori nudges Iris and says something under her breath.

"*Eh,eh!*" Iris says, then leans over to Shaye. "Don't mind those women. They're not nice people and they have ill-tempered daughters. The scarcity of women here made it possible for them to think they could treat the hearts of the men here with contempt and still have their pick among them. You and Jariel have probably damaged the chances of their daughters with the most eligible men, so who can blame them for being angry?"

Shaye frowns at the thought. "I'm not here to find a husband. I'm no threat to their daughter's chances."

Just as she says this, Mule, David, Philip and Tooth show up. The young women are genuinely glad to see them since it feels as if they are all old friends now.

"Where are the others?" Shaye and Jariel ask.

"All of them will come," Mule says, "After all those weeks of Tooth's cooking, who would miss an opportunity at such a feast?"

Tooth gives him a shove and they both laugh.

Iris watches the way Mule and the others are interacting with the young women, then glances up at the unhappy mothers and grins, but she doesn't say anything.

Shaye's focus follows that of Iris and sees the scowls have grown deeper than ever. "Perhaps we should move along." she suggests and they continue down the street. To her delight, Cori is attempting to be the translator for Jariel—and for the most part, succeeding.

They stop often for introductions and tasting, but they keep walking down the street until they get to the end of it then turn around to head up the other side, wandering up onto porches and down again, sipping and tasting, and eventually they run into fellow travelers Jude, Matthew, John, Loash, and Avallach. Each of the men greets them and asks how they are faring in homeplace. David makes a joke about their journey together and Shaye is amused. Her gaze sweeps down the street at all the people moving in the golden light, and it makes her feel warm inside. It almost feels as if her soul were smiling, at least until Ben comes into focus. He's standing on a porch with a cup in his hand and talking to another man when he turns and sees her. He sets the cup down, steps off the porch, and disappears into the crowd.

Mule watches the scene unfold, then tells her, "Don't let anyone take your joy."

She looks down and says nothing.

"Benjamin is my friend," Mule tells her while dusting crumbs of bread out of his beard. "He is a man with strong feelings and opinions . . . and pride." He shrugs. "Ben knows he acted foolishly yesterday—but he hasn't worked out how to ask for forgiveness. Give him time."

They're moving past Willow's house so Iris and Cori decide to rejoin Willow while the young people continue on. The music is louder at this end of the street. Children chase each other through the crowd playing tag, splashing in puddles, and squealing with delight. In front of an older, wooden home, several men are playing a game with small pebbles and an oblong platter with grooves in it where groups of pebbles go. David tries to explain it to the women, but it makes no sense to them. Further down the street, Jariel elbows Shaye and pokes her chin in a certain direction.

When she looks, Shaye sees the "odd" woman Jariel wondered about earlier, still wearing her baggy dress, still with her baby and three other children, all ravenously eating and loading whatever will fit into their pockets.

"*Eh,eh!*" she says before she gives Jariel a smile.

# CHAPTER 29
# Man from the Forest

### In Aegea

He awakens but doesn't open his eyes. *What woke me up? I must have been talking to myself.*

At first, he's only aware of the fact that he's cold and he shivers. A blanket pulled up to his chin warms him, and he dozes again. Later it's the sound that catches his attention. *Water, splashing down.* He realizes that he's thirsty. He opens his eyes.

An old Genon man leans over him. In the candlelight the lines of concern on his face look as if they were carved there. "Are you awake now?" the old man asks in Genon. "Can you understand me?"

The man on the cot nods, and finally manages to unstick his tongue from the roof of his mouth. "Water," he whispers.

Old Menoh leans down with a corsha gourd ladle containing water and lifts the man's head off the pillow, tilting the gourd only a moment at a time to ensure the man has time to swallow each sip.

The man is so thirsty he feels as if he could drink non-stop for days. But when he tries to take hold of the gourd, he realizes he can barely lift his arm more than a few inches off the bed. It feels as if it weighs as much as one of his legs. *How about the other arm?* His other arm feels even heavier! Then he realizes he can barely move his legs at all and he groans. "What's wrong with me?"

"You've been sick for many days, sometimes burning with fever, sometimes barely breathing. You must keep still and allow your body to mend itself. In time, your arms and legs will remember how to move. It would help if you could take some broth. Could you?"

His head feels heavy as well. "Yes."

The lines in the old man's face soften a little. "That's a good thing." When the man on the cot shivers again, Menoh unfolds another blanket and places it on him. "You're wet with sweat and it's making you cold."

The man nods.

"Tell me," Menoh asks, "You kept whispering, 'I kept them safe, I kept them safe.' Whom did you keep safe?"

The man's eyes sweep around the room. "Where am I?"

"Do you remember *anything* about your journey here?"

He fights the urge to panic. "No."

"I don't wonder. The fever had fully taken you by the time they found you. You would have died in another day or so, but the Maker must have had other plans. Some men found you and did what they could, then brought you here as fast as they could. You are in Aegea, my son—probably further than you have ever been from home."

He remembers getting very sick but cannot imagine that he's really in Aegea. *They surely would have killed me. This must be the fever,* he tells himself. *I'm crazy with the fever.*

### 

The aroma of the broth awakens him. He opens his eyes and the old man is still there. But now, two other men are with him. Young men. And one of them has a color of hair that he's never seen before. It's like a sunset—a sort of golden red. *This cannot be real . . .*

Seeing the look of consternation and panic in his eyes, the old man follows his gaze to Ty. "*Eh, eh,*" he says, then speaks in the Command Dialect of Aegea. "It's your hair. I don't think he's ever seen hair like yours before."

Ty exhales as if he'd been holding his breath. "Of course he hasn't. "Because he's not *from* here." He nods to Basil who moves closer to the stranger and speaks in Genon.

"When they found you, you were injured and very sick. Do you remember?"

"No . . ." he answers. *I must still be dreaming, ready to die.* But then a small glimmer of a memory does comes back. "Perhaps I . . . remember. Did someone try to hold me under the water?"

"Yes," Menoh tells him, "but not to harm you. You were burning with the fever and they had to cool you down by placing you in a stream. I'm told you put up a mighty struggle, but they held you there for a while."

Old Menoh cradles the young man's head and lifts it off the bed. "Here, son. Drink some of this broth. I don't think the fever is finished with you yet. Your body needs nourishment if you are going to live."

Then the memories all come crashing in on him. He takes a deep breath as he looks away. "Why should I live?"

"Indulge an old man," Menoh says, tipping the broth to the man's lips.

It has a strange flavor, but some of the spices of home. Despite his determination to let nature take its course so that he can die, he realizes how much his stomach aches for food and he can't stop himself. He takes a few more sips.

"My wife, Fiona, made this just for you, from bones and vegetables. I can tell you for certain," Menoh says with a hint of a smile, "you do not want to insult her cooking. You should drink all of this."

# CHAPTER 30

"It's part of our nature to want to control all the aspects of life. But life isn't always as controllable as we'd like, is it? Life and love have a way of breaking free of our command no matter how hard we try to rein them in. I'm saying maybe it's not always a bad thing when they do."—*Aberta Harris during Jariel McClaren's Planning Day festivities*

## At the western end of the Aegean Plateau

It's the middle of the night and the man's fever is raging again. It's Ty's turn to watch over him so he wrings out another set of cloths from the cold water and places them on the man's head and body.

The man's eye's open but he's delirious. "I saved them. No harm came to them while I was with them." he says in Genon.

Ty leans forward. "Who is it that you kept safe?"

"I kept them safe. They are safe now."

"I know," Ty says, patting the man's shoulder.

The man falls silent and Ty gives up on a response before the man starts to hum a haunting sort of tune. At the end of it, he speaks, in a whisper. "No harm will come to either of you while I'm watching over you."

## In Homeplace

Willow sits at the table, mending an old dress by lamplight and looks up when Shaye enters the room. "It won't be daybreak for more than an hour," she says quietly. "You should probably rest some more."

Shaye stretches, then takes a seat on the opposite side of the table. "I used to get up early every day and help Mosha—the woman who raised me. We cooked and kept the kitchen."

"Your father and mother are both gone?"

"My father died when I was three. A fever took my mother when I was ten."

Willow's thick-knuckled fingers work the fishbone needle in and out of the cloth, pausing only when she moves the piece around to the next section of the patch. As she's turning the cloth, she sighs and says, "Every life has its tragedies, doesn't it?"

"Yes, but Nathan says the Maker has a way of working things out for our good, even when it doesn't look like it could ever be so."

Willow takes the last stitch, then knots the thread on the back of the cloth and bites it off. She holds the work at arm's length to inspect it before she glances up at Shaye. "What do *you* believe?"

"At the beginning of this year, I was so sure about everything . . . I thought I could see the hand of the Maker in so much. I had plans, I was sure of myself, and I felt like I could find my way in this world. . . . Now everything is flipped over." She scoots a small bundle of thread around the table with her finger while she talks. "My life has taken several unexpected turns and I'm no longer sure of anything. I used to have such a sense of the Maker's presence and love . . . and I guess I somehow thought had earned those things. But does anyone ever *earn* them? Does anyone *deserve* them? Perhaps . . . I understand now that I never did . . . and I'm hopeful that Nathan was right, that everything good comes from the Maker and He is working even when we cannot see it. Maybe our part is to trust Him."

The old woman sighs and places her hand on Shaye's. "Maybe, in time, both of us will see some good again."

### 

## At the western end of the Aegean Plateau

During the night, Ty became so worried about the man from the forest that he awakened Old Menoh again and for several hours the old man wasn't sure the stranger would live through the night. They changed cold compresses on him for hours before the fever broke again. It's nearly dawn now.

Ty touches the man's skin. "He's staying cool."

"Go and wake up Basil," Menoh tells him. "You need to rest. The danger is passed for now."

## In Homeplace

Shaye stands outside, eyes closed, letting the newly risen sun kiss her face. She and Willow talked till sunup, but she's not tired. The baby inside her is leaping around and she places her hand over it. *Good morning, my love. It's a new day for all of us. A new day for a new life. I have much to do today. Jariel and I must find work—but you will behave, won't you?*

Willow comes to the window and breaks into her reverie. "Come inside, child. The air is too cool this time of the morning. Jariel is awake, so come in and eat."

Shaye opens her eyes and, for the first time, she sees a hint of a smile on Willow's face.

*Perhaps the Maker will turn even my mistakes and sorrows to the good.*

## The End


Thanks for reading my book! If you enjoyed it, would you take a moment to write a review for your favorite retailer?

Thanks again!
Terry L. Craig


Follow the continuing story in:
***Under an Open Sky***
Book 3 in the *Scions of the Aegean C* series

## About the Author
## Terry L. Craig

Born in the Southwest, Terry has lived all over the US and spent many years living in the Caribbean. She is a people-watcher and a comparative thinker who is fascinated with words, art, and ideas. She has a passion to share spiritual life in a way that allows the reader to weigh the values of different ideologies from a non-threatening perspective.

Terry is a follower of Jesus, a wife, mom, and grandma who currently resides in North Carolina with her professional pilot husband (her lifetime love) Bill. The development of true friendships and healthy community life are high on her list of life's essentials.

You can learn more about/connect with Terry L. Craig at:

**www.terrylcraig.com**

Or, you can check out her author pages at:

Wild Flower Press, Inc. (**www.wildflowerpress.biz),**
Amazon.com
Goodreads
Google+
Smashwords
Terry L. Craig on Facebook

## Other Books by Terry L. Craig

- *Scions of the Aegean C Descent into the Wilds,* Book 1 of this series

- *The Fellowship of the Mystery* trilogy,
  1. *GATEKEEPER*
  2. *SOJOURNER*
  3. *SWORDSMAN*

  (Terry says that nearly every month that goes by, she is amazed to see technologies and events—written into the Fellowship of the Mystery trilogy many years ago—unfolding before her eyes.)

- An Apologetic study on Universalism entitled, *What Mama Never Told You about the Afterlife*

All of Terry's books are available as paperbacks and as eBooks through Amazon.com, Smashwords, Apple iStore, Barnes & Noble and many fine retailers.

### Upcoming

- *Under an Open Sky* will be Book 3 in the *Scions of the Aegean C* series

  Check in at Wild Flower Press, Inc. www.wildflowerpress.biz or at Terry's website at terrylcraig.com for updates on the release of *Under an Open Sky.*

# Other Books Published by Wild Flower Press, Inc.

### Fiction

- The *Within the Walls* trilogy by Stephanie Bennett is a series of futuristic novels chronicling the life of Emilya, a virtual travel agent in 2070.
    1. *Within the Walls,*
    2. *Breaking the Silence*
    3. *The Poet's Treasure*

- The *Fellowship of the Mystery* trilogy by Terry L. Craig is apocalyptic fiction from an uncommon perspective.
    1. *GATEKEEPER*
    2. *SOJOURNER*
    3. *SWORDSMAN*

- *Scions of the Aegean C, Descent into the Wilds* by Terry L. Craig is Book 1 in the *Scions of the Aegean C* series with more to come in the future. Check our website for updates.

### Non Fiction

- *Passport for the Journey, 21 Day Challenge* by Tonya J. Brown is a Devotional / Journal for use by individuals or groups.

- *What Mama Never Told You about the Afterlife,* by Terry L. Craig is an Apologetic study on Universalism.

All our books are available as paperbacks and as eBooks through Amazon.com, Smashwords, Apple iStore, Barnes & Noble, CreateSpace, and many other fine retailers.

**www.wildflowerpress.biz**